David—Handsome, loved hero. After alone has the power to r tered nation.

Sunu—This fiery young Child of the Lion decides that his true calling is not as an armorer but as a warrior for David in the struggle against the ruthless, marauding Philistines.

Mara—Daughter of Jonathan, granddaughter of Saul, princess of Israel, she possesses the passion, the beauty, and the defiance to subdue the fiercest warrior.

Joab—A mighty man of Israel and one of David's most devoted allies, he will nonetheless disobey orders in the name of personal vengeance, earning the everlasting curse of his beloved king.

Kaptar—A royal son of the Nile and a Child of the Lion, he has survived the murder of his mother and the betrayal of Egypt at the hands of a ruthless oppressor. Now he sets out on a treacherous journey to reclaim his birthright . . . and exact his revenge.

Nefernehi—Her marriage to Kaptar is a matter of political expediency, but not so the burgeoning passion she feels for the one man who could lead her country back from the brink of a bloody abyss.

The Children of the Lion series by Peter Danielson
Ask your bookseller for the titles you have missed

Volume XVIII

THE SHINING KING

PETER DANIELSON

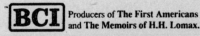

BCI Producers of **The First Americans** and **The Memoirs of H.H. Lomax.**

Book Creations Inc., Canaan, NY • Lyle Kenyon Engel, Founder

BANTAM BOOKS

NEW YORK • TORONTO • LONDON • SYDNEY • AUCKLAND

THE SHINING KING

*A Bantam Book / published by arrangement with
Book Creations Inc.*

Bantam edition / March 1995

*Produced by Book Creations Inc.
Lyle Kenyon Engel, Founder*

ISBN 0-553-56147-2

Published simultaneously in the United States and Canada

*Bantam Books are published by Bantam Books, a division of Bantam
Doubleday Dell Publishing Group, Inc. Its trademark, consisting of the
words "Bantam Books" and the portrayal of a rooster, is Registered in
U.S. Patent and Trademark Office and in other countries. Marca Re-
gistrada. Bantam Books, 1540 Broadway, New York, New York 10036.*

PRINTED IN THE UNITED STATES OF AMERICA

OPM   0 9 8 7 6 5 4 3 2 1

The Beauty of Israel is slain upon the high places:
How are the mighty fallen.

II Samuel 1:19

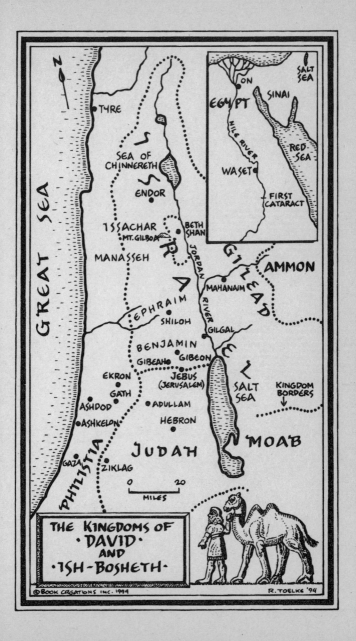

THE KINGDOMS OF
· DAVID ·
AND
· ISH-BOSHETH ·

GREAT SEA

TYRE

SEA OF CHINNERETH

ENDOR

ISSACHAR

MT. GILBOA

BETH SHAN

MANASSEH

JORDAN

GILEAD

AMMON

MAHANAIM

EPHRAIM

SHILOH

RIVER

GILGAL

BENJAMIN

GIBEAH

GIBEON

EKRON

JEBUS (JERUSALEM)

SALT SEA

KINGDOM BORDERS

GATH

ASHDOD

ADULLAM

ASHKELON

HEBRON

MOAB

PHILISTIA

JUDAH

GAZA

ZIKLAG

0   20
MILES

EGYPT

ON

SALT SEA

SINAI

NILE RIVER

RED SEA

WASET

FIRST CATARACT

© BOOK CREATIONS INC. 1994

R. TOELKE '94

THE SHINING
KING

Prologue

The scholar had walked far. Thirst dried his lips, and his throat was scratchy. He leaned wearily on his staff. Behind him the road wound its way down Council Hill, through the deep valley called the Hinnom, and upward to the first of the dwellings on the outskirts of the city. A benevolent sun created a stark contrast of gleaming white structures and deep shadows, turning the city into a brilliant mosaic. On the temple mount, Solomon's testimony in stone to the glory of God caught the light and sent it shimmering back into the heavens.

It was good to rest, good to feel the sun on his upturned face. The sky was cloudless. The day was one for filing away in memory, to be taken out and treasured when the winds of winter blew from the Great Sea and chilling rains lashed the terraced orchards on the slopes.

" 'Praise waiteth for thee, O God,' " the scholar whispered, voicing words once sung by the Shining King, by David himself. " 'The little hills rejoice on every side. The pastures are clothed with flocks.' "

Fat sheep with soiled, yellowed coats ready for fleecing ambled closer. The scholar had regained his breath, but he waited as a shepherd boy approached behind his flock.

A smile of recognition burst onto the boy's face. "Rabbi!" he said with enthusiasm. "Uncle." He bowed to show his respect.

1

"Son of my sister," the scholar said cheerfully. "You are well?"

"God is good," the boy said, nodding.

"And your mother?"

"She will be most pleased to see you, Uncle. Will you walk along with me and my charges?"

"With pleasure. But give me a moment."

The scholar let his eyes measure the city spreading across its three hills. There was Solomon's great cedar palace with its adjuncts, the houses of the Forest of Lebanon, wherein lived the king's Egyptian wives.

The boy's eyes followed his uncle's gaze. "It is only the city," he said, for he saw it every day when he took his flock into the sparse pastures on the semibarren hills.

" 'Only the city,' " the scholar repeated with a smile. "You do not find it beautiful?"

"I like the orchards and the trees," the boy said. "The city is too large and by far too noisy when I go there with my father."

"It was not always thus," the scholar said.

The boy waited. He had seen that look of intense contemplation on his uncle's face before. He glanced up at the sun. There was plenty of time. He sank down and settled back against a large rock, holding his shepherd's staff erect. "It seems to me it has been there always," he remarked.

"Not always," the scholar said. "And never so glorious." He looked down at his nephew. "What was the city called when Joshua led the children over the River Jordan?"

"It was called Jebus because it was the home of the Jebusites."

"Good, good, you remember. And was Joshua successful in taking the city of the Jebusites?"

"No, Rabbi."

"No. He was not. The lands all around were given to the tribe of Judah, but the Jebusites held the fortress atop the hill." He nodded. "And had the city other names?"

The boy frowned in concentration. "I know not, Rabbi."

The scholar smiled. "Do you know the name Shalem?"

The boy swallowed nervously. "A Canaanite god, Rabbi."

"So the name of the city is composed of two words of Canaanite origin—the name of a Canaanite god and the root word meaning to establish or raise up. Thus Yerusalem: the established city of Shalem."

"Can it be that the city of the Shining King was named for a heathen idol?" The suggestion was so near blasphemy that it incensed the boy.

The scholar laughed and motioned with an outflung arm at their surroundings. "We took it all from them," he said. "We came up out of Egypt and slew or drove away those who held the lands. Is it not justice that they should have left something behind? A name? A memory?"

He fell silent. The boy waited.

"When Saul was slain, and his sons with him, the Jebusites were secure in their fortress," the scholar continued. He pointed. "The city was much smaller then, covering only the Ophel area on the slope—there, below the great wall. Thus it was when David was in Judah, having returned from his exile among the Philistines. Thus it was when Abner, kinsman of Saul and commander of the Army of Israel, went over the River Jordan with Saul's only surviving son. Do you remember his name, nephew?"

The boy's brow furrowed; then his face brightened. "Yes," he said with satisfaction. "This son, the youngest of four, was first called Esh-baal, and that was one of the things that angered Samuel. He felt it wasn't suitable for the anointed king of Israel to name his son after a Canaanite idol."

The scholar straightened, taking pleasure in the landscape. His nephew's sheep were grazing peacefully a few yards away. It was only a short walk to the house of his sister, and there was no hurry.

Sensing that his uncle was content to linger, the boy pointed toward the city atop the hills. "Uncle, tell me the story of how the fortress of the Jebusites came to be called the City of David."

The scholar nodded. "It is a story worth the telling, but it cannot be told without preamble. The events that brought David to Jerusalem had roots in the quarrel between Saul the king—the Tall King—and the prophet Samuel."

"I know of that," the boy said. "Saul was anointed by Samuel, but the king usurped the functions of a priest of God after having disobeyed the will of God."

"The will of God as interpreted by Samuel," the scholar amended. He smiled at his nephew. "Can we doubt that God spoke to Samuel?"

The boy swallowed hard. There were times when his uncle's flirtation with blasphemy made him decidedly uneasy.

"No, we cannot," the rabbi said, answering his own question, "for the holy texts are explicit. Perhaps Saul spent too much time among the Philistines so that his mind was poisoned by their heathen philosophies. Perhaps he was truly possessed by devils." He shrugged. "The inevitable result of his being abandoned by Samuel and by God came when Philistine General Galar's Army of the Five Cities crushed the might of Israel at Gilboa, leaving the lands of the Rachel tribes north of Judah helpless and open to bands of the enemy, who looted and killed at will."

"Why was Judah spared?" the boy asked.

"Because it was David's land, and the Philistines considered David to be their vassal."

The boy opened his mouth to protest but thought better of it—although he could not accept the image of the Shining King as a servant of the Philistine lords. All he could do was point mutely to the city, the City of David.

"What you indicate is true without question," the scholar said fondly. "God smiled upon David, and he *accomplished much. But how did such wonders come about? David had only those men who had followed him into exile when he fled to escape the wrath of Saul. He was but one man, and his forces were small. Even when he left the land of the Philistines and established himself at Hebron, where he was accepted by his own tribe as their king, he faced terrible odds in his attempt to reunite the Hebrews. The Philistines' chariotry had proven itself virtually invincible in crushing Saul's army at Gilboa. The enemy's heavy infantry was arrogantly victorious, a matchless force."*

"But David had supporters, Uncle," the boy said.

The rabbi nodded. "That is true. He had his followers. He was respected among his own tribe in Judah, and he had his friends. Eri the armorer had been a companion and a trusted adviser. Eri and his father, Urnan, both masters of the weapons maker's art, were at his side once again."

"The Children of the Lion," the boy said in awe. "Descended from old Belsunu of Ur, whence came Abraham."

The scholar beamed. The boy had learned well. "And why are they so called?"

"Each male child has as a birthmark the imprint of a lion' s paw. Usually placed low on his body."

"And why is it called, this lion's trace, the mark of Cain?"

"It is said, Rabbi, that Cain was the first worker in metals." The boy smiled sheepishly. "Other than that I don't remember."

The scholar explained in a patient voice, "When Cain killed his brother, God laid a lion's limb on him to brand him forever before driving him away into strange lands. To commemorate mankind's first encounter with death and to remind succeeding generations of the repugnance of Cain's crime, all those who followed in his line would feel the touch of the lion's paw before birth and be condemned to roam the known regions of the earth while *working at their forges fashioning what Cain had wielded against Abel: weapons of death."*

"It seems a harsh punishment," the boy said thoughtfully.

The scholar shrugged. "Yahweh is Yahweh. He giveth and He taketh away. He gave David strength and courage and the ability to inspire men through his musical and poetic artistry and his leadership, but he denied the Shining King his most cherished goal."

The boy waited for his uncle to continue, but instead the scholar pointed to the sun, now low in the western sky. "Perhaps we should go," he said.

"Yes," the boy agreed.

The scholar looked over his shoulder. The red rays of the setting sun turned the white prospects of the city a rosy gold. "Forty years," he mused. "God gave David forty years in which to secure his kingdom. Wars and death he knew, but in the end . . . this."

"Tonight, Uncle, will you tell us how David bested the Jebusites and took the city?"

The scholar smiled fondly. Lessons were taught through the telling of stories. It was good to see his nephew so eager to hear of God's love and His wrath when He was defied by mere man.

"That and more," he promised. "I will speak of the Shining King and of his troubles with Saul's remaining son, and of the Children of the Lion who fashioned his weapons and fought at his side."

"And Egypt," the boy said. "Will you speak of old Egypt, where the son born of a princess and the armorer Urnan also bore the mark?"

The scholar smiled. "That, too. That, too." He rose. "Now, nephew, let us guide your rather odorous charges toward shelter, for evening is near and I have traveled far."

CHAPTER ONE

A cold, light rain started falling just as the first light of dawn prevailed over the chilly night. Urnan, the smith of Shiloh, armorer to a dead king, pulled a sheepskin robe up to the chin of his sleeping companion. The rain dampened Urnan's coiled, graying black hair and glistened on the perfumed sable tresses of the woman who slept soundly beside him, her soft buttocks pressed tightly to the curve of his body.

It was morning of the third day since they had left the village of Endor just ahead of the advance units of General Galar's army. With the rain came a smell of burning. To the north, pillars of smoke marked the destruction of Endor. Urnan eased out from under the sheepskin robe, lifted his face to the sullen sky, and stretched the stiff muscles of his powerful arms and legs. Fighting was hard work, and he had wielded his

sword more than once as Saul led the Army of Israel
from a position of advantage in the Gilboan hills onto
the Plain of Jezreel, where the warrior maiden Deborah had once defeated an enemy of Israel.

Urnan considered building a campfire, then decided against it. The Philistines would be moving fast,
each man eager to seize his share of the bounty of war,
to gather slaves, and to claim that ancient right of the
victorious warrior: possessing the women of the van-
quished.

Heavy mist blew into Urnan's face and ran down
the sun-bronzed planes of his cheeks. The dark, fore-
boding skies echoed the blackness of the lost hopes of
Israel; the rain was Israel's tears.

Saul, the Tall King, was dead. Noble Jonathan, the
son who was to have followed him to the throne, was
dead as well, as were his brothers. The Army of Israel
was scattered, and far too many of its soldiers,
sprawled untidily in death on the Gilboan hills and the
blood-drenched plain, would feed the sharp-beaked
carrion feeders of the air and the skulking jackals of
the night.

Behind Urnan, the woman stirred and awoke. He
turned and looked down into a pair of dark, sultry eyes.
She was Jerioth, whom some called the Witch of Endor. Like many others, she had been widowed during
Saul's struggles against the tyrannical Philistines. Her
olive skin was as smooth as the heart of a ripe fig; her
long lashes were dewed by the mist. Her smile lifted
Urnan's heart out of the morass of grief and despair.

"You're awake." He knelt beside her, cupping her
cheek in his right hand.

His iron-hard calluses were scratchy on her skin.
She reached up to hold the hand hardened by work at
forges in Israel, Judah, and—long ago—in Egypt.

"Hungry?" he asked.

She nodded.

He unwrapped the meager rations gathered hastily

before their flight from Endor. She took a handful of dates, smiling as she chewed.

Urnan, too, reached into their sparse stores. He was eating gratefully when he heard something, a telltale sound of danger. He touched his lips to caution Jerioth to silence. Their makeshift camp was but an arrow's half-flight off the road leading toward the south and east.

Crawling to a place of vantage, Urnan peered down through concealing brush. A gleaming Philistine chariot drawn by two prancing white horses rumbled along the rocky road. Sharp, strong blades attached to the vehicle's wheel hubs made sparkles of light. Behind, moving at a quick pace, came a small company of Philistine heavy infantry.

Jerioth crept to Urnan's side. Seeing their enemy, she clung to his arm, her fingers digging into his flesh.

"Galar's troops," Urnan whispered, voicing the name of the general in command of the Army of the Five Cities with a vehemence that bespoke his hatred. Each of the barefoot infantrymen sported the bright blue feathered crest of the city of Ashdod and a layered leather vest to protect his upper torso.

"Royal guard," Urnan added, identifying the unit by its blue kilts decorated with a patch of red between white stripes and tassels that bounced rhythmically from the front hem. Each man carried the short, efficient Philistine sword and a heavy leather shield.

Urnan waited a long time before leaving his place of concealment. When he was at last satisfied that the unit of Galar's royal guard was not being followed by additional troops, he led Jerioth toward the east. There lay the River Jordan. To reach the destination he had in mind it would be safer to cross over the Jordan and follow the river south. These lands west of the river lay open to the Philistines. They swarmed the highlands and the central plateau like rabid scavengers, with no one to stand against them. Once, from his temple at Ramah, Samuel had rallied Israel in a time of troubles;

but Samuel, too, was dead, having preceded Saul and
his sons to Sheol by two years. There was no king in
Israel nor a prophet to call down God's blessings on
those who cringed and suffered as the Philistines
looted, raped, killed, and burned. The Army of the
Five Cities had split into small units after destroying
Saul's army at Gilboa, the better to strip the land.

Urnan stopped abruptly. Mere paces ahead, sleeping on a grassy slope beside the rude track leading
toward the river, lay another group of Philistine infantry, about a dozen of them. The smith shivered invol-
untarily. He had barely missed leading the woman he
had rescued from the destruction of Endor into enemy
hands.

The narrow escape convinced Urnan that he
should travel by night.

Taking great care, he led Jerioth back through a
grove of trees. He could smell water. They left the road
in case the river crossing was guarded. A sound caused
Urnan to halt again, and Jerioth, following close behind, bumped into him. He stood with his head cocked.
The sound came again—a smothered cry, a moan of
anguish and pain. Urnan guided Jerioth into concealing thick brush, signaled her to be quiet, and crept forward.

What he saw made the gorge rise in his throat.

Two Philistine infantrymen sat on an outcrop of
stone, watching and making ribald suggestions to a
third soldier who labored between the pale, outspread
legs of a young girl. Urnan could clearly see the girl's
large, dark eyes. They were glazed with pain and near
madness.

Once before he had come upon such a scene.
Many years had passed since he returned to his home
in Shiloh to find the woman who was his wife and the
mother of his son, Eri, being raped by soldiers under
the command of a Philistine officer—an officer named
Galar. The scene in the glade before him now burned
his consciousness and aroused all the old fury. He

stood erect. He did not stop to remember that his last single-handed charge against Galar's men had resulted in years of slavery, in being separated from his son. In his mind the girl who was being ravaged became his beloved and long-dead Shelah.

He burst into the clearing with his sword in hand, a weapon of his own making, a blade of iron honed to a peak of deadliness. The two spectators were stripped to the waist, waiting their turns, their upper-body armor lying on the rocks with their weapons. One died leaping for his sword as Urnan's blade, driven by all the strength of a smith's powerful right arm, drilled into the back of his neck and severed his spinal cord.

The second man yelled in defiance as he raised his hastily recovered sword. But Urnan's momentum carried him under the Philistine's wild swing, and the sharp tip of his sword buried itself in the Philistine's stomach at the vulnerable point between the vee of ribs. The smith thrust the blade upward and twisted, then freed it as the lifeless body slumped to the ground.

The third man, his reactions slowed by the intensity of his lust, pushed himself away from the shocked, staring eyes of his victim. He was crawling on hands and knees when Urnan nearly decapitated him with a two-handed downward chop of his sword.

Weakened by his swift and sudden exertion and the fury of his emotions, Urnan bent over, gasping for air. Through his labored breathing he heard the girl making an odd sound and turned to her. It was only then that he saw the evidence of the force that had been used on her. He knelt beside her.

"I am a friend," he said as she cringed from him.

The girl could have been no more than thirteen. She made gagging sounds in her badly bruised throat as if trying to speak. One of her hands came up slowly to touch her side over her heart. There was an odd distortion of her torso just below her left breast. Urnan put his hand there and pressed gently. She screamed as he felt bone grind on broken bone. She rolled onto her other side and tried to crawl, using her one good arm.

"You have nothing to fear," he said, putting his hand on her. "I am a friend."

The girl was making pitiful noises, like a wounded animal caught in a snare. Her feet were digging into the dust, slipping as she tried to scrabble away.

"Jerioth!" Urnan called. "Come quickly!"

She emerged from the brush and walked around a fallen body. Her eyes were wide, her mouth set grimly.

"The child is hurt," Urnan said.

Jerioth made a sound of sorrow and shock as she knelt beside the girl and arranged her torn garments to cover her womanhood. Not even Jerioth's soothing voice calmed the child, who continued, for a moment more, to try to crawl away. Jerioth reached out and touched her tenderly—just as the girl cried out, spit up blood, shuddered, and was still.

"She's dead!" Jerioth said in disbelief.

"Her ribs were broken badly," Urnan said. "From the blood, I'd say her lung was punctured. Perhaps even her heart."

Jerioth stared at him, her mouth open, her eyes wide, accusing. "How can you speak of it so calmly?"

"Would it change anything if I screamed out my rage to the heavens?"

Jerioth could not respond. She was kneeling in the dust, her hand on the shoulder of the dead girl. Urnan saw the pain in her eyes. It could have been a reflection of his own outrage. He lifted his head and in a hoarse, strained voice roared against death. His words ran together. The tendons of his throat strained with his effort.

"Yahweh!" he wailed. *"Yahweh!"*

Jerioth got to her feet and took his arm in her hands. His muscles were tense, as hard as iron.

"What kind of God are you?" Urnan bellowed. "What kind of heartless God are you to desert those whom you call your chosen people?"

"Hush, hush," Jerioth was saying, but her words had no effect. Urnan's tirade continued until the force of it made his throat hurt, and he at last fell silent.

Jerioth was weeping. Urnan turned his face down to hers and felt chagrin. "I'm sorry," he said.

"No. It's all right."

"I do not ordinarily choose to do battle with gods."

Jerioth smiled through her tears. "You told me you were not a Hebrew."

"I'm not."

"And yet you dispute with God as if you were. You reminded me of my father during one of his—he called them discussions—with God. He said that if God had not intended us to speak to Him He would not have given us a voice. He was a devout man, but he believed in sharing his thoughts with Yahweh."

"And his reward for such defiance?"

Jerioth smiled. "He lived to a ripe age."

A horse suddenly neighed nearby. Urnan's head jerked toward the sound, and he felt his stomach clench. Had his incautious outburst called the enemy down upon them? He motioned Jerioth to silence and moved away quickly. Three fine horses—those of the rapists, undoubtedly—were tethered to bushes. He smiled and called to Jerioth.

"We walk no further."

"For that I thank God."

"I wager there will be food there," Urnan said, pointing to a heap of goods that had been looted by the three dead Philistine soldiers.

Jerioth walked over and sorted through the plunder. She put aside a container of sun-dried dates, a ceramic jar of honey, a full wineskin, and a bag of coarsely ground flour. She tossed away a brace of gold drinking cups.

Urnan laughed. "You have a low opinion of the yellow metal."

She shrugged. "You can't eat it."

"But it will buy more food than we'll find here," he said, bending to pick up the cups. He fashioned packs for the food and valuables, loaded them onto the spare horse, and made ready to help Jerioth to mount.

"We must bury the girl," she said.

"Perhaps her people will come for her."

"We can't leave her like that."

Urnan looked into her eyes. "Not far from here lie the bodies of thousands of the sons of Israel. Can I bury all of them?"

"You can give this one little girl a decent grave."

"And leave her family to wonder what happened to her?" Urnan asked. "It will be kinder to let them discover her as she lies. At least they will know, and it will give her father and her brothers reason to hate those who inflicted such horrors upon her and to be all the more ready to rise up and fight when the time comes."

Urnan lifted Jerioth onto her horse. Her face showed her anger. He would have acceded to her wishes had not the sound of a Philistine trumpet come from the west. "Perhaps we can ask those who come to relieve their dead comrades to help us bury all of the dead," he suggested dryly.

Jerioth made no further protest.

On its journey southward from the Sea of Chinnereth the River Jordan meandered through a narrow valley thick with vegetation where now roamed wild boars and once, in the not-too-distant past, lions. Steep banks allowed for few natural fords; the dead Philistines had been posted to guard one such crossing. Urnan found a way down the bank and urged the horses into shallow water tumbling over exposed stones. Once on the eastern bank he sought the cover of dense brush and pushed on into the land of Gilead. Ahead lay Jabesh, whose inhabitants Saul had saved from Ammonite domination in the early days of his reign. Urnan's planned route lay southward into Gad, almost to the great Salt Sea and the Wilderness of Judah.

His plan was threatened when a dozen armed men leaped from the brush to seize the reins of the horses.

The smith's first reaction was to reach for his sword, but the feel of a sharp iron spearpoint at his throat dissuaded him. The men were not Philistines, but that didn't mean their intentions were peaceful. Bandits were known to frequent the areas east of the Jordan.

"Aha. Three fine Philistine horses," said one of the heavily bearded men.

"And what have we here?" asked another as he plunged his hand into one of the packs and pulled out a gold cup.

"He isn't dressed like a Philistine," remarked a third.

"And yet his horse has a harness of Philistine design, and he has looted Israel."

"Not true," Urnan said. "It was Philistine soldiers whom I relieved of these horses and the contents of the packs."

"Oh, ho! A great warrior."

"Are you not men of Israel?" Jerioth asked angrily. "You speak as if you are, but you act not like men who fear God."

"God we fear," said the leader of the troop. "Philistines and dogs of Philistines we kill."

"I am neither Philistine nor a sycophant of Philistines. I am Urnan," the smith said, lifting his chin.

The bearded leader cocked his head. "Lie to me and the beasts of the fields will gnaw your bones tonight. I know of only one Urnan—he who was once known as the smith of Shiloh, he who was a friend of the king."

Urnan nodded. "I was with Saul at Gilboa."

"Get down off your horse," the bearded man ordered.

Urnan obeyed. He jerked away angrily when the bearded man grabbed his tunic.

"If you are the smith of Shiloh, you will have proof of it," the leader said.

Urnan lifted his tunic to reveal, above his tightly wound loincloth, the purple trace of a lion's paw.

Satisfied, the bearded man said, "I am Joktan of Jabesh-Gilead. I welcome you, smith. It would please me if you will come with us to our town."

"I cannot. I have urgent business in Gilgal," Urnan said.

"In the race to reach Gilgal—or any town west of the Jordan—the Philistine will win. Will you hurry there to meet your death?"

"I hope to avoid that fate, but I will go."

"I had thought, since you were Saul's friend, that you would join us as we pay him his last honors."

"The time to honor him was before the Army of the Five Cities slashed the flower of Israel to pieces and left him lying dead on Gilboa," Urnan said.

Joktan bristled. "I wouldn't speak so haughtily were I you. It was you who left the king to be desecrated. While it is true that we of Jabesh-Gilead did not join him in his fight, we were not content, as were you and the men of Israel, to leave his dismembered body on display."

Urnan was astonished. "You have Saul's body?"

"And those of Jonathan and his other sons."

"I pray that your God will bless you for this," Urnan said.

"We heard of Saul's fate from those who fled the battle, and we did not hesitate to act," Joktan said, looking up into the blue of the sky. "The human jackals from the plains stripped the bodies of the dead where they lay. They found Saul and his sons and removed their armor, placing it in the temple of their heathen goddess, Astarte. They cut off the king's head and those of his sons, hanging all on the wall of Beth-shan." Joktan put his forefinger under his right eye. "Saul, the

king, saved me from having this eye taken by the Ammonites. I would not see his body become food for the
raven. I would not see him and his sons mocked in
death by Galar of Ashdod."

"You will give them the proper rites?" Jerioth
asked.

Joktan looked up at her and nodded. "We carried
them to our town. We will burn them, to prevent the
Philistine Galar from recovering so much as a bone to
prove his great victory. We will bury the ashes under a
tree that grows in Jabesh, then we will fast seven days
in honor of a king. Come with us."

Urnan studied the man's face. "Tell me, Joktan,
have you a grandchild?"

The Hebrew laughed. "Not one grandchild—many
grandchildren."

"And if one of them were in danger, what would
you do?"

"I would fly to save him, of course," Joktan said.

"I have but two grandchildren," Urnan said. "The
mother of one of them has, I fear, been possessed by a
devil, for she has left her home and now sits by night
on the bench of the prostitutes in the town square at
Gilgal with my granddaughter on her lap."

Joktan shook his head in pity. "I understand. I
think the king would understand, as well. May God
clear a path before you."

Urnan and Jerioth had ridden for an hour before
she said, "You have not mentioned to me that which
you told the man of Jabesh-Gilead."

Urnan sighed. "I pray each night that it isn't true,
but that is what I was told by someone who saw her
there."

"The woman is your daughter?"

"No, she is the wife of my son, Eri."

"I am sad for you, but I will not pry into your
private sorrow."

He looked over at his companion, this woman he

barely knew, yet about whom he knew everything. They had first met when, riding in service to Saul, he had stopped in the village of Endor seeking lodging and food. Jerioth, who had been widowed when her husband was killed in battle, had been recommended to him as someone who occasionally offered accommodations to travelers. The need that overwhelmed them almost upon meeting—he a handsome man entering his middle years and she a sultry and sensuous beauty —was unexpected yet somehow inevitable, one of those rare comings together of a man and woman whose hearts keep the same rhythm. He did not see her again until, months later, he brought Saul to see her to divine the shade of Samuel—an occurrence fraught with consequences.

Urnan now reached across the distance between them as they rode side by side and touched her on the arm. "I will have no secrets between us."

Jerioth listened intently as he spoke of the childlike Sarah, first wife of Eri, and of how Sarah lost her sanity after witnessing the butchering of her family by the Philistines; how she stayed hidden in some dark, arcane place within her own mind for years until he, Urnan, used the Egyptian magic he had learned from his friend Prince Kemose to bring her to her senses. Learning only then that Eri, in his loneliness, had turned to his house slave, the Ammonite Baalan, and made her his second wife—she subsequently bore him a son, Sunu—Sarah, forever locked in the mind of a fifteen-year-old, became incensed.

"She was jealous of Baalan?" Jerioth asked.

"And of the boy from Eri's loins."

"The poor little fool," Jerioth said.

"Yes, I weep for her, but it is the child about whom I am most concerned. Sarah was given nothing but love, yet I was told that she ran away from her home to marry a young man, taking my granddaughter with her."

"How do you know she is in Gilgal?"

"A man of that city told me, just before the battle at Gilboa."

Jerioth kicked at her horse, urging it to a faster pace. "Hurry, then," she said. "We must get there before the Philistines arrive."

CHAPTER TWO

The scourge of Philistine occupation had slowed, but advance parties of looters were not far to the north when Urnan and Jerioth followed in the ancient footsteps of Joshua ben Nun at a River Jordan crossing. Jerioth, well versed in the sacred traditions, told Urnan that the warrior who had taken over command from Moses had established Gilgal when he and the people encamped east of Jericho before attacking that city.

"He marked the place by taking twelve stones out of the Jordan," she explained. " 'Gilgal' means a circle of stones."

"For the twelve tribes of Israel?" Urnan asked idly, his mind on what lay ahead in the town.

She shrugged. "Or for the twelve cycles of the moon."

As they neared Gilgal the smoke from Philistine

destruction could be seen in the north. They breasted a tide of refugees fleeing the town in panic. Once Urnan was forced to draw his sword and kill as three men tried to seize the horses. He held the bloody blade before him in warning as they advanced to the town square.

There was the town's well; there was the bench of the prostitutes. It was deserted.

Urnan and Jerioth dismounted, staring at the empty bench. Urnan seized a passing man by the sleeve. The man struggled to escape, frantic to flee the oncoming Philistines. Urnan held his sword in the man's face and demanded, "The prostitute who sits on the bench with an infant girl on her lap, do you know her?"

The man scowled. "Do I look like someone who frequents prostitutes?" Even in the face of the Philistines, a good citizen and a godly man would be insulted by such a suggestion.

A woman came toward them. She was weeping. Urnan halted her, asking the same question.

"I am deserted and alone," she wailed, "and you expect me to take account of a fallen woman?"

Again and again Urnan accosted bolting citizens. The town was emptying fast. Fires had started in one quarter, and the wind caused acrid smoke to swirl and eddy in the square. Through the smoke came a man laden with two sheepskin bags. He seemed to be in no hurry. Urnan stepped in front of him, and the looter dropped the bag in his right hand to replace it with a short sword of inferior make.

"Find your own bounty," the man snarled.

Urnan's upper lip curled in disgust. "Stealing from your own in a time of trouble is not my concern."

"Should I leave it all for the Philistines?" the man countered defensively.

"Do as you wish. I search for the prostitute who sits on the bench with a child on her lap," Urnan said.

Looking relieved that the formidable-looking

stranger wanted nothing more than information, the
looter said, "Ah, the silent one."

"You know her, then?"

"Yes—if, indeed, the silent whore is the one you
seek."

"She has a child."

"Yes, a girl child."

"Do you know where she lives?"

"Wherever she finds a roof and a bed," the man
said. "Now, by your leave, *lord*"—he delivered the title
with great sarcasm—"I will go about my business."

Urnan seized the man by the hair and placed his
keen blade at his throat. "You will dampen the dust of
the square with your blood if you don't help me find
the woman."

"All right, all right," the man acquiesced quickly,
taking a half-step backward. "If I were you I'd look
there." He pointed toward the quarter of town where
the fires were growing. He laughed. "Hurry, lord, or
there'll be no place left to look."

Urnan helped Jerioth to mount, and they trundled
off. In a narrow alley they encountered a family
dressed in rags: a crippled man, a wizened woman, four
emaciated children below the age of ten. As Urnan allowed them to squeeze past, he asked once more about
the silent prostitute.

"There," the woman said in a hollow voice, pointing.

The structure she indicated was a crumbling, one-
room mud-brick hovel nearly completely open to the
elements. The front door was ajar, sagging on its
leather hinges, the windows had no protecting coverings, and the roof was caving in. Urnan's heart leaped
as a child inside the hut began to whine in a voice
strained by much wailing. Hurrying to the dwelling, he
pushed his way into a room littered with vile clutter. It
took a moment for his eyes to adjust to the murky interior. When they did, he saw a huddled heap on a filthy
pallet. Ragged coverings were piled atop the figure.

Only her pale face showed. He took a step toward the bed, then halted. On the cluttered floor, dressed in a thin shirt that did not fully cover her nakedness, sat a child less than a year old.

Jerioth, coming inside behind him, moved quickly to scoop the little girl into her arms. Urnan was stunned by the squalor of the place, by the filth that soiled the face of the child. Jerioth pulled a rank, decaying mutton bone from the infant's hands. She could tell by the marks that the tainted bone had been well gnawed by a dog.

Urnan bent over the bed. Sarah's flushed face was wasted and gaunt. He touched her cheek gingerly with his hand; she burned with fever. Overcoming his revulsion, he took one of her filthy hands in his. Her fingers had lost all their flesh. It was like holding the hand of a skeleton.

"Sarah," he whispered. "Sarah, I have come for you."

Her eyelids flickered. Her eyes opened only a crack, for her lashes were gummed together by some vile secretion.

"Sarah, can you hear me?" Urnan asked.

She struggled to open her eyes. Urnan wet his fingers with water from a clay pitcher sitting beside the bed and washed away the sticky residue from her lashes. Her eyes had a look that was familiar to him—the blank, empty stare that had been hers before he had used the technique of mental control taught to him by his old friend Kemose, a technique Urnan had first seen demonstrated when the Egyptian prince had used it to facilitate their escape from their Philistine slavers and the copper mines on the island of Kittem.

"Sarah, damn you," Urnan said to his daughter-in-law in quick anger, "I won't let you do that again. You will not be allowed to flee into the shelter of nothingness. You have a child now."

The hollow eyes looked at him without seeing. He put his face close to hers and spoke in a soft, monotonous voice. He felt her hand tense in his. Awareness suddenly burned in her eyes.

"Urnan?" she asked weakly.

"It is I."

She strained to lift her head. "Urnan . . ."

Sarah fell back. Her hand went limp in his. She took a long, shuddering breath, expelled it in a gusting sigh, and was still. She had found the ultimate release from a life that had held more horror than she was capable of facing.

Urnan closed her sightless eyes and turned away, fighting the sense of despair that threatened to overwhelm him. He watched Jerioth, who was using a rag and water from the pitcher to wipe the worst of the dirt from the little girl's face. It would take more than a pitcher of water and one small rag to clean the rest of her.

Smoke billowed into the dingy room through the windows. The flames had reached a house just two doors down the narrow street.

"Urnan, we must go," Jerioth urged.

"Yes, soon," Urnan said.

He glanced out the rear door at the weed-grown garden behind the shack. With quick, purposeful motions, he wrapped Sarah's body in the soiled, vermin-infested bedding and carried it outside. Using his sword and a large, sturdy section of a broken storage jar, he began to dig a shallow grave.

Jerioth came to the back door. "Hurry," she said.

"Yes. Yes," Urnan answered. "Go and check on the horses."

She went to the front door only to come face-to-face with a bleating nanny goat, its udders swollen with milk. Jerioth talked coaxingly to the frightened animal, holding out one hand. As if needing reassurance from a human, the goat approached and allowed her to seize a frayed length of rope hanging from its neck.

"Good girl," Jerioth soothed, patting the goat. "Good girl." She put the child down, led the goat into the room, emptied the water from the pitcher, and squeezed rich, hot milk from the goat's udders. The little girl was trying to drink from the pitcher with Jerioth's help when Urnan came back into the hovel, though more milk was spilling onto her soiled, sodden shirt than was going into her mouth. Smoke filled the room suddenly, causing her to cough.

"We can go now," Urnan said solemnly.

"It is done, then?"

"Yes."

"May she find peace."

"Yes," Urnan said.

"We must take the goat, as well."

Urnan looked at Jerioth blankly.

"For the child."

"Her name is Leah," Urnan said. "My son chose the name."

"It is a good choice. It's the name of Jacob's wife."

"Yes, I know," Urnan said, taking hold of the goat's lead and turning toward the door. "Shall I carry the child?"

"Take care of the goat. I'll carry the child."

"Her name is Leah," Urnan repeated. His face was frozen, his eyes dulled more from the sadness of finding Sarah in such a place than from her death.

"It's a good name," Jerioth said softly.

Urnan helped her onto her horse. Fires were reaching for the sky all around them as they crossed the square past the well and the bench of the prostitutes. Once clear of the town, Urnan turned and looked back. They had escaped just in time. Even as they were leaving Gilgal to the south, a band of loot-laden Philistine infantry was entering from the north.

Urnan and Jerioth rode to the east, toward the river, for it would be necessary to fill their waterskins before setting out into the wilderness south of Jericho. They made camp on the bank of the River Jordan, where Jerioth bathed the baby, and herself, thoroughly.

"I feel as if I should throw away all my clothes,"

she complained, sitting beside a fire with nothing more than a sheepskin robe covering her. Her clothing was spread on bushes to dry. "I keep thinking I feel things crawling."

Urnan, who had been partially successful in putting thoughts of Sarah out of his mind, was able to laugh. "Where we're going, the crawling things will die of thirst."

Jerioth smiled—at Urnan's levity and his restored spirit both. She looked over at the baby. "She's a fine little girl," she said, nodding at Leah, who was sleeping happily naked atop a soft fleece.

Urnan knelt beside the baby and touched her soft, dark hair with a forefinger. "She has Eri's hair and her mother's nose."

"She looks quite healthy."

He snorted. "Sharing bones with the dogs is nourishing?"

"Before your daughter-in-law fell ill she must have taken good care of her. She's fat and sassy. Did you see her lapping up that goat's milk?"

Urnan chuckled. "At least there's nothing wrong with her appetite."

At a village on the northern end of the Salt Sea, Urnan traded gold taken from the dead Philistines for meat and fruit. Jerioth fed Leah by first chewing the food, then placing the pulped residue in the child's mouth with her fingers. It made Urnan think of his first wife, Shelah, who had fed the baby Eri the same way.

Leah was a lively, wide-eyed, smiling child who withstood the rigors of travel without so much as a whine. In the evenings, when Urnan set up camp, she was eager to explore, moving with surprising swiftness on her hands and knees. Within days she had captured Jerioth's heart and was pleasing to the eyes of her proud grandfather. Urnan rode with Leah perched on a thick fleece in front of him as they traveled down the west shore of the Salt Sea into the burning wastes of the Wilderness of Judah.

Now they were alone, with no danger of encountering elements of the Philistine army. The nanny goat bleated in protest of the burning sun but followed dutifully, even when Urnan removed her lead. They camped at night sheltered in dry wadis. Their meager supply of water had to be shared with the animals, but each day's ride brought them closer to the hidden valley were Eri had established a secret armory in the days before Saul was king, when the Philistine rulers allowed no smiths in Israel.

Sentinels spotted them before they neared the entrance to the valley. Urnan was greeted warmly. His first question concerned Eri, for the last he had heard, his son was with David, who had gone over to the Philistines. He was overjoyed to learn Eri was in the valley. Escorted by a growing number of men, Urnan answered questions about the state of affairs in Israel as they rode. His heart soared when he saw the smoke of the forges. Weapons were being crafted to rearm the men of Israel. Now all that was needed was a leader to replace Saul.

They reached one of the forges. There Eri, naked to the waist, his well-developed biceps and chest muscles gleaming with sweat, was putting the finishing touches on an iron sword that would more than match the best the Philistines had. Hearing his name, he turned. His detached expression turned to one of shock and surprise at seeing his father sitting astride a handsome horse. Gathering his wits, Eri cooled the sword by thrusting it into a vat of blackened water, put it carefully on a rack, then met Urnan with open arms as his father dismounted. There was no shame in him as he wiped the tears spilling from his eyes with the back of his hand.

"Thank God!" Eri breathed, clasping Urnan to his breast. "We have heard terrible things."

"They are all true," Urnan said.

"Saul is dead, and Jonathan," Eri said sadly, "and the army destroyed?"

Urnan nodded. "At Gilboa. He let them lure him down from the mountain onto the plain."

"Ah, God . . ."

"You have not heard all of the sadness," Urnan said. "Sarah is dead."

"I cannot grieve for her," Eri said with surprising sharpness.

Urnan stared uncomprehendingly at his son. "But here is your daughter," he said as Jerioth came around from the other side of the horses with Leah in her arms.

Eri took a step backward. The baby gurgled happily.

"Look, little one," Jerioth said. "Here is your father." She made to hand Leah to Eri.

"No!" Eri snapped.

Jerioth looked at him inquiringly.

"My hands are soiled," he said quickly. "From my work."

At that moment Baalan came running up, with Sunu directly behind her. After greetings and many questions and excited talk, she took Leah from Jerioth's arms and crooned baby-talk to her, for she was more than willing to call Leah her own.

"Please," Jerioth said weakly, looking at Urnan, not quite knowing how to voice her wishes.

Urnan cleared his throat. "Jerioth has become quite fond of the child. She will be happy to help you care for her, Baalan."

"If she will," Eri announced, "let the child be hers."

There was a long moment of strained silence. Baalan looked stricken. At last Urnan nodded. "As you wish," he said.

There was much information to exchange. It was done over a hastily arranged feast, where father and son took turns talking and a group of the fighting men of Israel crowded around to hear. Moans of anguish accompanied Urnan's account of the battle at Gilboa and its aftermath. Angry mutterings promised resistance to the renewed occupation of Israel.

"Tell me, my son," Urnan finally asked when he and Eri had some moments to themselves, "how is it you cannot bear to look upon your daughter?"

"Because Sarah conspired with the traitor Mered to sell Baalan and Sunu into slavery—and her treachery nearly succeeded. Though I tell myself that the child is flesh of my flesh, I can think of her only as the issue of Sarah."

Urnan was shocked upon hearing of Sarah's perfidy, but he defended her. "She had but a child's mind. When one is very young, it is difficult to think of anyone other than one's self. That is the way she died—as a lost child."

"Let the past go to the grave with her," Eri said.

"So be it," Urnan said sadly. He brightened when Jerioth and Baalan came into the shaded area under the brush arbor where the men were feasting. "I am in need of the services of a Levite priest," he said, winking at Eri.

"To confess your sins?" Eri asked.

"To make this good woman my wife," Urnan said, standing and taking Jerioth's hand.

Tears came to Jerioth's eyes. Though she was a necromancer and had the ability to call up the shades of the dead—an activity that had been outlawed under the rule of Saul and frowned upon by the priesthood—she was a God-fearing woman, a devout Yahwehist. So great was her love for Urnan that she would have endangered her soul by continuing to live in sin with him, had that been his wish. But his decision filled her with joy.

"I am to have a mother," Eri teased, rising to give Jerioth a hug. "And you a grandmother, boy," he said to Sunu, who was standing sheepishly nearby. "Come, pay your respects to your grandmother."

At fourteen, Sunu was officially a man. He had not yet achieved his full growth, but already he was an inch taller than his father or his grandfather, who stood at a fair height. He was an attractive lad, strong of limb and solid of frame like his fathers before him. The blood of old Ur was diluted in him by that of a Hebrew grandmother, Eri's mother, and his own Ammonite mother, but he had been born in Israel. His God was Yahweh. If he had been asked, he would have said that he was a Hebrew—but when he bathed in the sun-heated waters of the Salt Sea, the stamp of the lion's paw was there for his companions to see, a perfect purple impression on his hip.

Sunu shyly draped his arms loosely around Jerioth's shoulders. She laughed and kissed him on the forehead. "Have you no questions for me, who will be your grandfather's wife?"

"Only one, lady," Sunu said.

"And what is that?" she asked.

"Can you cook? My grandfather is terrible at it."

"Give her a chance to get settled," Urnan admonished with a laugh.

"You will live with us, of course," Baalan said. "Our house is much too large for the three of us, and Leah can then be a part of her father's family."

Eri's brows knitted, but he remained silent.

"If you're sure . . ." Jerioth said.

"Of course I'm sure," Balaan insisted. "The men are always away either making war or preparing for it. I will be glad of your company."

"Urnan?" Jerioth asked.

"If it's all right with Eri and Baalan, it's certainly all right with me."

"As Baalan said, it is a big house," Eri said with a grin. "It will be good having you, Father. And you, Mother-to-be."

*   *   *

The wedding ceremony took place with what was, for Jerioth, pleasing dispatch. One of the few priests who had survived Doeg the Edomite's massacre at Nob performed the rite, which was followed by much feasting, much wine, much singing and calling out of good wishes. Eri's house was built with two wings, so there was privacy for the newlyweds. Oddly, Jerioth was shy when she came into the bedchamber clad in clinging, diaphanous white. Urnan laughed when she blushed at his touch.

"It's different," she said in explanation.

He kissed her tenderly. "You know, it *is* different," he said in amazement. There was a sweet element of reverence about it, a newness. Their union was total and highly satisfying, as it had been in the past, but something had been added.

"It was as if I were in bed with a different woman," Urnan said with wonderment as they lay side by side after their lovemaking, breathing hard and warmed by their exertions.

"For you, husband, I will be a different woman every night," Jerioth said.

Urnan groaned. She lifted herself on one elbow and looked at him questioningly.

"Every night?" he said in mock panic.

She laughed and hit him, rather hard, on his muscular shoulder.

He grinned. "Well, maybe every other night."

CHAPTER
THREE

Singly and in small groups, men of Israel sought refuge in Eri's desert stronghold. With the refugees came depressing word of conditions in the north. The Army of the Five Cities controlled all of Israel west of the River Jordan. Among the Rachel tribes, where once Samuel and then Saul had led the resistance, there was no leader to keep the hope for freedom alive.

"But there is David," said young Sunu to a group of men who lounged in the shade of an arbor near the forges.

A clean, hard smell was in the air, the scent of heated iron and burning charcoal. The concealing cliffs echoed a song of power and defiance, manifested in the ringing impact of iron hammer on emerging blade.

"True," answered a warrior of the tribe of Benjamin, "but David is a man of Judah. Moreover, he fought against Saul and the Kingdom of Israel. I, for one, would not follow the lead of a man who is nothing more than a Philistine vassal."

As it happened, Eri and Urnan had approached the group of young men in time to hear the exchange. "I doubt that David would consider himself to be a chattel of the Philistine," Eri put in.

"And yet even you, master," said the young Benjamite, "chose not to go with David, although he was your friend, when he accepted servitude under the Philistines at Ziklag."

"It must be remembered," Sunu remarked, "that David did not fight against Saul at Gilboa."

"As it turned out, he was not needed," said a glum-faced older man.

"I think, my friends," Eri said, "that we have not heard the last of David. My guess is he will now return to his homeland, to Judah."

"Will the men of Judah accept him as their king?" Sunu asked.

Eri shrugged. "Perhaps. It was in Judah that Samuel anointed him. As long as Saul was alive it was not possible for David to rule over his own tribe, for Saul would not have accepted an independent Judah under a strong king. It is possible now because there will be no opposition from Israel and because he is considered by the Philistines to be an ally."

"Is it true, Master Eri, that David is more skilled at the strategy of war than Saul was?"

Eri gave the question some thought before answering, "His victories have been many. But remember, he learned from Saul. He emulated tactics developed by Saul to harass the might of the Philistine army with a small, highly mobile force."

"We, too, can follow Saul's example," Sunu said with the intensity of youth. "From this safe place in the wilderness we can be an army without banners as was Saul's band in the beginning. We can drift like the mists of the morning, letting the winds blow us to the point of least resistance, where we can strike."

Eri was trying to hide his pride as he listened to his son. Sunu had studied the ways of war along with the wisdom of the priests. He was both a scholar and an artisan, for he had not let his studies detract from his training as an armorer.

"The Philistine army is like a tree nourished by long roots," Sunu continued. "The roots run all the way back to the coastal plains. We will travel with the winds and cut the individual roots until the great tree begins to wither."

"And who will lead this army of shadows?" asked the Benjamite.

"We have leaders." Sunu looked up at Urnan. "My grandfather fought with Saul."

Urnan smiled sadly. "Unfortunately, this graying hair does not cover the head of a great leader. I am an armorer."

"But you fought with Saul," Sunu persisted.

"In a losing cause," Urnan said. He was both pleased and saddened by Sunu's eagerness to fight. As for himself, he had seen enough of war. His years made him a member of a small minority; not many men lived to count almost threescore years. Life had not always been kind to him. He had lost two women whom he loved. Now that he had found another love, he was not eager to leave her to pursue the dubious rewards of a soldier. "If there is fighting to be done," he added, "I will leave it to the younger ones while I stay with my family and exercise the skills that I have been given by having been marked by the lion."

"Father, how say *you*?" Sunu asked Eri.

"Certainly the time will not be soon when we can meet the Philistine on equal terms," Eri replied. "Sunu's suggestion to follow the examples of both Saul and David, to hit the enemy where he isn't expecting it and withdraw quickly before he can deploy superior force, is, I would say, the only hope we have."

There was a sudden stir on the outskirts of the settlement. Everyone turned and watched as guards escorted two men over to Eri and Urnan. The newcomers were ragged and soiled, but their bearing was that of soldiers.

"We seek the armorers Urnan and Eri," said the taller of the two.

"You have found them," Urnan said.

"We come to you, master, from Mahanaim in Gilead, from Abner, cousin to our dead king, and from Saul's sole surviving son, Ish-bosheth."

Eri's eyebrows shot up. "Both Abner and Ish-bosheth live?"

"Yes, master. They live to avenge the death of the king and his sons. They live to reestablish the Kingdom of Israel with a son of Saul's blood on the throne. In the name of God, they beg you to move your armory east of the Jordan, where it will be secure behind the natural barrier of the river, and to join with them in rebuilding the Army of Israel."

"We will consider this," Urnan leaped to answer before Eri could speak. "In the meantime, my grandson will see to your refreshment."

"For that we will be grateful."

Eri and Urnan watched for a few moments as Sunu led the visitors back to their house; then they walked off alone, facing the red sun that sank to touch the hills of Judah to the west. The coming night forecast its chill with a small wind.

"My problem with this proposal is my doubt about the leadership of Ish-bosheth," Urnan said after a long silence. "Of all Saul's sons, he is the least likely to have the ability to rule wisely."

"True, but there is Abner to strengthen his backbone," Eri said. "Abner is a good man, a strong man, a fighter."

"But it is not Abner who would sit on the throne of Israel."

Eri halted and faced his father. "There is this: The

men from Gilead spoke of having the armory shielded
by the natural barrier of the Jordan."

Urnan shook his head. "So thought the Canaanites when Joshua's horde appeared on the eastern
bank. No, the trackless wastes afford more protection
than a rather small river. We have been safe here behind the shield of the arid wilderness."

"And yet we owe it to our children and our children's children to free the land."

Urnan looked at his son wryly. "My boy, when
you're older you will find that dying for posterity is a
chilly comfort compared to being in the arms of the
woman you love each night."

Eri laughed. "My father has great wisdom."

"Thank you."

"And the passions of a man half his age."

"For which I thank God."

"What are we to do, then?" Eri asked.

"As we are doing. An army must have weapons of
iron. We will continue to produce them, and we will
supply them to men who are ready and willing to fight
when that time comes."

"You're thinking of David, aren't you?" Eri asked.

"David or Ish-bosheth," Urnan said. "To the Child
of the Lion, it does not matter who wields the product
of his armorer's skill."

"But you don't think that Ish-bosheth is the man
to deliver Israel from slavery."

Urnan shook his head sadly, but tempered his de-
nial by saying, "More and more, Eri, I find myself
thinking like a Hebrew, leaving the final decision up to
God. Oh, I question Him. I ask Him why He saw fit to
have the bodies of Saul and his sons hanging on the
wall at Beth-shan. Jerioth tells me that in my sometimes heated monologues addressed to the God of
Abraham I sound like a Hebrew, and perhaps I have
become so in thought. At any rate, be it God, fate, or
some mindless mechanism of time about which we can

have no inkling, it is not for us to say what will happen."

Eri walked on in silence. The sun was gone now, leaving only a red blaze of fire in the sky far away over the Great Sea.

"When my new mother called up the shade of Samuel from Sheol, he predicted the future," he said. "Perhaps . . ."

Urnan sighed. "I have speculated along those lines myself. Saul called upon the Witch of Endor and learned that he was to die. I have often wondered if the outcome of the battle would have been different had not Saul been convinced in advance of his defeat."

"It does make one think," Eri agreed. "If my mother called up the shade of Saul or Jonathan or even old Samuel, and the shade said that the Philistine would reign triumphant for a thousand years, there would be no reason for us to continue the struggle."

Urnan laughed. "If I thought a shade would so state, I would have Jerioth call him up quickly. Then we could all relax, settle in here, and develop trade with all the nations about us, including the Philistines. We could grow fat and rich because we were supplying needed weapons and tools—with the protection of our former enemies."

"And you would be in your own bed each night," Eri said. "I think you're growing soft, Father."

"That I will admit," Urnan said. "But come, it's going to be dark soon. I don't want to risk breaking a leg trying to negotiate that abominable path down the cliff without the use of my eyes."

In addition to Saul's surviving son, another man felt he had a claim to the throne in the cold, stone-walled room of the citadel at Gibeah. The town itself was deserted. In the streets where children had recently played, a hungry jackal skulked, finding only scraps of leather to fill its empty stomach.

The footsteps of one man rang in the empty halls

of the royal palace, once the pride of a people. There in Saul's throne room was Mered. Mered the traitor. Mered the captain of hundreds, who, jealous of Jonathan's and David's elevation above him in the Army of Israel, had sold his loyalty to Galar of Ashdod, general of the Army of the Five Cities.

As he sat awkwardly on the hewn-stone seat of power, Mered's thin lips pouted. Things had not been going as he had planned. On the excuse that someone in authority had to stay in Gibeah to attend to the king's business, he had not taken part in the battle at Gilboa. When he had heard of the defeat and of Saul's death and that of his sons, Mered was jubilant. He had the word of Galar of Ashdod that he, Mered—who had informed the Philistines of the civil war between Saul and David and who had personally told Galar that it was time to strike the final blow—would rule all the lands of Israel in the name of the conqueror.

Mered had been waiting patiently. He had chuckled when his subjects deserted Saul's capital, fleeing before the rumored coming of the Philistines. He had laughed gleefully because the citizens of Gibeah had no other place to go. They would of necessity quickly return to pay homage to their new king.

He was no longer laughing now, weeks later, for the town was still deserted save for the hungry jackal— and there was no sign of Galar to keep his promise of placing a crown on Mered's head.

Mered decided to travel northward. Hastily throwing together a kit for his journey, he set out from Gibeah in late morning on horseback. He soon encountered Philistine troops engaged in looting and only narrowly escaped with his life by ultimately convincing the soldier in charge that he, too, was in Galar's employ. He learned that Galar was in Beth-shan and headed there accordingly.

Upon arrival in that city he had great difficulty gaining admittance to the building chosen by Galar as his headquarters. Finally, though, he was permitted entry and now stood before the general. Looking at Galar, all of Mered's confidence evaporated. His planned angry demand that the Philistine keep his promise died aborning as he fell to his knees and groveled, whining praise and loyalty to the kings of the Five Cities.

"You waste my time, Mered," the general growled. "Speak your piece and be gone."

"Yes, O mighty warrior. In all humbleness, Great One," Mered said in a fawning, coaxing voice, "I would remind Your Honor that you promised to make me governor over Israel in return for my service to you."

"Service?" Galar asked, raising one eyebrow in disdain. "I did not see you leading my infantry into battle at Gilboa. I did not see your sword red with Hebrew blood. What service can a pig of the hills perform for Philistia?"

"High One," Mered squeaked, full of fear that his words would be taken wrongly but more terrified of not speaking at all, "in exchange for the information I sent you regarding Saul's plans and movements, I was to be named ruler over conquered Israel. Surely you remember, Great One."

Galar, a soldier, a man of action, had no use for traitors. Near him a young aide put his hand on his sword and looked at the general inquiringly.

"No, no," Galar said with a smile. "The pig of the hills is correct. I did make a vow to him. Bring me the *crown*, then, that was on Saul's head under his helmet."

The aide saluted, made a quick exit, then returned with a soiled and bloody piece of cloth in his hand.

"Come forward, Mered," Galar commanded.

Mered scurried to kneel just steps from the general. Galar held the cloth gingerly. "From Saul's head to yours, Mered," he said, smirking at the aides who were trying to conceal their grins.

"What is this, lord?" Mered asked as Galar placed the stained, bloody band around his forehead. He jerked the material from his forehead and looked at it, recognizing it as the headband Saul wore to keep his helmet from chafing. He blanched.

"There is your crown. Wear it with pride." Galar laughed. "Perhaps Saul's shade will be drawn to the smell of his own blood and will give you advice on how best to rule. All of the pigs of the hills are yours to command, *King* Mered," he continued with exaggerated formality. "You have but to ferret them out of their hiding places. Feel free to use my name."

"Lord, lord, what have I done to be treated so unjustly?" Mered wailed.

"Enough!" Galar said angrily. He made a motion of dismissal and turned to his aides. "Throw this pig of the hills out."

Mered was hauled out of the throne room by several guards and unceremoniously dumped into the courtyard, where he landed hard on the flat stones. Betrayed by the master to whom he had sold his honor, his God, and his country, his once-proud mien in tatters, Mered slunk out of Beth-shan and made his way back to Gibeah to seek comfort from his wife, Aiah.

Aiah was a good woman, a God-fearing woman. Without issue of her own, she had loved the childlike Sarah, first wife of Eri, who was the object of Mered's enmity. When Sarah gave birth to the girl, it was almost as if God had gifted Aiah with a granddaughter. And then, suddenly, without explanation, both Sarah and the child had disappeared. Mered had told Aiah that the feckless Sarah had decided to run away with a young man. It was only now, during Mered's absence, that Aiah was finally to learn the truth.

By dint of great persuasion—plus the fact that she garnered a good deal of loyalty—she had managed to keep two servants with her when all the other citizens of Gibeah fled. As it happened, one of the servants was the sister of the men whom Mered had hired to take Sarah and the child away and sell into slavery. The servant was an older woman, kind of heart, and it grieved her to see her mistress mourn. Once too often the servant had entered Aiah's room to find her in tears. Finally it was more than the gentle woman could bear.

"Weep not, lady," she consoled, taking advantage of their solitude that morning.

"Ah, I do miss them so," Aiah said. "She was such a lovely girl. And the child . . . Ah, if I only knew what has happened to them."

"You need not fear for them, mistress," the servant murmured.

"How can you say that? How can you know? We don't even know what sort of man took them away. Perhaps he deserted them. Perhaps he was a knave who lured her away only to profit by selling her into slavery."

"Not so," the servant said somewhat hesitantly. She did not dare tell Aiah that Mered was behind Sarah's disappearance and the order to abandon mother and infant in Gilgal. She measured her words carefully. "You can rest at ease, knowing that Sarah and her child are safe in a city quite far away."

Aiah's tears immediately dried. She approached the servant and looked her directly in the eye. "If you know anything at all about the whereabouts of Sarah and the child, you will tell me this instant."

"It is only that I have heard, lady, that they are safe in another place," the servant said nervously.

"Say more!" Aiah ordered sharply.

The servant was quite concerned. To tell more would be to reveal that it was her brothers who had taken Sarah and the child away and that it was Mered who had ordered the deed. She held her tongue.

Aiah's grief turned to anger. She seized a stout stick and belabored the servant woman painfully. Finally the servant capitulated, and Aiah at last learned the full truth.

When Mered returned several hours later, seeking solace in the arms of the one person in the kingdom whose loyalty to him was certain beyond question, he found a wife he had never known. Where he sought sympathy and comfort, he received a cold glare and colder words.

"Is it true, husband, that you ordered men to take Sarah and her infant from this house and abandon them in a far place?" Aiah demanded without preamble.

"How can you be concerned about that whore and her whelp when I am in deep trouble?" Mered asked, holding out his hands to her.

Aiah backed away. *"How could you?"* she screamed at him. "How could you take that poor girl away from everything and everyone dear to her and leave her alone in some strange place? She looked upon you as a father! That you could betray her trust and use her to further your lot by bowing to Galar is an abomination! God may forgive you, Mered. I will not!"

Just how abominably he had treated Sarah—first misappropriating the title to her family home and all its furnishings, then brutally beating her into submission and raping her before having her hauled away—he didn't dare tell his wife. "Be silent, woman!" he ordered, raising his voice.

Women were chattel. A wife had no appeal from her husband's decision. Mered would not be defied.

"I will not be silent!" Aiah cried. *"I will shout your crime from the rooftops! I will call down the curse of God on you! I will—"*

She was squelched by a backhanded blow that sent her sprawling against a wall. She sank to the floor and sat there weakly, looking up at Mered as if he had mysteriously changed places with a stranger.

"You fool," Mered growled. "I have been betrayed by Galar. I am not to be governor. I will not have the might of the Philistine army to back my authority. When they learn what has happened—"

"What are you saying?" Aiah asked, struggling to her feet. *"You? You* were to be governor?"

"So I was promised."

"By whom?"

"By Galar."

"And why should the commander of the Philistine army promise you so much when you have done nothing for him?"

"Little you know," he sneered. "I have been very valuable to Galar."

Aiah's face burned with her emotions. "How could you be valuable to Galar of Ashdod?" When Mered, realizing that he had already said too much, was silent, she persisted. "What service, Mered?" Her mouth fell open as she remembered all the times he had questioned Sarah about the activities of Eri and Urnan. "By all that is holy, surely not treason! You? A traitor?" she gasped.

"Never say that," Mered snapped. "Never let anyone hear you say that."

She nodded. "No matter. What matters is what you did to Sarah and the child."

"Damn that whore and her bastard! What did I do with them? I'll tell you. I ordered them taken away and abandoned. When last I heard, she sat on the bench of the prostitutes in Gilgal."

Mered turned away, loosened his sash, and hung his sword on its peg on the wall.

"Tell me again," Aiah said as if not able to comprehend.

"She works as the whore she is," Mered said angrily. He whirled around to see that Aiah had loosed his sword from its sheath. He laughed haughtily. "Fool, what would you do with that?"

With a cry of anguish, Aiah plunged the sword to the hilt into Mered's soft stomach. He cried out, his eyes wide with pain and shock, while Aiah, stunned by her action, took her hand off the hilt of the weapon and stepped back. Mered, gasping in terminal agony, used both hands to pull the sword from his stomach. He staggered toward his wife and made one last, desperate slash, opening Aiah's abdomen. Clasping both hands over her bleeding stomach, she sank to the floor. Mered, too, slid to a sitting position, his back against a wall.

"I am slain," he moaned. He needed comfort. He held out his arms to Aiah, who sat mutely, holding in her intestines with both hands.

"I am slain," he repeated. "You have killed me and I you."

She nodded.

"Come, let us die as we have lived—together." He stretched his arms out farther.

"You took from me two people I had learned to love with all my heart," Aiah said in a hoarse whisper. "You delivered Sarah into everlasting shame, and only God knows what will become of the child. I will not be with you, Mered . . . not even in death. You are no longer my husband."

"Aiah . . ." he begged, feeling the dullness of death growing in him.

Thus he died—alone, reaching out to a wife who now felt nothing but contempt and hatred for him. She watched the glaze of oblivion form on his open eyes. His mouth gaped and his tongue protruded as he slid along the wall to lie on his side.

Aiah's own light began to fail. She begged forgiveness from Yahweh in a weak, faltering voice. Her last words were a prayer for Sarah and her child.

CHAPTER
FOUR

Ziklag, the town given to David by the Philistine lord who had engaged his services as a mercenary, was situated in a green and fruitful land on the southern border of Judah. The men of David's small army were eager to be home as they marched southward from the Gilboan hills through the last of the rains—and they were thankful that the Philistine high command had refused to allow them to participate in the battle against Saul.

When they came in view of the town, a groan of despair went up from the ranks. Fires smoldered in burned-out dwellings. Dead animals littered the green pastures.

David spurred his horse and hurried into the town. It was deserted except for a few old ones.

"The Amalekites," an old woman gasped as she

clutched David's arm. "They came in the night and carried away our sons and daughters and all the cattle and everything of value."

At first, when the lords of the Five Cities told David's employer, King Achish of Gath, that David's services as a mercenary would not be needed at Gilboa —lest in the heat of battle he remember his kinship with the Hebrews and desert those who paid him— David had been angry. He had loved Saul with all his heart, yet his reward was the loss of the princess Michal, his first wife, and self-imposed exile to escape the increasingly suspicious Saul's continual efforts to kill him. He would, in fact, have fought against Saul at Gilboa had he been allowed, for his blood was heated by what seemed to be an opportunity to end the long struggle with Israel's king. But he had had time during the march to Ziklag to join most of his men in giving thanks to God that circumstances had delivered him from the sin of shedding the blood of his own people.

Actually, David's consuming rage was directed more toward his situation than toward Saul and the men of Israel who followed Saul's orders. That rage demanded the outlet it had been denied; he found opportunity as he walked through his ravaged town. Among those who had been taken by the Amalekites were his two other wives.

He had only to state his intention to inflict vengeance to revitalize the army. Even though the men were weary from the long march, six hundred immediately set out from Ziklag. Upon arrival at the brook Besor, only four hundred men were still on their feet. The swift pace had thinned the ranks by one third, but those who followed David southward fought against exhaustion because somewhere ahead of them were the Amalekites—and with the enemy each man had a wife, a son, a daughter, all destined for slavery in the filthy desert camps of the nomads.

It was dark when David halted. He was having a

meal of bread, figs, and raisins when two soldiers came to his fire supporting a third man dressed in the rags of a slave, too weak to walk without help.

"We found this one on the field as we scouted ahead," said one of the soldiers.

"To whom do you belong?" David asked.

The slave lifted his head, and there was dignity in his stance as he struggled to stand erect. "I am no man's slave," he said proudly.

"You speak with an odd accent," David said.

"I am Sekmut of Egypt, lord. I was on a diplomatic mission when the Amalekites seized me unlawfully and sought to enslave me."

"Has mighty Egypt fallen so low that her emissaries are not given safe passage?" David mused. "There was a time when a pharaoh would have come thundering up out of Egypt like a devouring lion to remedy such a situation. His men-at-arms would have numbered thousands—ten thousands. The wheels of his chariots would have sent the Amalekites scurrying for their pathetic dens in the desert."

"Alas, lord, that time is past," Sekmut said. "The Two Lands are divided. In the south the priests of Amon hold sway. In the north my master, Paynozem, rules in name only, for he is a vassal of the dogs of the desert, the Libyans."

David was not—at least for the moment—interested in the troubles of old Egypt. "Give him food," he ordered his aides.

They did so with alacrity, and David watched as Sekmut ate hungrily.

"I have had nothing for three days and three nights," Sekmut said, pausing for breath. "I am in your debt, lord."

"Repay me by guiding me to the camp of the Amalekites," David said, "those who burned Ziklag to the ground."

"Give me your word, lord, that you will not kill me

or return me to those who called themselves my masters and I will do so," Sekmut said.

"You have my word."

So it was that David, leading four hundred men, descended upon the Amalekite camp at twilight like a wolf on the fold. The enemy warriors were eating, drinking, and dancing in celebration of their successful incursions into Philistia and Judah, though a few escaped on camels as the Hebrews avenged in blood the burning of Ziklag. When all those who had not fled lay lifeless in the dust, there were joyful reunions. David's two wives flew into his arms, neither of them the worse for her brief captivity. Sons, daughters, and wives embraced their saviors. The spoils of the Amalekites became plunder for David's men. A great herd of cattle was driven back to Ziklag.

With the dry season now well established, David sat in the sun watching children at play. All around him, Ziklag reverberated to the sounds of industry as the residents repaired the damage done by the Amalekites.

David had not had a chance to talk with Sekmut the Egyptian on the return march; therefore, he summoned him now and invited him to sit beside him on a bench. The Egyptian's face was no longer gaunt. He wore a Hebrew robe.

"Tell me more of Egypt," David said. "We were there once, as you know—all the children of Abraham."

"So it is written," Sekmut said. He passed his hand over his forehead. "What shall I tell you, lord? Shall I speak of the shame of falling under the rule of foreigners?"

David shook his head sadly. "We Hebrews know that feeling all too well."

"In that case I will tell you of the beautiful princess who came to the north from the ancient city of On to give herself as wife to a barbarian from the desert.

She came on a barge shining with gold. Fifty and two handmaidens danced on the deck of the splendid vessel. When the princess herself appeared—dressed in white, wearing the crown of upper Egypt on her ebony hair—men had to close their eyes lest they be made sightless by such beauty."

David reached for his harp. It was second nature for him to strum music to accompany a story, usually his own. He listened as Sekmut continued, and his fingers brought forth sweet, soft sounds.

"She had a son, the Beautiful One who came from the south—a strong son with the blood of kings in his veins, a son whose face was bronzed by the olive-dark skin of his father, who was a smith."

David's lyrical fingers paused in their movements. His drifting attention became sharply focused, and he listened intently to Sekmut's next words.

"And on the left hip of the sun-blessed son of the princess was a paw print, as if a lion had touched him with a brand of fire."

"The mark of the lion," David said, astonished.

"So it was said. It was said that the princess Tania—"

"Hold!" David said. "The name of the Egyptian princess was Tania?"

"It was, lord."

"She was the cousin of Prince Kemose, high priest of Amon in the southern city?"

"The same, lord." Sekmut's eyes narrowed. "I am puzzled as to how the fame of the princess and her royal cousin has spread into these hills."

"Tell me the boy's name," David ordered.

"He is called Kaptar. Does his name mean something to you, lord?"

"His name? No. But I know the boy's father. He is Urnan, the smith of Shiloh. He served Saul as armorer. I have heard him speak more than once of his Egyptian wife and his great friend the priest Kemose. And you say the son, Kaptar, is his?"

"Of this there is no doubt," Sekmut said, "for the princess Tania proclaimed it throughout the land, saying, 'My son, Kaptar, is the seed of Urnan the armorer.' "

"The ways of God are strange," David remarked. "I will send word of this to a secret place in the Wilderness of Judah. If Urnan survived the battle at Gilboa, perhaps he will be there. He will be both pleased and saddened to know that he left a son behind in Egypt."

"You will have to tell him, lord, that Princess Tania is dead."

"How so?"

"Musen, the Libyan prince whom she married, gave out the news of her death, saying that she died of fever after giving birth to Musen's son, who was named Namlot. The Oracles say that Namlot will sire a king, and the way things are in Egypt, that is very much a possibility."

David beckoned an aide and instructed him to send a messenger to Eri's wilderness armory immediately. He was interrupted in his purpose by a sudden stirring; a soiled and ragged man was being escorted to him by a brace of guards.

"My lord David," the newcomer gasped, prostrating himself.

"Rise and speak," David said.

"Lord, I have seen a great slaughter," the man said, still lying prone before him.

"Speak, man," David commanded irritably.

"This I have for you." The man lifted his torso just enough to hand David a golden bracelet.

David stared at the object. "This graced the arm of the king."

"In truth," the man confirmed. "It was from his dead arm that I took it after I did his bidding."

"His bidding?"

"I am one of the few who came away alive from Gilboa."

"I pray you, tell me," David said.

"All of the men of Israel are fled, or they lie dead on the field of battle—among them Saul and Jonathan."

"How do you know this?" David asked, leaning forward, a hard light in his eyes.

"I am no braver than others," the man said, as if in explanation. "When the army took flight, I, too, ran, coming only by chance upon the king where he sat with his back against a boulder. He had run himself onto his own sword, but he lived, and his pain was great. He called to me, and I said, 'Lord king, here am I.' 'Who are you?' he asked, and I said to him, 'Sire, I am an Amalekite.' "

David's eyes hardened.

"He begged me, saying, 'Stand close to me and deliver me from my pain.' He said, 'Stand upon me so that your blow will be true and slay me.' I put my foot on him and did as he wished, for it was obvious that he could not live with his wounds so grievous. When he was dead, I took the bracelet that you hold in your hand, lord, to show that it was, indeed, the king."

David lifted his face to the heavens and emitted a great wail. He continued to howl his anguish as he rent his clothing in a traditional showing of grief. Around him the others took up mourning for Saul and for Jonathan and for the house of Israel, fallen by the sword of Philistia.

Suddenly David's sorrowful wailing ceased. His eyes were hard as they sought out the messenger's. "Who are you?" he demanded.

"Sire, I am merely an Amalekite soldier who followed Saul."

David rose to his full height, drawing back his shoulders, his head elevated. "Were you not afraid to lift your hand in violence against God's anointed king of Israel?"

"No, lord," the Amalekite said, "for I did a mercy at the king's own request."

"You *should* have been afraid," David said coldly. "You should have cowered on the earth and begged the king to rescind his request to you." He sighed and motioned to one of his mighty men, who stood nearby. "You have brought it upon yourself, Amalekite," he said. "From your own lips we have heard you admit that you slew the anointed king."

He made a small motion to his warrior, who lifted his sword. The blade made a hiss and then a solid thunk. The Amalekite's head fell from his neck and rolled over once, twice, to lie on one cheek in the dust, the visible eye staring vacantly.

In the middle of the night David sought solace in the arms of his younger wife. Her charms cloyed. Drawing his cloak around him, he picked up his lyre and walked to a promontory above the town. There, alone, he sang to the stars, to the pale, gibbous moon:

"Ye mountains of Gilboa, let there be no dew, neither let there be rain, upon you, nor fields of offerings: for there the shield of the mighty is vilely cast away, the shield of Saul, as though he had not been anointed with oil. . . .

"Saul and Jonathan were lovely and pleasant in their lives, and in their death they were not divided: They were swifter than eagles, they were stronger than lions.

"Ye daughters of Israel, weep over Saul, who clothed you in scarlet, with other delights, who put on ornaments of gold upon your apparel.

"How are the mighty fallen in the midst of battle! O Jonathan, thou wast slain in thine high places. . . . How are the mighty fallen, and the weapons of war perished!"

*   *   *

David's voice had matured from the sweet tenor of youth—the first time he had entered Saul's throne room as a boy and soothed the devil-possessed madness of the king with his songs—to a deep richness. His song soared, then settled; in the town below, it was heard by men waking in the night, and they, too, mourned, although they had fought against Saul more than once. A king was dead, a king of Israel, and nothing would ever be the same again.

David lifted his face to the stars and let his harp fall silent. "What shall I do, Lord my God? Shall I go up into Judah? Whither shall I go now, Lord?" he asked aloud, fairly pleading.

The answer formed in his mind, but it was as if he heard the words with his ears.

"*Unto Hebron.*"

David repeated, "Hebron. Hebron."

Tucking his harp under his arm, he made his way down from the slope and returned to his house. His wife Abigail, who had been the wife of Nabal, the rich man of Carmel in the Hebron mountains, met him with an oil lamp in her hand.

"My husband is restless," she said.

"No longer," David said. "Now I will sleep."

"Come," Abigail said, taking his arm to lead him to her bedchamber. "I will warm you."

"Leave me," David ordered. "Soon the sun will come. Wake the household and prepare it for travel."

Abigail obeyed. First she awakened Ahinoam the Jezreelite, David's second wife.

"But it is too early," Ahinoam complained.

"We are to be ready to travel with the sun," Abigail said.

Ahinoam wiped the sleep from her eyes and sighed in resignation. Her life as a wife of David had not been without its moments of tumult, that was for certain. She and Abigail had accompanied David in his wandering and into exile at Ziklag, where she had been kidnapped by the Amalekites. But David had come to save her before any harm came to her. She had the utmost faith in her husband. She did not bother to ask where they would travel but began immediately to prepare for the journey.

CHAPTER
FIVE

Abiathar, who had escaped Saul's massacre of priests at Nob, found his way to the armory in the Judean wilderness with some difficulty. Worn out and dehydrated and feverish from the sun, he was delivered into the hands of Baalan and Jerioth, who pampered him back to health quickly.

He requested an audience with Eri and Urnan as if the smiths were men of royal blood. "As you know," he began formally, "I was with David during his wanderings and, indeed, in his exile at Ziklag."

"You must have many wonderful stories to tell," Urnan said in an effort to make Abiathar feel comfortable.

"By the grace of God, I do," the priest said with a smile. "I can speak of miracles and things of wonder that could only have been wrought by Yahweh." He lifted his hands. "But that, sirs, is not the purpose of my presence here."

"Are we to understand that you represent David?" Eri asked.

"To assure you that I speak for him," Abiathar said, "he told me to remind you, Eri, that once you solved an odorous problem for him by suggesting that certain items of value only to David be stored in wine."

Eri laughed and turned to Urnan. "Truly, this man has David's confidence. He refers to the bride-price that David paid to Saul for Michal. Saul demanded the foreskins of one hundred Philistine warriors, but the foreskins rotted faster than David could collect them. I suggested that he store the, um, tokens in wine."

"We are satisfied that you speak for David," Urnan said, nodding.

"He is the anointed of God," Abiathar said. "The sacred oil was poured on his head by Samuel himself. So it is that I am here on the business of David, King of Judah."

Urnan's eyebrows shot up. "So soon?" he asked. "We have heard that David and his men now dwell in Hebron, but is he indeed king?"

"Very quickly the men of Judah came to him and exalted him king over the house of Judah," Abiathar replied.

"Could it be, priest," Urnan asked, "that the men of Judah were eager to name David king because of his alliance with Philistia?"

"He is God's man first," the priest said defensively, "and then he is a man of Judah."

"But can you deny that Judah will enjoy a certain amount of security from Philistine attack because the lords of the Five Cities consider David to be their vassal?"

"Neither I nor my king can be held accountable for the opinions held by the lords of the Five Cities," Abiathar said. "Can you deny that it will be a gain, and not a loss, if, by thinking so, the Philistine Galar keeps his scavenging hordes out of Judah?"

"I cannot," Urnan said. "Does David know that there is another king over the Jordan?"

"As you know, Saul had four sons, three of whom died at Gilboa: Jonathan, Abinadab, and Malchishua. His fourth son, Ish-bosheth, survives, having fled the battle at Gilboa with Abner, the commander of Saul's army. Yes, the King of Judah is aware of the ambitions of Ish-bosheth. Indeed, even now emissaries are traveling over the Jordan to negotiate with Abner and the son of Saul in an effort to unite the isolated units and clans of the Twelve Tribes."

"A worthy cause," Eri said. "Tell me, priest, is my old friend well?"

"The king is well. He sends you personal greetings, Eri, and asks me to express his sadness over the death of the prince of Israel who was friend to both of you."

"Jonathan," Eri said sadly. "Ah, if he had lived to fight at David's side . . ."

"Or to fight against David for the seat of power?" Urnan asked.

"Let us leave politics to those best suited to deal with it," Eri said with a bittersweet smile. He faced Abiathar again. "Tell me, priest, what other messages do you carry from David?"

"It is the king's wish that the alliance he once enjoyed with the Children of the Lion be renewed. His words were these: 'Tell them, priest, that Israel needs them. Tell them that their skills and the products of those skills are vital if we are to once again drive the Philistines out of Israel. Tell them that they will be secure in Hebron with me.' "

"He has chosen his capital well," Eri mused. "When I last saw Hebron, it was a well-fortified town."

"It is, sir," the priest said. "And its location atop a defensible hill was one reason the Lord told David to make the town his stronghold. When the Philistine re-

alizes that David is not his puppet, not even the Army
of the Five Cities can dislodge us from our high place
in the heart of Judah."

"Abner and Ish-bosheth would point out that any
attempt to cross over the Jordan by the Philistine army
would be perilous," Urnan said, "that their lines of
communication and supply would be fatally extended.
They would say that our armory would be safer in Gilead than in Judah."

"I think we must all work to avoid that which
would be most harmful to Israel as a whole," Eri said.
"I speak of war between David and Abner."

The priest smiled. "You have expressed the heart
of the problem, sir, by naming Abner as the leader of
the Trans-Jordanians instead of Ish-bosheth. Abner,
being Saul's cousin, is fiercely loyal to Saul's memory,
but it is the opinion of David that he is not convinced
of Ish-bosheth's ability to rule a united Israel. By working together we can win Abner to our side—and do so,
hopefully, without shedding the blood of brothers."

"By 'we' you mean our weapons and David's
army," Urnan said.

The priest nodded. "I know you both loved Saul.
For you, Eri, he was the friend of your youth; for you,
Urnan, he was companion, friend, king. But Saul is
dead, and David is the anointed of God. Israel needs a
strong king—not one who is incapable of ruling in his
own right, not one who can be secure on his throne
only if he is supported there by the arms of a powerful
man like Abner. We can all be grateful to Saul for
showing us the way, for proving that we can stand
against the Philistines and drive them from our nation.
We can follow Saul's example of unifying all Hebrews
—without falling prey to the devils that possessed
him."

Urnan silently took Abiathar's measure, then said,
"I will give you my thoughts in plain words, not with
the unctuous skill of speech possessed by the profes-
sional emissary. You state that David is the anointed of

God, according to Samuel. I have always been suspicious of men who take it upon themselves to speak for God. Perhaps it is my non-Hebrew blood that makes me wonder why God spoke only to Samuel in this matter, why he and he alone heard the divine voice and was chosen to name a king for Israel."

He held up his hand to forestall the priest's objections, then continued, "Saul, too, was anointed by God through Samuel, and God must have been on Saul's side because he drove the enemy back to the coastal plains. Perhaps God did desert Saul. I cannot testify one way or the other on that matter, but I do know that Samuel deserted him in a time of need not only for Saul but for the entire nation of Israel." He shrugged. "I do not hear God's voice, and therefore I have to rely on my own reason and what I hope is some degree of honor. Saul was my king. He was just to me and mine. I will not turn against his son or against Abner, a man who was loyal to Saul."

Abiathar's face was gloomy. "I will carry your words to David." He turned to Eri. "Does your father speak for you?"

"I am an armorer," Eri said. "It is the function of the armorer to forge arms, not covenants. I come from a long line of weapons makers. It is said that we are descended from Cain, who was cursed by God. My ancestors supplied arms to Abraham, but through the ages the Children of the Lion made weapons for others —for satraps and tyrants, for a priest-king of Egypt. Tell David that we will supply weapons to his army to the best of our ability, but we will not deny the same to the Trans-Jordanians, who, after all, have the same cause: to drive the Philistines from the land."

Abiathar nodded, his expression sad. "I will deliver your words."

"Rest here for a few days," Urnan urged in a kindly tone, knowing he had disappointed the priest. "When you have fully recovered from your ordeal, we will send you into Judah with a guide to make your way less difficult."

"You are kind, sir," Abiathar said, bowing.

That evening, after a meal featuring a pie of baked doves—the game provided by Sunu, who had taken the birds with a sling as they came in for water at the spring near the armory—it was Eri who again brought up the subject of kings. "I've been thinking. . . ." he said.

There was a long pause. Sunu went on eating. Jerioth and Baalan cleared the table and came back with a plate stacked high with sweetmeats. Urnan took a handful and chewed slowly, savoring the richness.

"If Israel is ever to be united, it will be under David," Eri finally continued, reaching for his own portion of sweetmeats.

"He is accepted by his own tribe," Urnan said. "But in my opinion his service with the Philistines will prevent his acceptance by the tribes of the north—by Ephraim, Benjamin, Manasseh, and the rest."

Eri shook his head and sighed. "If only Jonathan had lived. Despite Saul's conviction that David hungered for the throne, David would not have usurped it from Jonathan. He would have become Jonathan's good right hand and together—"

"But Jonathan *is* dead," Urnan said pointedly.

"Ah, what would he have to say about a possible confrontation between David and Ish-bosheth?" Eri mused.

"I think blood would support blood," Urnan offered.

"Can you be sure?"

Urnan shrugged.

Jerioth spoke in her low, sultry voice. "If Jonathan could speak to you, would each of you abide by his advice?"

"Without question," Eri said.

"He was a wise man," Urnan agreed.

"Baalan," Jerioth said, turning to her daughter-in-law, "would you please help me darken the windows?"

"What is this?" Eri asked, puzzled.

Urnan laughed. "You wish to consult Jonathan, do you?" he asked. "Well, son, perhaps you'd best be careful about what you ask for in the future, because I have a feeling that you're about to have your desire fulfilled."

Eri suddenly remembered that his stepmother was known as the Witch of Endor, that she was a necromancer. He shivered. "She can truly do this thing?" he asked softly.

"I saw Samuel, dead Samuel, as clearly as I see you," Urnan said. "And he told Saul that he was a dead man."

Eri shook his head. "I'm not sure I want this, Father."

Urnan glanced at his wife. "It seems you're not to have any choice."

Baalan watched with wide, frightened eyes as Jerioth prepared a burner and filled it with unfamiliar herbs and fragrances. Smoke drifted up and was sucked into horizontal motion by drafts coming in through the chinks around the doors and the shaded windows. An aura of unreality settled over the darkened room. Jerioth was staring into the swirling smoke, her eyes unblinking, unnaturally large. Her throat was moving, but no words emerged from her full lips.

Suddenly another presence was in the closed room. Eri felt it, and the hairs stood up on the back of his neck. He glanced at his father. Urnan was staring as if he had been addressed by the Egyptian magic practiced by Kemose.

A strong, manly face materialized in midair. "Who calls?" asked a deep, masculine voice thrillingly familiar to both Urnan and Eri.

"Jonathan, is it truly you?" Eri breathed, awestruck.

The shade turned dark, empty eyes toward him.

"David is the anointed of God," the voice whispered, sounding as if it came from a far distance, down the ringing, empty corridors of an empty cave.

"But he allied himself with the Philistine," Eri said.

"Forgive him. He was our friend. Go to him." The face flickered, faded, then became visible again as it turned. "And you, old friend, master armorer, adviser to my father, the king, you are not wrong in supporting my brother, for he, too, has the blood of Saul. He, too, wants to cleanse Israel of the Philistine. Go to him, Urnan. Only you can convince him and the brave Abner to cast their lot with the king anointed by Samuel in the name of the one God."

"Jonathan?" Eri said urgently as the shade melted into a mist and disappeared.

"He is gone," Jerioth said.

"Mother Jerioth, is it a trick?" Eri demanded. "Do you put things into my mind as my father can when he uses the Egyptian magic?"

"What you heard came not from me," Jerioth said.

"Then we are to be separated?" Eri asked, turning to his father.

"What the shade said makes sense," Urnan said. "If we can be instrumental in creating an alliance between David and Ish-bosheth, traveling in different directions will be a small price to pay."

"I will not abandon this place until I am more certain of the future than I am at this moment," Eri said.

"Leave most of the craftsmen here," Urnan suggested. "They will continue to bleed iron from the stones and fashion it into blades to kill Philistines. Take with you to Hebron the tools and the men necessary to maintain the weapons of David's army. For my part, I will set up a shop east of the River Jordan to show Abner and Ish-bosheth that I come in good faith."

"You will not go without me and our daughter,"

Jerioth said. She had come to think of Leah as her own, and neither Eri nor Baalan disputed her claim.

"To be away from you, wife, is a price I am not willing to pay," Urnan said, smiling and taking her hand.

"Then it is decided," Eri said. He rose. "I'll go tell the priest that he will not have to travel through the wilderness alone with only one man to guide him."

"No one has asked for my opinion," Sunu spoke up, sounding slightly put out. "If anyone cares to know, I will fight with King David of Judah."

Eri nodded in approval.

Baalan's face paled. She cast a quick, frightened glance at her husband before giving her son an incisive look. "Judah has soldiers," she said, "but she has few craftsmen who can fashion a blade of iron that will stand up to the weapons of the Philistines. Let me hear no more talk of fighting, Sunu. Your place is with your father at the forge."

"I promise that I will fight no more than three days in each week," Sunu said, smiling fondly at his mother. "On all other days except the Sabbath I will be at my forge."

"Such big talk," Baalan countered, "from one who but yesterday was running to me to soothe a scraped knee."

Sunu drew himself up to his full height. He was an inch taller than both Eri and Urnan. "Mother, you have not been looking at me lately."

Baalan shook her head wordlessly, gazing at her son with a mixture of pride and fear.

CHAPTER SIX

The healing rays of the sun god, Ra, warmed the old bones of Kemose, King of Upper Egypt and high priest of Amon at Waset. He lay motionless on soft cushions arranged comfortably on a gilded couch in the courtyard of the royal residence. His torso was bare. Even in ill health and at his advanced age he was an impressive-looking man; he had not gone to fat as did many men his age who had access to unlimited amounts of food and drink. He turned onto his side. Old scars, marks of the lash he had felt more than once during his time of slavery on the island of Kittem, scored his back.

Two of his wives, their eyes outlined with kohl, their cheeks red with rouge, sat at a table in the shade of a striped canopy, playing at a child's board game. Their flutelike voices were muted in respect for the sleeping king. There were no children. Kemose would leave no seed when he was at one with eternity to sail across the heavens in the bark of the sun god.

At the slap-slap of hurriedly moving sandals coming down the corridor and into the king's chamber, Kemose stirred. His oldest and most trusted minister—a priest whose natural baldness no longer required that he shave his entire skull—came into the room.

"Is he awake?" the old priest asked the wives in a whisper so loud it could quite possibly have awakened the dead.

"He is now," Kemose muttered, rising on one elbow.

The minister bowed. "Great king, live forever!"

"We are alone here," Kemose said. "There is no need for formality."

"Yes, sire, forgive me." The old man fell silent.

Kemose looked heavenward and rolled his eyes impatiently.

"There is news," the minister said hurriedly. "From the delta."

Kemose frowned. The last news he had received from the cities of the delta had cost him dearly, for it had been word of the death of his cousin, Tania. "I am not sure I want to hear any more news," he said.

"Great king . . ."

Kemose sighed and closed his eyes. He let his head fall back onto the pillows.

"The news is this: Your brother, Paynozem, live forever, is dead."

"By the beard of Osiris," Kemose whispered as he sat back up. "The details, old man. Speak!"

"Great king, details are not to be had. The messenger has traveled far, but his words are few. He was dispatched while the king's body was still warm. He knows only that Paynozem collapsed at a state banquet and that his son, Amenemopet, will take the throne and will perform the ceremony of the opening of the mouth when Paynozem is placed in the abode of eternal rest."

Kemose knew little of his brother's son. "Tell me about Amenemopet."

The priest swallowed nervously. "Great One," he said softly, "our relations with the court of Paynozem have not been, ah, intimate since the death of your cousin, may she live forever."

Kemose stared at the minister. "When the cat is ill, the mice play at will," he said. "You're telling me that we have no intelligence from the court of my late brother, that the priesthood of Amon—rulers of one half of the world's greatest nation—knows nothing of the man who will sit on the throne of Lower Egypt."

The old man bowed in confusion.

"I know, I know," Kemose said. "He is my nephew. It is I who should know him. I should have maintained contact with Paynozem's court."

He was not a man to blame others for his own weakness. His health had begun to deteriorate even before word of Tania's death had been brought to him. It was not only for reasons of health that he found himself becoming disinterested in affairs of state, leaving the running of the kingdom to his ministers, but his once magnificent body was failing him in various painful ways. For weeks, during his last siege of incapacitation, he had been suffering the pain of the damned as poisons built up under the large teeth in his lower jaw, swelled his face to enormous size, and lanced agony throughout his entire system. Only in the last two days had the poisons finally eaten their way through bone and flesh to erupt into his mouth in vile-tasting putrescence.

Frustration and disappointment also played a part in his wish to step down from the high priesthood, but there were complicating factors that delayed his decision. He had always entertained a faint hope that it would be Tania's son, Kaptar, who inherited his titles and would sit on the throne of Upper Egypt. Indeed,

he had worked for years to lay the groundwork for
Kaptar's succession, only to be thwarted by a powerful
clique of opposition among the Amon priesthood who
said that Kaptar's Mesopotamian blood from his father, Urnan the armorer, made him ineligible for the
throne.

It would have been so simple—and so satisfying—
to declare Kaptar coregent, to hand over the responsi-
bilities of power to a young, vital man with the energy
to cope with the chaotic conditions that prevailed in
the Two Lands. Had not old Ikkur, high priest of the
twin temples built by the great Ramses beyond the
First Cataract, prophesied that Kaptar would be instrumental in reuniting the two kingdoms?

Kemose was tired. The suppurating cavities in the
bone below his worn, painful teeth were healing, true,
but he had been severely weakened by the long period
of exquisite pain, a pain that could not be dulled by all
the potions of the physicians nor by the potent fer-
mented products of the brewer's art.

"Great One, we must send a representative," the
priest said.

"Yes," Kemose said. "Bring Kaptar to me. If my
guess is right, you will find him in the royal armory."

"It will be done," the priest said, bowing backward
out of the royal presence.

Kaptar was exactly where his uncle had expected
him to be. Kemose had succeeded in giving his nephew
one title and the position that went with it: armorer to
the king. Unlike Kemose, whose faculties had been
dulled by pain and ill health, the thirty-one-year-old
son of Urnan and Tania knew that he would never follow his uncle to the throne. He had long since dis-
counted the prediction made by old Ikkur—the priest
who was living out the last days of his life in a deserted,
vandalized temple in the land of the black barbarians—
that he, Kaptar, would be the man who reunited Egypt.
He was content to work at his forge, to use the strength
of his arm to pound out iron blades for the king's army,

and to fashion delicately beautiful golden jewelry for the ladies of the court—many of whom rewarded his generosity with gifts of their own in the form of warm, loving arms; softness and heat; ecstatically lubricious secret depths; and an unacknowledged family consisting of one daughter and two sons, both of the latter bearing the mark of the lion.

Coming into the king's chamber, Kaptar was saddened to see Kemose so pale, so thin, so sapped of vitality. He sat on the edge of his uncle's couch and took his hand.

"You sent for me, Uncle?"

"I am sad, son of my cousin."

"The physicians say the malevolence has burst forth from your teeth, and now you will be relieved of pain," Kaptar said optimistically.

"Pain," Kemose said. "Pain is nothing to one who has felt the agony of the slaver's lash on his bare back, the agony of despair when there is no hope—agony for which the only remedy is escape, either literally or through death. Pain? Ha!"

"What troubles you, then?" Kaptar asked.

"It troubles me that when this arm was strong"—he lifted his shrunken right arm with difficulty—"I did not use it to lay about me and remove all those who oppose you as my rightful heir."

"Uncle, that is debris from the past. It floated away down the sacred river many inundations ago. I am content. I will serve the man who succeeds you—and that will be many years from now—as I have served you."

Kemose lifted Kaptar's tunic and touched his finger to the purple paw mark of the lion high on his nephew's side. "As an Egyptian you will be loyal. As the son of your father you will not be content without the smell of charcoal and hot iron in your nostrils. In that you will be true to the blood of both your parents."

"Yes," Kaptar said.

"You are wrong in one thing, though," Kemose added. "It will not be years before I go to the house of the dead." He held up his hand to stop Kaptar's protest. "Before I go I must ask a thing of you."

"You have only to speak."

"Paynozem is dead."

"May he live," Kaptar responded automatically.

"You will be our representative at the crowning of his son and at the final ceremonies of his ascension to godhood."

Kaptar's heart sank. The last thing on earth he wanted to do was to travel to the city where his mother had died. For a long time that had not been true. For many miserable months he had burned with the need to return to the north and kill his stepfather, the Libyan Musen—the man who had robbed his mother of eternity. His basic common sense had prevailed over his desire for vengeance. He was only one man. Once he had dreamed of leading an army down the Nile, but that possibility was long past. Even if he could somehow get close enough to Musen to drive his blade into the Libyan's black heart, he would not live to savor his revenge. He chose life not only for selfish reasons, however. Without him his uncle, the man who had been a father to him, would be alone.

"Uncle," he said, "ask me to go into the desert, as we once did together, and slay a lion with my bare hands, but please don't ask me to go to the city of On. Don't ask me to smile and pretend that I do not wish Musen's death."

"I have never understood your violent hatred of the man," Kemose said. "True, he is an enemy of Egypt. True, he married your mother after your father was exiled from Egypt by Paynozem. It would be natural to have a distaste for Musen, but your venom is, I feel, overdone."

Kaptar was silent.

"I thought you might be interested in seeing your brother," Kemose said with a sly smile. It gave him

pleasure to refer to the delicious secret that was shared
only by the two of them: The boy whom Musen called
his own and had named as his heir had been fathered
not by the Libyan but by an Egyptian commoner, a
man deliberately chosen by Tania, who traced his lin-
eage back to the time of Ramses the Second. Thus had
Tania cut off the seed of the man who aspired to put
his son on the throne of not only Lower Egypt but of
the Two Lands.

Kaptar was troubled. "There is something, Uncle,
that I have never told you."

Kemose lifted his eyebrows in question. "It is not
like you to keep secrets from me."

"I did so for your own good . . . or so I thought,"
Kaptar explained. "You were ill when I came back
from"—he paused—"my mother's entombment."

"Let me be the judge," Kemose said sternly.

"This is why I must not go near Musen. It was he
who killed my mother."

Kemose's eyes widened. "How do you know this?"
he demanded, his voice regaining some of its old thunder.

"There is more," Kaptar said. "You recall that my
mother told me in a letter entrusted to Cefut, the high
priest of Amon at On, that Musen was not Namlot's
father."

"Yes, yes," Kemose said impatiently.

"What I did not tell you is this, and the information comes again from the priest: Not only did Musen
himself kill my mother, he dismembered her body and
fed it to the crocodiles of the sacred river. He has
doomed her *ka*, her soul, to wander forever between
reality and the netherworld."

Kemose's face went deathly pale. He struggled for
breath and seized his heaving chest with both hands.
Kaptar dampened a cloth in a bowl of cool water and
applied it to his uncle's forehead.

"By all the gods," Kemose gasped, "tell me it isn't
true!"

His uncle's severe reaction was just what Kaptar had feared it would be, what had kept· him silent all these years. But the damage was done, and so he proceeded.

"The body of a prostitute was prepared in the house of the dead, wrapped in royal swathing, and placed in the separate tomb that Musen assigned at the last moment," he told Kemose.

"She—Tania's body—is not in the tomb prepared for Musen?"

"It is not."

"Then it must be true," Kemose said. "Otherwise the Libyan would not give up the prestige of being entombed with a royal princess." He stared at Kaptar, his face ashen. Sweat was breaking out on his forehead and his naked chest. "So said the priests of Amon?"

"So they told me. So you see that if I come near Musen, I will have to kill him."

"No, no!" Kemose said, lifting one hand. He was recovering from the pains in his chest, although he was still filled with horror. His cousin, his loving and beautiful cousin, companion of his youth, friend of his adulthood, would never find peace in the afterworld. Eternity had been denied her. He lifted himself on one elbow. "You must go. Furthermore, you must ingratiate yourself with Musen. Nothing must be allowed to happen to the boy, to the child Musen calls Namlot, for he is Egypt's revenge. You understand that, don't you?"

"I fear that the sight of Musen will make me lose my reason and that I will be forced to kill him."

"No, you must not! Would you negate the great service done for Egypt by your mother for the sake of momentary satisfaction? Think of her sacrifice. She left her beloved home to become the wife of a man she loathed. She did it for Egypt. She realized even better than I that the Libyans would be victorious one day. She knew that a king of Libyan blood would be on the throne of Lower Egypt not long after the death of Paynozem and that one day the Libyan dynasty would rule

all of the Two Lands. By her actions she deprived them
of their victory. She took a common Egyptian soldier
into her bed and accepted his seed, and in doing so she
assured that an Egyptian king would sit on the throne."

Kemose suddenly laughed in delight—though the
laugh abruptly broke off in severe coughing. When he
had regained his breath, he said, "Don't you see the
exquisite irony of it? Bringing about the death of one
Libyan, Musen, would be satisfying, true—but to deprive them of the throne?" He chuckled again. "De-
lightful."

"But they won't know," Kaptar argued. "They
won't know that Namlot has no Libyan blood. Paynozem's son will be king in the north. If Namlot ever
takes the throne he will have a Libyan queen, and
there will be Libyan blood on the throne as the dynasty
continues."

"No, because you will see to it that Namlot does
not take a Libyan wife. Look, nephew, these barbarians
can be more respectful of our traditions than we at
times because they want so badly to possess the great-
ness of being Egyptian. With you in the court to remind them of the traditions, you can perpetuate Tania's
revenge. Remind them that the legitimacy of a king
comes only through marriage to a royal princess. Paynozem had daughters. The man who follows me here in
Waset will probably have daughters. It will be up to you
to see to it that young Namlot takes a wife with the
blood of the old pharaohs—and to protect your
brother until he wears the crown."

Kemose coughed again, putting his hands to his
chest. "Perhaps," he whispered, "it would be well if you
called my physician."

Kaptar stayed while the physicians fussed over
Kemose. At last, wearier than he had ever been,
Kemose ordered the priests from the chamber and
called Kaptar to his side.

"They lie to me, nephew," he said. "They tell me

that the pain I feel is not from my heart but from something that I have eaten." He laughed weakly. "Something I have eaten? With these?" He opened his mouth and pointed to his worn, blackened teeth.

Kaptar did not flinch at the stench.

"My time is soon. You must go."

"If your time is soon, my place is here at your side," Kaptar protested.

"One of my last official acts will be to provide you with a royal dhow and a military honor guard to see you safely downriver," Kemose said. "Prepare yourself to leave with the morning sun."

"This is truly your wish?"

Kemose nodded. "My wish, my legacy to you, and my order to you. You will be supplied with the means to live well in the north. You will be a man of some wealth."

"Let me stay with you," Kaptar said, making one last plea.

Kemose shook his head sadly. "Obey me, nephew."

Kaptar nodded. "Yes."

"Soon I will join Tania. Perhaps I will see your father."

"Yes," Kaptar said, fighting to hold back his tears.

"If so, I will tell my old friend Urnan that the son of his loins is a *man*."

CHAPTER
SEVEN

Father, son, and grandson parted with emotional embraces. Eri's group, including his son, Sunu, would head westward, toward Hebron. Urnan and Jerioth, with the child Leah, would be heading toward the north.

Eri and Urnan had orginally planned to leave Sunu in charge of the wilderness armory. He was young, but he was a Child of the Lion, and his skills and knowledge would have been sufficient to keep the armory in operation in the absence of his elders. But Sunu would have none of that scheme. He had insisted on going with Eri and Baalan to Hebron. Since he was a man, almost fifteen years old, Eri did not impose his will.

Eri watched his father, daughter, and stepmother cross the barren plain. He was troubled. To contact Abner and Ish-bosheth in Mahanaim, Urnan would have to travel into the areas under Philistine domination and cross over the River Jordan in the vicinity of Jericho or Gilgal.

"God will protect them," Baalan said, reaching across from her fine horse to touch Eri's arm.

"So I pray."

Urnan and Jerioth were less splendidly mounted. Deeming it unwise to risk an encounter with the enemy while riding Philistine horses, they rode utilitarian beasts of burden. Urnan's legs almost brushed the ground as his donkey crossed the terrain at a steady, brisk pace.

Eri lifted his hand in salute as Urnan pulled his animal to a halt on the crest of a hill to turn and wave one last time before disappearing from sight. With a resolute sigh, Eri kicked his horse to a walk and led his band onward.

The journey to Hebron was a short one. It was pleasant to ride from the barren aridity of the wilderness into greenness, to see fields of grain and orchards of olives and fruit on the hillsides. At roughly a half-day's ride from Hebron a mounted troop of soldiers halted the caravan, which consisted of six smiths trained by Eri and Urnan, two servants, and several pack animals carrying weapons and the tools needed to set up an armory in David's city. As it happened, the leader of the patrol from Hebron was a young officer whom Eri knew well.

"The king will be filled with joy," the officer told Eri.

He was not wrong.

A runner had ridden ahead to bear news of Eri's coming, and David was waiting at the gates of Hebron for his old friend's arrival. He was wearing a kilt and tunic much like that worn by Philistine officers. He stood with his strong legs spread, his arms crossed on his chest. His hair was long, gathered at the nape of his neck and secured with a leather thong.

"He is a king," Baalan said in a voice filled with admiration.

"So Samson must have looked," Eri said.

His old companion was considerably more mature than when last they were together. His arms bulged with muscle, and it was easy to understand how, even as a boy, David had slain a lion with nothing more than his shepherd's staff and his bare hands.

Eri pulled his mount to a stop, lifted his left leg over the horse's neck, and slid to the ground.

"God is good," David said earnestly, and there were tears in his eyes. He stepped forward, and Eri felt the strength of his arms as they embraced.

"Ah, my old friend," David said, smiling as he looked into Eri's eyes. "I don't have to ask if you are well."

"Nor I you," Eri said.

David's eyes looked past Eri. He walked over to stand at the head of Baalan's horse. "Baalan, wife of my friend, you are as beautiful as ever. I welcome you to Hebron."

"We are honored," Baalan said.

"And this is the young lion," David said, putting his hand on Sunu's shoulder. "There is no mistaking that he is your son, my friend."

"I will be honored to serve you," Sunu said, his voice deep with emotion.

David smiled. "And I will be honored to have you, young lion."

He turned and lifted a hand. A young soldier leaped forward. "Take the wife of my old friend to my house," David instructed. He turned back to Baalan. "My wives, Ahinoam and Abigail, will welcome you. I will send your husband along later, but first we have much to share."

As the young soldier led Baalan's horse away to David's house, Eri looked around. He spotted an open space with plenty of room to construct arbors to shade the forges. "We will set up shop there," he told Sunu, pointing. "Will you see to the unpacking of the equipment?"

"I will, Father." Sunu beckoned to the smiths, and the caravan moved off toward the area chosen by Eri.

David turned to Eri, slapping him resoundingly on the shoulder. "Now, my friend, what have you brought me?"

"For the King of Judah, for the man who will take up the work of Saul, I have swords and spearheads and the iron tips of arrows."

"Ha!" David cried gleefully.

Eri held up his hand. "For a vassal of the Philistine, however, I have nothing more than greetings."

David threw back his head and roared with laughter. "Then, my friend, let us have a look at these weapons and determine if you still have the skill you once possessed." He put his arm around Eri's shoulder. "Not that I doubt you, but your blades must be strong and keen to cut through the shields of Galar's infantrymen."

Eri nodded. His question had been answered.

"Understand, however, that we will not challenge the might of the Army of the Five Cities immediately," David continued. "For a time it will serve our purposes to let the Philistines continue to look upon me as an ally. There is challenge enough in bringing together all the men of Judah. Once that is accomplished, we must include all others who will fight for the freedom of the seed of Abraham."

Eri clasped David's arm. "It pleases me to stand with you once more in united purpose. Count me, King of Judah, as one of your own."

"That title is new to me," David said with a sheepish smile, "and not all men use it. It will never be necessary between you and me. I will pray to God that I am worthy of your confidence."

"You have chosen well in establishing yourself here," Eri said, taking in the town as they walked to where Sunu had led the pack animals.

"If it ever came to it, we could hold off a sizable army," David said. He turned to look at Eri and halted his steps briefly. "Forgive me. In my joy at seeing you again I have forgotten to inquire about your father."

"He is well."

"Thank God. I feared that he perished with Saul."

"No. Though he was with Saul when the king died."

"Did Jonathan fall beside his father?" David asked, continuing on.

"No, Jonathan was fighting on another part of the field."

David's voice thickened. "How I do miss him."

"Yes," Eri said. "I, too."

"What a king he would have made."

"Yes."

"But Urnan is well?"

"He's married again."

"Good for him!"

"A woman of Endor."

"Ah, there must be a story there."

"A long one," Eri said, "one that begins before the battle of Gilboa."

"I look forward to hearing it."

They reached the area Eri had chosen. Men of Hebron were busily unloading the pack animals, and Sunu was directing the smiths in setting up their forges. An arbor was already being raised.

After admiring the weapons from the forges of the desert armory, David led Eri to his home, where a feast had been laid. Following the meal, while David strummed his lyre, Eri told the story of how Urnan and Jerioth had met—and of all that had followed.

"Ah, no!" David groaned, learning of the prediction of the shade of Samuel. "How terrible it must have been for Saul to go into battle knowing that he was doomed, knowing that he would lose not only the fight but his life."

When Eri finished his tale, having arrived at an

account of Urnan's coming to the armory in the wilderness, David was reflectively silent, his harp stilled.

"You said that you wanted union with all men who would fight for the freedom of Israel," Eri said.

David nodded.

"Even now my father goes to Mahanaim. To Abner and Ish-bosheth."

David's eyes narrowed.

"He is your friend, my father," Eri said.

"So I always counted him."

"His interest, too, is in throwing off the Philistine yoke."

"By backing the last surviving son of Saul?"

"By doing what he can to see to it that the sons of Abraham fight the Philistines and not each other," Eri said.

"Well, Abner is a good man," David said grudgingly. "He's a brave and loyal man."

"I think so," Eri said.

"I could work with Abner."

"And Ish-bosheth?"

David looked up from his lyre. "That will be up to Ish-bosheth. The next king of Israel was to be Jonathan, not a man named originally for a Canaanite god. You know that he was christened Esh-baal."

"I can see why the name was changed," Eri said dryly. "It wouldn't do for the son of a king of Israel to be called after a heathen god."

"I'm not sure which is best," David said with a shrug. " 'Bosheth' means shame. How can a king be called a man of shame?"

Eri sipped wine before saying, "There can be but one king if the Philistine is to be driven from Israel."

"Eri, I did not ask Samuel to anoint me in the name of God, and you, above all others, must know that I was loyal to Saul, even when he sought my death."

"I know, I know. And I also know this: A king is much more than a title." He remembered Baalan's words when she saw David standing outside the gates of Hebron. A king was not merely a political leader. He had to lead with the strength of his sword arm and his skill in battle. He was at the forefront. He could not stand on a hilltop and let a man like Abner stand in for him.

"As you said," Eri continued, "Abner is a good man. Perhaps he will also be a sensible man. The people of Judah have accepted you as God's anointed. Since Judah is not occupied by the Philistines, it will make an effective base of operations for movement northward into the lands of the Rachel tribes—first Benjamin and Ephraim and then on to Manasseh and Issachar and the rest."

David laughed. "I have missed your optimism and enthusiasm, my friend. With you at my side—" He stopped and eyed Eri. "Am I to understand that Urnan's mission will be to effect some sort of compromise between me and Ish-bosheth?"

"The tongue can be a sharp weapon, but it does not cut flesh. No blood is shed while men are talking. If I may make a suggestion?"

"Of course."

"After giving my father time to feel out Abner and Ish-bosheth following his arrival in Mahanaim, a royal visitation from the King of Judah?"

"Not without invitation," David said firmly. "Ish-bosheth would see an unannounced visit as aggression."

"An emissary, then."

David nodded. "A man I can trust implicitly."

"Yes."

"Then choose your time," David said with a grin.

"Me?"

"Who else?"

"I am an armorer, not a diplomat."

"A man I can trust implicitly," David repeated.

Eri shook his head ruefully, made a mock bow, and said, "I hear and obey, O king."

David grimaced. "That's settled, then."

Once again he strummed his lyre and seemed to retreat inside himself. The women came edging back into the room as he began to sing his lament for the fallen.

"Ye daughters of Israel, weep over Saul, who clothed you in scarlet, with other delights, who put on ornaments of gold upon your apparel. . . ."

When David's lament ended, there was a long silence. He abruptly brightened, telling Eri excitedly, "But I have forgotten altogether, good friend! Have you ever suspected that you might have a brother in old Egypt?"

Eri grinned. "Well, my father was in Egypt when he was much younger. Knowing him, I would not be surprised."

"Well, a brother you have, and he is not the sprout of some concubine or woman of the streets. He is Urnan's legitimate issue, the son of a princess of Egypt."

Eri lifted his wine cup, his eyebrows raised in surprise and interest. "This is a tale I must hear."

Sekmut the Egyptian was immediately summoned. Once more he told of a princess who had loved and lost, who gave birth to a son after his father had been driven out of Egypt not knowing that he had sired a child.

"The mark," Eri said, fascinated, "is it like this?" He lifted his tunic and exposed the purple paw mark on his side.

Sekmut leaned close. "Exactly. But higher on the hip."

"A brother . . ." Eri murmured. "My father must hear of this." He frowned. "And of the death of the princess Tania." He turned to David. "Perhaps I will go to Gilead before I had planned."

Baalan smiled at her husband. "Please give me some notice so that I can be ready."

He touched her cheek fondly. "You won't have to journey again, for this time I will travel fast and alone," he said. "I know of no safer place for you, the one thing I treasure most dearly in this life, than with the king here in Hebron."

Eri's solitary journey would take him through country ruled by the Philistines. His mount, like Urnan's and Jerioth's, was a lowly ass; his dress was that of a hill country farmer. He had delayed his departure for a day to have some time alone with Baalan.

He carried David's instructions in his head. "Tell them," David had said, "that the men of Judah have anointed me king over them and that I welcome alliance with all who would join the fight against our common enemy. Make it clear, as diplomatically as possible but unquestionably, that the Army of God will be under my command and my command alone."

Eri had told David how the men of Jabesh-Gilead had removed the bodies of Saul and his sons from the walls of Beth-shan. Hearing this, David had instructed, "Then first go to Jabesh. Give the men of that city my praise for their bravery and for their loyalty to Saul. Tell them our intentions—and tell them that should they choose to fight at David's side, he will return to them the same loyalty shown by Saul when he was king." He had paused, looking away. "And Eri . . ."

"Yes?"

"Where Jonathan is buried? Under the tree?"

"Yes."

"Kneel for me. Say a prayer for his soul in my name."

"I will," Eri had vowed.

Although distances in the land promised by God to Abraham were not great, the mountains and rugged terrain made travel difficult. Eri rested with David's family near Bethlehem, then entered the land of Benja-

min east of Jerusalem. He passed near enough to Gilgal to see the tumbled walls and other destruction left
by the Philistines. Somewhere in the town, in a tiny,
littered, weed-grown garden behind a foul hovel, lay
Sarah, the love of his youth, his first wife. He could no
longer bring himself to condemn her for her actions.
Life had been unkind to her, making her so weak that
she could not endure the misfortunes that had been
her lot. He saw now that Urnan was right: She had
been nothing more than a child and no more responsible than a six-year-old for her actions in trying to doom
Baalan and Sunu to a life of slavery.

He had plenty of time to think as he rode northward through Gad, past Penuel and Succoth. In thinking of Sarah he was painfully reminded that he had a
daughter—a daughter whom he had, in effect, dis-
owned when he allowed Jerioth and Urnan to take her
as their own. The fault was not with the child. Some of
the grim old Yahwehists claimed that the sins of the
fathers were visited upon the sons. Eri was highly respectful of the God of his mother, and when he prayed
at all it was to Yahweh, but he could not accept the
tenet that Sarah's mistakes should somehow bring cen-
sure to Leah, child of her womb.

At last he reached Jabesh-Gilead, where, as a representative of David, he was made welcome. During
the feast that was prepared for him, he extended
David's greetings to the elders and repeated David's
praise of their courage and loyalty to Saul.

"Saul's son lives," said Joktan, the captain who
had led the raid to recover the body of Saul and his
sons.

Eri was not surprised to find that the Trans-
Jordanians were loyal to the memory of Saul. "To
match Saul's achievement of driving the Philistine from
Israel," he said, "all Hebrews must fight together. The
men of Gilead must stand side-by-side with the men of
Judah. I am here to ask Saul's son and his general,
Abner, to stand in solidarity with David of Judah."

"We stand with Abner and with Saul's son,"
Joktan said. "I pray God that I will never be asked to
lift my blade against any man with the blood of Abraham in his veins."

That was the extent of the commitment from the
men of Jabesh. They would follow Abner and Ish-
bosheth, but they agreed with David that the Philistines
should be driven from Israel.

Eri took his leave, and as he had promised David,
he knelt under the tree where the ashes of Saul and
Jonathan were buried and prayed to God in the name
of the king of Judah. Then he departed for Mahanaim
to see his father.

The trip was a short one through fertile countryside. He entered the city without fanfare, a simple hill
farmer on his donkey. He found Urnan by following his
nose and ears to a smithy where charcoal glowed and
hammers rang and heated iron gave off its special odd
but not unpleasant odor. He stood behind Urnan for
several minutes, watching in admiration as a molten
length of iron was shaped skillfully into a blade. When
at last Urnan plunged the iron into water to temper it,
Eri stepped forward.

"Not a bad blade," he said, "but it must be both
strong and keen to slice through the leather body armor of the enemy."

Urnan's head jerked around in surprise. "But
you're in Hebron!"

"I was until some days past."

With a cry of joy, Urnan swept Eri into his arms.

"It's only been a few weeks," Eri protested.

Urnan shrugged as he pulled back. "You're my
only son."

"Not so," Eri said with an impish smile.

Urnan looked puzzled.

"There is an Egyptian emissary in Hebron," Eri
said. "He knew the princess Tania."

"By God!"

"Tania gave birth to a son eight months after you

left Egypt, Father. His name is Kaptar. He bears the mark of the lion and is court armorer to Kemose, King of Upper Egypt."

"Is it true?" Urnan asked, stunned.

"So says the Egyptian."

"Kaptar? You say his name is Kaptar?"

"In addition to his skill at the forge, he is, the Egyptian said, an accomplished warrior. Some say he will sit on the throne of Upper Egypt when Kemose is dead."

"A king! I have sired a king! By God!"

Eri laughed. "This news that I have an Egyptian brother is more of a surprise to you than to me, isn't it?"

"Indeed, it is. Tania thought she was barren." Urnan removed the thick leather apron that protected his front. "Ah, Eri, you should see Egypt." He laughed. "Perhaps we will see it together. After all, if I have a son who is a king, the least I can do is visit him." He was silent for a few moments. "And Tania. I think she would have aged well. She's a mature woman now." He chuckled. "Though no doubt hiding the silver in her hair under a wig as black as the underworld."

Eri put his hand on his father's shoulder. "The Egyptian had news of the princess," he said solemnly.

Something in his son's voice warned Urnan. "Tell me quickly so that be it pain or joy it will be over."

"Father, she lies in her tomb."

"Ah, God!" Urnan moaned, feeling a stab of loss as vivid as if he had held Tania in his arms only moments past. He was silent for a long time before speaking. "Well, it has been many years, and we have been as the dead for each other because of the tyranny of distance."

"You loved her very much."

"I called her my lotus blossom. My blossom of the Nile." He sighed deeply. "And did the Egyptian speak of the political situation in the Two Lands? Of my friend Kemose?"

"The Two Lands are separate. A weak king sits on the throne of Lower Egypt. For all practical purposes the Libyans control the rich delta and the oases, but Kemose rules in Upper Egypt."

"So to greet my old friend and the son whom I have never seen I would have to make my way through the land controlled by the Libyans—by Musen, I assume."

"I don't think you're going to be traveling anywhere for a while," Eri said.

"I know, I know," Urnan said. "Work. There's work to be done."

"For Ish-bosheth?" Eri asked, waving his hand to indicate the shop.

"For Abner's army." He shrugged. "The armorer works where he is needed."

"I bring a message from David for Abner and Ish-bosheth."

Urnan chuckled as he eyed his son's ragged attire. "You don't look like an ambassador from a king."

"Perhaps I will when you take me to your house, where I can wash away the dust of the road and change into clothing that is more befitting."

The walk to Urnan's house was a short one. Jerioth greeted Eri with genuine warmth, which he returned in equal measure. Then he squatted to put his face on a level with Leah's. She was learning to walk by holding on to Jerioth's robe.

"And how is Leah?" Eri asked.

"Tell your father that you're fine," Jerioth said.

Leah put a thumb into her mouth and shook her head.

Jerioth smiled at Eri's questioning look. "We talk to her about her father. She is blood of your blood, flesh of your flesh. She will come to love you."

"Do you think so?" Eri asked uncertainly. The little girl had Sarah's face in miniature, including her snapping brown eyes and gleaming black hair.

"We will see to it," Jerioth promised.

"Refresh yourself," Urnan said. "I'll tell Ish-bosheth and Abner that you're here. I'll be back for you in a short while."

"Give me a chance to prepare him some food," Jerioth said.

"That I will, dear wife."

In fact, Urnan was back before Eri had finished eating, saying that Ish-bosheth would see him immediately.

Wolfing down the remains of his meal, Eri rose and accompanied Urnan to the finest structure in Mahanaim. There Saul's son, a slim and refined man who lacked the stature of the Tall King, sat on a thronelike chair in a large, elegant room. Abner, whose appearance bespoke exactly what he was—a man of action, a mighty warrior—stood by his side. As Eri and Urnan entered, a court attendant stepped forward and said in a loud voice:

"You are in the presence of Ish-bosheth. Bow down before the King of Gilead and of the Ashurites and Jezreel and Ephraim and Benjamin and of all Israel."

Father and son approached the throne and knelt.

"You may rise," Ish-bosheth said.

"You come from David." Abner's voice held the rough accents of the soldier.

"David, King of Judah, sends his condolences for the death of your father and your brothers," Eri said. "He sends you these greetings in peace, with a plea that you, Ish-bosheth, and you, Abner, join him to drive the enemy from the homeland of our late king and, indeed, from all of Israel."

Before Ish-bosheth could say anything, Abner declared, "We would welcome the men of Judah as a valued part of the Army of Israel."

Eri glanced at Urnan quickly.

Ish-bosheth then spoke. "Perhaps the shepherd who styles himself King of Judah thinks that we men of

Israel should subjugate ourselves to him." He laughed to show his contempt for the suggestion.

"If I may speak?" Eri said.

"Isn't that why you are here?" Abner asked gruffly. "To speak for David?"

"It is," Eri said with a nod. "I think you will both agree that David has some experience in fighting the Philistines."

"And in fighting his own people," Ish-bosheth added.

Eri continued. "He was Saul's good right hand until the unfortunate break between them—a break, you are well aware, that was precipitated by Saul as a result of his delusions. David's victories over the enemy are still praised in song by the women of the Twelve Tribes."

"Speak plainly," Abner growled. "Are you trying to tell us that David demands command?"

"I would not put it so bluntly."

"Then how would you put it?" Ish-bosheth asked.

Eri shrugged. "David, King of Judah, invites you and all others who reside over the River Jordan to join the Army of God in driving the Philistines from Israel."

Ish-bosheth opened his mouth, but Abner put his big, rough hand on the king's shoulder. "Tell David," he said, "that the tail does not wag the dog. Tell him that little Judah, which is only one of the Twelve Tribes, is welcome to join the rest under the command of the son of Saul the King."

"I will," Eri said.

"Rest with us before you set out on your return journey," Abner said. "A Child of the Lion is always welcome here."

Eri bowed his head in acknowledgment and backed out of the royal presence with Urnan at his side.

"I feared this," Urnan said quietly when they were safely outside.

"Abner is the strength," Eri remarked. "Does his

antipathy for David come from grief at the loss of his cousin, his king?"

"Like Saul, he sees David as a usurper."

"A strange people, these Hebrews," Eri said, sighing.

"Their own God calls them a stiff-necked people."

Eri chuckled. "It is no surprise. Tell me, Father, will you and Jerioth return to Judah with me?"

"No. I'll stay here for a while. Saul listened to me. Perhaps with help from the God of Abraham I can gain the confidence of his son."

"These people," Eri said, shaking his head. "One powerful enemy isn't enough for them. They have to seek others among their own kind."

"Knowing David as I do," Urnan said, "I can't see him starting civil war."

"No, he will not, but he is, remember, one of these stiff-necked ones. He will not suffer slights or aggressions from either Abner or Ish-bosheth."

Urnan shook his head and asked in a bemused tone, "How is it that we who bear the mark of Cain, we who fashion the tools of war, are now cast in the role of peacemakers?"

Eri laughed. "I have no answer for that."

"I've been thinking of Egypt," Urnan said. "I long to see the Nile again. And now I have another son."

"As you suggested, one day we will go there together."

"So be it. But for the moment, there is new wine waiting to be tasted. We will drink to our sons—all of them: you, my Eri; a prince named Kaptar; and our Sunu."

Eri smiled and clapped his father on the shoulder. "Gladly."

CHAPTER EIGHT

Joab, the second son of David's half-sister, Zeruiah, watched with interest as the young armorer Sunu straightened a blade that had drawn blood more than a few times. Joab was a true man of Judah: solid of build, powerful of arm and leg, stocky at a height that made him as tall as David but not as tall as Saul had been.

Sunu was stripped to the waist, but his leather apron protected his muscular belly and chest against flying needles of iron and sparks from the white-hot blade on his anvil. He tapped the edge once, twice, three times with his hammer, putting on the last delicate edge, then plunged the blade into a large amphora of blackened water. A satisfying cloud of steam rose from the hiss of cooling metal.

"A bit of polishing now," he said, holding the sword up for inspection.

"You are young to be so skilled," Joab said.

"And you are young to be a captain of hundreds," Sunu countered.

Joab laughed. "Older·than you, smith."

Sunu busied himself with a polishing stone. "The king has a title for such as you."

"Yes, well . . ." Joab shifted his sandaled feet.

"You are one of David' s mighty men."

"I was not the one who came up with that designation."

"I am honored to serve you," Sunu said.

"An arm as strong as yours could wield a sword to good effect."

"I am an armorer, but I am not totally ignorant of the use of the weapons I fashion."

"It is said that your father fought at David's side and that your grandfather was at Gilboa with Saul and Jonathan."

"It was my father who scaled the heights at Michmash with Jonathan," Sunu added.

"Yes, by God, it was!" Joab said excitedly. "I remember now. In truth, your father should be called a mighty man."

Sunu put a finishing touch on the gleaming blade and tested its edge with his thumb. "It must not be too keen lest it be fragile—but I think you'll find that this will slit a Philistine throat easily enough."

"I am grateful," Joab said.

"Just don't chop wood with it—and try to keep from blunting it on the larger bones of a man's body."

Joab laughed. "In the heat of battle, smith, one does not always have time to aim for the softer portions of the enemy."

"Well, it can be sharpened again, I suppose." Sunu brushed his hands on his leather apron. "Are you preparing to go up against the Philistine?"

"A reconnaissance only," Joab said. "A small

force. We're to go up into Benjamin and observe conditions. Those who come to us from the north tell us the Philistine has emptied the land of cattle and food and that the people have no choice but to leave or starve. Most of them go over the Jordan."

"To join Abner and Ish-bosheth?"

"Perhaps. But I like to think that there are men of Israel who will recognize a king when they see one."

"As you may know, my father has gone to Mahanaim to confer with Abner and Ish-bosheth in the name of King David."

"I wish him well." Joab hefted his weapon and held it vertically, hilt at the level of his chin. "This blade hungers for Philistine blood, not that of my brothers."

"When do you leave on this reconnaissance?"

"With the sunrise tomorrow morning."

"In the event of a clash with the enemy you will need the services of an armorer," Sunu said.

"I would welcome the presence of one of your trained men."

"One of us will be with you."

To Joab's surprise, it was Sunu himself who joined the troop of seasoned veterans who gathered at the city's gates before the sun showed its crimson lip over the eastern hills. He rode a splendid black horse and led two pack animals carrying a small but serviceable anvil and the other units of a portable forge.

"Have you obtained permission?" Joab asked.

"I am of age," Sunu said stiffly.

"Of course, so you are. I wonder, however, if it is wise to risk so valuable a craftsman on such a routine reconnaissance."

"When my father was not as old as I, he helped Saul return the Ark of the Covenant to Israel."

"All right, mighty man," Joab said with a fond grin. "We go."

He led his force past Gedor and Bethlehem, and

all along their route they were greeted by men coming up from their fields and women from their looms and kitchens to call out to them, to inquire of David.

"There is a king in Judah!" they shouted.

"Smite the Philistines!" they cried.

"David is the anointed of God," they whispered.

"Tell the king we stand with him," they pledged.

Sunu had heard the tellers of tales sing of the triumphant return of the Army of God from the battle of Shocho, where David slew Goliath, the giant of Gath. All along the way, the singers said, the people came out of their houses and stood on the side of the road to cheer the victors, and the women cried out praise for both Saul and David.

"David! David! David!"

He heard the name over and over. His chest swelled with pride, for he had become a part of something noble and lofty.

"Yes," he whispered to himself, "there is a king in the land once more."

The city of the Jebusites, unconquered by Joshua, still held firm in an uneasy alliance with the Philistines. Its strategic, hilly location effectively controlled the main roads to the north.

"That bedamned fortress," Joab complained. "It separates Judah from the Rachel Tribes in Israel."

"And not even the Philistine care to storm its walls," Sunu said.

"One day," Joab promised, as he glared at the tall, forbidding ramparts, "one day we will come calling on these Jebusites."

Chephirah, northwest of the old city of the Jebusites, had been razed by the conquerors. A few people had returned and with salvaged building materials had erected a dozen crude dwellings. Joab did not slow the column. He answered questions as he rode past.

"Yes, David is king in Judah. Yes, David will

come. Yes, David will smite the Philistine hip and
thigh."

They came to Gibeon, a city on a hill north of
Jerusalem. Destruction and ruin gave evidence of the
passage of a Philistine army. An old woman held out
her hands.

"We hunger, great ones. The Philistines left not
enough to feed the ravens."

"Give her food," Joab said to his second-in-command. And to the old woman he urged, "Go to the
south, Mother. Find David at Hebron in Judah."

"God will bless you," the old woman said.

Joab looked at the sun, low in the west. "We will
camp here. There will be water in the Pool of Gibeon."

He ordered his second-in-command to situate the
men. To Sunu he said, "Ride with me, smith. Let us see
what the enemy leaves behind when he visits a town in
Israel."

A thin, cowering dog watched their progress
through littered streets lined with fire-gutted buildings,
their walls tumbled in. The stench of ashes and death
was heavy in their nostrils. Joab pulled his horse to a
stop in the town square.

"In the days of old, Joshua made peace with the
men of this city," Joab said, "but Adonizedec, King of
Jerusalem, allied himself with five Amorite kings and
set out to punish Gibeon for its alliance with the Children of the Lion. Joshua came up from Gilgal and slew
them in a great slaughter. Before the fight was finished,
the day was growing short, so there, in the sight of all
Israel, Joshua said, 'Sun, stand thou still upon Gibeon,'
and the sun stood still." He shook his head. "Now what
the Amorites could not do has been done by the Philistines."

The cringing dog sidled up toward Sunu's horse,
brown eyes limpid, mouth open in apparent supplication. Sunu opened his pouch and threw the animal a
sizable hunk of bread.

Joab lifted a clenched fist. "They have much to answer for, these Philistines."

The sound of a horse moving at a run reached them. Joab turned his mount around to face the on-coming rider, who jerked to a halt with his horse snort-ing and breathing hard.

"Captain!" the soldier said urgently. "Abner is at the pool!"

"How many men?" Joab asked.

"Too many to count," the messenger replied.

"Ride quickly. My orders are to avoid contact. Tell my men of Judah to keep to one side of the pool."

The messenger wheeled his horse around and rode back. Joab seemed to be in no great hurry. He looked at the lowering sun.

"There will be no battle today," he said. He smiled wryly. "Unlike Joshua, neither Abner nor I are close enough to God to be able to command the sun to cease its plunge toward night."

The Pool of Gibeon was an ancient work, a well carved from solid rock to a depth equaling the height of six men. Its circular, rock-rimmed opening was even greater in width than in depth. Seventy-nine steps spi-raled down the side of the well, each step worn by the passing of countless thousands of feet over the centu-ries.

Joab and Sunu left their mounts in the encamp-ment and walked to look across the open pit. Joab rec-ognized Abner. The man who had been commander of Saul's army stood, legs spread, on the opposite side.

"Hail, Abner," Joab called.

"Greetings to you, Joab," Abner called back.

"We have no quarrel with you," Joab said.

"Nor I with you."

"My men are thirsty from a long march," Joab said. "We will send water bearers to the well."

"Let them come in peace," Abner said, "for we, too, are in need of water."

Joab sat down on a rock. Sunu sat beside him. Soldiers from both sides went down the stairs to the bottom of the pool and came up carrying bloated waterskins. Abner sat opposite them. No further words were exchanged as the sun fell behind the hills and the soft twilight drew a veil over the scene.

A short while later, as Sunu and Joab sat beside a small fire, chewing on hot, half-cooked slabs of rich mutton, the young armorer asked, "Will there be a fight?"

"I pray not."

"What will you do?"

"We will converse with Abner in the morning."

"And?"

Joab shrugged. "What can I do but ask if he is friend or foe to my king?"

It grew cold during the night, but Sunu was wrapped snugly in fleeces. He awoke with a feeling of mixed dread and anticipation. Around him the camp was coming alive; the smell of burning wood and roasting meat was in the air.

Joab was at breakfast. When he was done, he cleansed his lips and hands, girded himself with his weapons, and walked slowly to stand beside the Pool of Gibeon. On the other side of the pool, Abner's army was fully awake.

"It is a morning, is it not?" Abner called from across the way. He stretched and took a deep breath. "Bless God for such sweetness."

"Let us pray that we will never taint such a day with the stench of Hebrew blood," Joab said simply.

"My king does not seek the blood of his brothers," Abner said.

"Nor does mine," Joab remarked. "The desire of my king is that you and all those who follow you will join us in fighting our common enemy."

"Under whose command?" Abner asked.

"Under the command of the king anointed in God's name by Samuel," Joab said.

Abner's face took on a grim seriousness. "But that king is dead. Now we men of Benjamin pay our allegiance to his son, Ish-bosheth."

"Abner, as a comrade-in-arms, I beg you to reconsider," Joab said. "Is Ish-bosheth the anointed of God?"

"He carries the blood of the anointed."

"I beg you. Follow David, not some false king whose only claim is the death of his father."

Abner shook his head sadly. "We must not shed blood here, not in this place so recently devastated by the Philistine. Go back to David, Joab, and beg him, as you have begged me, to cast his loyalty with the son of Saul."

Joab was silent. Tension hung over the field as the sun waxed hotter in the eastern sky. Suddenly, from Joab's right, an arrow traveled its path of death across the pool and buried itself in the breast of one of Abner's soldiers. A great shout of anger went up from Abner's army.

"Hold, hold!" Joab roared, turning to his troops and raising both arms. "The next man who lets fly an arrow will die at my hands!" He turned back to face Abner.

"My man is dead!" Abner shouted, his face contorted with anger. "We will have a life for a life!"

"An eye for an eye," Joab agreed. "That is the law."

"No! No! No!" chanted the men at Joab's back.

"Is Joab in command of his troops or is he not?" Abner sneered.

"If you must have blood," Joab said with resignation, "let it happen in this manner: Choose a dozen of your finest. We will send twelve of ours. Let the side that is victorious win the day and the dispute between us. The side that loses will pledge allegiance to the winner's king."

"I agree to only a part of that suggestion," Abner said. "I will not sell my loyalty based on what is merely a variation on the old practice of single combat. The premise is a lie. When David fought Goliath, the Philistines did not keep faith with the bargain but tried to avenge his death."

Joab nodded. "You speak with wisdom. Very well. The outcome will settle this day only." He turned and began to pick his finest warriors.

Sunu felt his heart begin to pound even before he had made his decision that he would be one of Joab's twelve. Never before had he faced an enemy in battle, but he was a man, and it was time to discover whether or not he could do a man's work. He came to stand before Joab.

"I am one of the twelve," he said simply.

"You're not much more than a boy," Joab said. "Too much depends on this test."

"David was younger than I when he faced Goliath."

"David was the anointed of God."

"Let me go, Joab," Sunu pleaded. "I must go."

Joab nodded. "So be it," he said, for he was not much past Sunu's age, and he knew how vital it was for a man newly sprouted to find himself. Facing an armed enemy was part of the process of maturing. Actually, the boy would have a better chance of survival in a staged combat than in the appalling confusion and numbing din of a pitched battle.

"I, too, will be one of the twelve," said a young man who was perhaps a year older than Sunu.

Joab shook his head. "Ah, not you, too," he growled. For the volunteer was Asahel, his younger brother. For a moment he hesitated, but he could not play favorites. He could not refuse to send Asahel into harm's way and accept the willingness of others.

Sunu and Asahel walked side by side as the men of Judah approached the field where the bloody drama would be staged.

"Hold your shield higher," Asahel whispered.

"I will hold it so as to best protect me when the time comes," Sunu said.

"There is still time to go back," Asahel said. "You are too young. My brother will appoint a more experienced man in your place."

"Do you see that man, there?" Sunu pointed his sword at the largest of the Benjamites. "He is mine."

"Fool," Asahel spat. "Take the one on the end. He is young and not much taller than you."

"You make your choice," Sunu said. "I will make my own."

Opposite stood their counterparts, the twelve chosen Benjamites. Behind their brothers, the grim, bearded men of Abner's army leaned on their spears. It was quiet, so quiet that only the step of sandals on the rocky earth and the creak of leather armor could be heard as Joab's twelve took their positions. Both Joab and Abner took a single pace forward. Each raised a hand and, as one, let them drop.

Sunu had to fight a wild urge to turn and run in the opposite direction. A haze engulfed his mind. He could feel his knees moving, could sense the pounding of his feet on the hard earth as he moved forward. There was an ocean of sound in his ears, but he could not identify it as the combined roar of the two armies as they urged on their champions. A high, shrill, continuous cry came from close at hand. It penetrated through the haze, and he looked askance at Asahel, who was running by his side. Joab's brother was keening a cry like that of a bereaved woman.

To his left the faster men of Joab's force collided with the onrushing Benjamites. The clash of iron on iron, a familiar sound, cleared Sunu's head. Suddenly he saw the world through the eyes of an eagle, saw it more clearly, more vividly than ever before. He let his eyes center on the black maw that was his personal opponent' s open mouth. He noted the position of the man's sword, the tilt of his shield. Just before he would have smashed head on into the Benjamite, impaling himself on a rigidly held sword in the process, he used the reflexes of youth to dart to one side. The larger man swung his weapon, and the deathly wind of its passage stirred Sunu's hair as he bent low and with one slash of his weapon hamstrung the enemy. With a hoarse cry of pain and devastation the Benjamite fell, his right leg useless. He rolled to his knees and tried to stand, but fell again. And as his leg failed him, so did his life; Sunu, with a barked grunt of effort, bypassed his opponent's sword to land a two-handed blow to the back of his neck. The man dropped facedown and was still.

So quickly had the man died that Sunu was stunned. He bent his head, watching blood well up from the fallen Benjamite's neck. Sounds began to penetrate again: the roar of the two armies as they yelled to their own, the clash of iron, the thwack of blade on leather shield, and the different, duller impact of sharp iron in flesh.

"Help me!"

The words brought Sunu around quickly. Asahel had lost his sword. He was trying desperately to counter a hail of blows with his shield. Abraded leather flew with each impact.

Sunu leaped forward. The Benjamite left off belaboring Asahel and faced this new threat. Once again Sunu danced to the side, but this time the enemy was too quick. Swords clashed. There was power behind his opponent's blow. Sunu found himself backing away, fighting for his life. His shield was growing heavier and heavier, and fire burned in the muscles of his right arm. The iron sword of his enemy penetrated past Sunu's shield, and a sharp pain on his left breast told of a hit. He knew a moment of fear that almost paralyzed him, but he recovered quickly. Hot rage filled him. He had known the shock of accident, the quick, burning impact of a glowing ember flying from the forge, a finger mashed by the hammer; but never before had he felt the white-hot penetration of a blade into his flesh. It was the ultimate invasion, that hit of the enemy's iron, an insult that could not be endured, a threat to a life he had never valued as highly as he did at that moment.

He felt the tendons of his neck straining as he screamed out his hatred. His arm no longer ached with tiredness. His feet were as agile as those of a goat on a mountain. Before his skilled attack the older, heavier warrior fell back. And then it was over with a suddenness that left Sunu gasping for breath, surprised and overjoyed to be alive. He felt his blade strike bone as he bypassed the shield, and for a quick moment he was reminded of his advice to Joab on how to avoid dulling his blade. Yet even as that thought flashed past, he was parrying a thrust and coming up under the enemy's shield to drive his blade home into the softness of the man's belly.

Asahel had recovered his weapon and now ran to Sunu's side. Men lay sprawled on bloody, barren, rocky earth. Those who stood were all of Judah. A roar of victory came from Joab's army.

"We have won!" Asahel crowed.

Sunu could not speak. He looked across the blood-drenched field to a sea of sullen, angry faces, and he knew that it was not over. Suddenly the men of Benjamin, as if they thought as one, gave vent to a terrible battle cry and surged forward.

"Run!" Sunu shouted.

Asahel hesitated. Sunu grabbed his arm. "Run, fool!"

They ran with the yells of the Benjamites closing behind them. Joab's army was coming to meet them, the men eager to extend the victory gained by the original twelve. Sunu's momentum carried him past the men in the fore. He turned and found himself at the rear. The clash of battle was terrible in his ears. He worked his way to the flank of the army and then, in a seemingly endless, mind-numbing, energy-draining maelstrom of violence, became a part of the battle, dodging under a horizontal swing of a sword, brushing aside a spear with his weapon, slashing a man's throat to take a great gush of blood on his shield; before the man fell, he swiveled and drove his blade into the side of another man. He smashed and parried and felt blood running down his own side from a second wound —and then the enemy was turning, running, fleeing the field.

Out of the corner of his eye he saw Asahel. Joab's brother was off in pursuit of one of the Benjamites.

"Come back!" Sunu shouted. "Come back! It's over!"

He ran after Asahel, who was scampering up a slope, making his way around huge boulders. Ahead of him the lone figure of the Benjamite stopped and turned.

"Abner!" Sunu whispered.

Asahel was bent on catching up with the most powerful warrior among the Benjamites. "Asahel!" Sunu bellowed. "Stop! Come back!"

If Asahel heard Sunu's plea, he did not acknowledge it.

When Asahel, brother of Joab, had followed Sunu's urgings to run for the security offered by the Army of Judah, he, like Sunu, was carried all the way through the onrushing ranks to the rear. Unlike Sunu, he had felt no great urgency about fighting his way back to the front. When at last he came onto the field of battle the fighting was almost over. The enemy was fleeing. He saw Joab, bloodied and panting with exhaustion, standing within a circle of dead. He saw Sunu looking very much the victorious warrior. And he cringed inside, remembering how he had been forced to call on Sunu, who was nothing more than a boy, to save his life.

He knew, did Asahel, that he had not acquitted himself well—he, the brother of a great warrior. Shame became determination. He ran onto the field, leaping over scattered bodies. A great slaughter had been done there that day, and the dead were men of both Judah and Benjamin. The enemy were fleeing up a rocky slope, pursued by the men of Judah. As he stood at the foot of the slope he watched the pursuers disappear over the crest. He knew he could not catch up to them; there would be no glory for him that day. He lowered his sword and shield.

Then, just ahead, halfway up the slope, he saw movement. A man had been crouching in the shadow of a large boulder. The form was familiar.

"Abner!" he breathed in great excitement.

Perhaps there was a way to salvage the day, a way to earn honor to replace the shame of having to call on a boy to save him. He leaped up the hill, his legs young and strong. He was much fresher than the man he pursued, for he had not been in the thick of the fight. He reached the top of the hill and bounded down as Abner crossed a dry wadi.

"Hold, Benjamite!" Asahel cried. "Let us finish what you began this day!"

Abner turned. His face was soiled with sweat, dirt, blood. The blood, however, was not his own. His sword had tasted the flesh of many that day.

"There has been enough killing," Abner declared.

"Not quite enough. The total is short by one!" Asahel shouted boastfully, leaping down the last few feet to land in the sand of the wadi.

"You are just a boy," Abner said wearily. "I have no stomach for further bloodshed. All those who lie on the field beside the Pool of Gibeon were the seed of Abraham, all God's chosen. Leave me. Don't force me to kill you."

But Asahel was running across the sand. Abner held up his hand. "We do not have to fight. Too many are already dead."

Unheeding, Asahel leaped toward the general, his sword flashing. With a sigh, Abner defended himself.

He held back on his blows, fighting defensively, until it became clear that he had but two choices: to die or to kill. He put an end to it swiftly and mercifully, cleaving Asahel's skull with his sharp blade.

Halfway up the hill Sunu's foot slipped on loose gravel. His ankle gave way and he fell heavily, rolling down the slope and slamming into a boulder. He lost his breath and was lying there gasping when Joab materialized and knelt over him.

"Where are you hurt?" Joab asked.

It was a while before Sunu could answer. When he finally drew air into his burning lungs, he gasped, "Asahel!"

"Where?" Joab demanded, standing erect.

"Up the hill! Go quickly!"

Joab scrambled up the slope. From the top he saw Asahel's crumpled form lying in the wadi and feared the worst even as he went bounding and sliding down the steep backslope. He knelt beside his brother, saw the white ooze of brain matter mixed with blood in a great depression at Asahel's temple. When he put his hand on his brother's face he felt the waxen stillness of death. He lifted his eyes heavenward and moaned out his anguish as his bloody, bruised hands rent his garments. He continued his display of grief until Sunu came down the hill to stand beside him.

"I tried to follow him, to help him," the young smith said. "But I lost my footing."

"God, O my God, tell me the name of the man who did this to my brother," Joab prayed. "Show me his face that I might exact vengeance."

Sunu spoke without thinking. "The man he was chasing was Abner."

Joab's face was terrible to look upon. "Then on this ground, on this day, I swear by God that I will not rest until I see Abner's head opened as was that of my brother. Hear me, Sunu ben Eri: This I vow."

"I hear," Sunu said.

*   *   *

On the field of battle the moans of the injured filled the air as their comrades did what they could to bandage wounds or give some small comfort to the dying. With Joab mourning his brother's death, his second-in-command was organizing the army to move. His biggest problem was the transportation of men too grievously wounded to sit a horse.

"We need a few Philistine carts," he said as he came up to the small group of men that included Sunu. His face brightened. "Ah, the young smith," he said. "I saw you, smith. Your blade was red with the enemy's blood." He nodded, impressed, then spread his hands and faced the others. "Did you see him, the smith?"

"We saw," a man said.

"In the battle of the twelves," someone said, "he killed twice. On the Field of Sharp Swords two fell before him."

"Helkath Hazzurim," said the second-in-command. "The Field of Sharp Swords. A fitting name for such a place." He nodded again and clapped Sunu on the back. "The king will hear of your prowess in battle, young friend. He will, indeed, hear of it."

Suddenly Sunu began to shiver as if with cold. For the first time he knew the full import of what he had done. He had killed twice in the battle of the twelves, and he had lost count of how many times his sword had struck home in the general engagement. He lifted his blade in a shaking hand. "I t-told J-Joab n-not to ch-chop wood or b-bone," he stuttered. "I—I—" He fell silent. He lifted his face to the heat of the sun and fought the tears, but he couldn't stop them.

"It's all right, son," the second-in-command said. "It's all right."

Sunu tried to pull away.

"You have nothing of which to be ashamed," the older man said. "Your reaction is normal for one who has just fought his first battle."

"But they were of us," Sunu said in a choked voice. "They were of our blood and of our people."

Joab had joined the group in time to hear Sunu's protest. "Neither we nor our king asked for this fight," he said. "The choice was theirs. It was Abner who disputed the man anointed in the name of God by Samuel. Those who are against God's will are against us."

Sunu knew that it would be futile to say more. For the first time in his life he felt alone, isolated. He had considered himself one with the people of Judah-Israel; but in the final analysis the only Hebrew blood in his veins was from his grandmother, Shelah, Urnan's first wife. Sunu's mother had come into his father's house as an Ammonite slave from across the River Jordan. He would not allow his small fraction of the blood of Abraham make him like these stiff-necked, bloody people who were not content with one powerful enemy but had to seek others among their own kind.

"I am going back to Hebron, Captain," he said to Joab.

Joab nodded. "We will all go home, smith, and you will ride at my side."

And in the company of victors, a hero among heroes, Sunu thought less and less about that which had troubled him.

CHAPTER NINE

Kaptar was dressed as a prince of Egypt when he disembarked at the royal quay in the city where Paynozem had ruled. An honor guard, Libyans all, stood stiffly as Musen himself welcomed the son of the woman he had robbed of eternity.

Smile now, Libyan, damn you, Kaptar was thinking as he forced his own lips into an amiable expression, *but one day I will wipe the smirk from your face.*

"Such pleasure to welcome the son of my beloved Tania," Musen said, "and such sorrow that we have been deprived of the earthly presence of the great god Paynozem."

"May he live," Kaptar said ritually.

"You are in time, Prince," Musen said. "You will, of course, be my guest. May I inquire of your uncle, may he live, Kemose the King?"

"He is well," Kaptar lied, "but overwhelmed with affairs of state and temple. Only duty would have kept him from paying tribute to his brother."

"Of course," Musen said. "But come, perhaps you do not remember your cousin."

A pale, hollow-eyed youth dressed in the finest of white kilts stepped forward.

"Amenemopet," Musen introduced, "son of Paynozem."

"Cousin," the pale one said, nodding imperiously. "It is good of you to come and grieve with us."

It struck Kaptar that Amenemopet did not have the look of sorrow. There was, in fact, a look of supercilious satisfaction on his face.

"Cousin Amenemopet," Kaptar said.

"You are not a true prince of Egypt," Amenemopet said with distaste. "Therefore, you are not to be familiar with me. Address me as Menkheperre if you must speak."

Musen looked at Kaptar with a long face. "Your cousin fancies that he already sits on the throne," he said.

"Keep your tongue, Musen," Amenemopet said, his voice going shrill, "or I will have my royal bodyguard cool your impertinence with a swim in the river."

The look in Musen's eyes should have given warning to Amenemopet, but he was effetely oblivious as he shifted his gaze to Kaptar and allowed a smug half-smile to distort his mouth.

Kaptar was making mental notes for his report to Kemose. He would give his uncle the opinion that the young prince would not sit long on the throne of lower Egypt if he continued to challenge and insult the commander of his army.

Official mourning subdued the activity in the royal quarters, but in Musen's house there was music, dancing, good food, much beer, and gaiety. Kaptar accepted Musen's offer of his choice of the lithe, nubile dancers, so his bed was warmed delightfully.

His report to Kemose would say: "There was no grief among the Libyans. Rather, there was a mood of celebration."

Now began the long, tradition-bound ceremonies that would see Paynozem to his tomb. In spite of her division, Egypt was still a rich country, and in the fertile delta prosperity extended from the extravagance of the court, with its ubiquitous gleaming gold, all the way down to the swarthy countryman tilling his small plot of land with a wooden plow and watering his crop with the bounty of the Nile lifted to his irrigation system by creaking waterwheels of ancient design. The city reeked with incense as hordes watched the procession bearing the king's mummified remains to the great, golden barge that would carry him across the water to his resting place.

Amenemopet performed the ceremony of the opening of the mouth, thus assuring his father life in the afterworld. Priests chanted as the dead king was carried to his tomb and placed in his sarcophagus. The tomb was sealed. Paid mourners wailed. The priests feasted and drank rich, foamy beer.

Amenemopet was installed as Menkheperre, King of the Two Lands—that claim being made in spite of the actual division of Egypt. The new god-king distributed food and beer to the masses, and the city rejoiced for that, if not for having a new king.

Late that night Kaptar was awakened by a slave girl. Feeling a soft hand on his shoulder, he groaned and was prepared to tell his bed companion that she asked too much.

"Prince Kaptar, the king would speak with you," the girl whispered.

He rose and quickly dressed, then was led through the women's quarters to a small room away from the main areas of the royal residence. There he found the new king pacing back and forth impatiently.

"It took you long enough," he snapped. It was unclear whether he was accusing Kaptar or the slave girl.

"I attend you, Great One," Kaptar said, bowing.

"You may sit."

Kaptar took a chair. Menkheperre continued to pace for a few moments, then stopped and faced his cousin. "These Libyans—" He paused, swallowing with difficulty. "Musen—" Again he seemed unable to continue.

"What concerns you, cousin?" Kaptar asked.

"He has the army, you know."

"Yes."

"He thinks I am king in name only, but I will show him." He lifted one frail arm and clenched his fist until his knuckles were white. "There are still fighting men in Egypt."

"Yes."

Menkheperre pulled his shoulders back. "It is said that you will follow Kemose to the throne in the south."

"Although that is my uncle's wish," Kaptar said, "there is opposition because my father was not Egyptian."

Menkheperre dismissed that statement with a wave of his hand. "You have the royal blood through the princess Tania. When you are on the throne, cousin, you and I will speak of the reunification of the Two Lands. You will find that I can be very generous. Since you yourself admit that you are not qualified to rule, that you are not a true Egyptian, I will appoint you governor of the southern lands and high priest of Amon at Waset, and together we will put these foreigners in their place. We will send them scurrying back to their dens in the desert."

Menkheperre's naivete astounded Kaptar. He was speechless as the young king continued, "It will be necessary, of course, to kill the child Namlot." He began pacing again.

Alarm flared in Kaptar. He had made a vow to Kemose to do his best to keep his half-brother from harm and see him seated on the throne of Lower Egypt.

"But don't worry," Menkheperre said. "I will attend to that." He paused in his pacing. "Have you been struck dumb by my brilliance?" He laughed. "It takes only a little Egyptian cunning to best the stupidity of the Libyans."

"It is my goal, like yours, to see the Two Lands one again," Kaptar said.

"Good, good. Here's what you must do. Go back to Waset. I am told that our uncle is in poor health. If he has not joined the gods by the time you get back, I'm sure that you can find some method to speed him along his way." He looked sad for a moment. "The old ones cling to life like a drowning child trying to mount a lotus pad. It is disgusting how they struggle to continue their suffering." He made a sound as if gagging. "Had I rotten teeth like our uncle, I would welcome the deep sleep of death and the release from pain that comes in the afterworld."

Kaptar had to fight to keep his poise. His cousin's speech had raised two questions. He did not reflect on the first, but he had the distinct impression that Paynozem had not died a natural death. His impulse was to say, "What kind of monster are you, you who would murder my half-brother and the uncle I love?" Instead he said, "You have excellent intelligence in the court of my uncle."

Menkheperre smiled. "Of course."

It was time to speak. "It will not be desirable to kill my half-brother."

The young king's eyes narrowed. "You are either with me or against me. Which is it to be?"

"There must be a middle course," Kaptar said. "I have told you that I will not follow Kemose to the throne, as you agree I should not, so your entire premise is based on a false assumption. Moreover, I would defend my uncle's life with my own."

"And would you fight for the Libyan brat? Your precious half-brother?"

"It is neither necessary nor desirable to kill Namlot," Kaptar said firmly. "At this time I will extract from you your promise that you will not attempt to harm him."

"You . . . will . . . extract?" There was anger and threat in the king's voice.

"My alternative is to go to Musen and tell him that he must take measures to protect his son."

Menkheperre hissed like a snake, and his face was flushed. "Leave me!" he shouted. "They are right in saying that you do not deserve the throne of Upper Egypt, for your heart is corrupted with your alien blood!"

Kaptar came to his feet. He was taller than his cousin by a head. "Great One," he murmured, "if I may offer you this advice—"

"You may not!" Menkheperre screamed. "Guards! Guards!"

Two muscular Egyptian soldiers burst into the room. Kaptar was unarmed. He waited warily as the two men stood, swords drawn, to hear orders from their king.

"My cousin has displeased me," the king announced with chilling calm. "Take him to the river and let him join his mother in the belly of a crocodile."

"You know about that?" Kaptar gasped in astonishment, wondering if his cousin knew the rest of the story.

"It is in my interest to know everything." Menkheperre nodded to the soldiers. "Take him now."

Kaptar would not make it easy for them. It took several men to subdue him, even though he was unarmed. Four other members of the king's personal guard helped to wrestle the muscular smith to the floor.

Menkheperre stood over him. "I want him taken far away. Take him upriver to the empty lands. Do not disobey me. Do not try to make your task easier. Bring to me an inscribed mud brick from the destroyed palaces of the Heretic to prove that you have obeyed. When you reach the empty land, do to him as Musen did to his mother."

So he knows about that, too, Kaptar thought. Then he felt the world fall away as one of the soldiers smashed the hilt of his sword against the back of his head. He became aware of motion, of being carried by four men. He had no strength in his limbs. He could feel the coolness of the night air, could hear the labored breathing of those who held his arms and legs. He felt only a dull contact when he was thrown into the bottom of a dhow. The smells of the river—dampness, the residual odors of long-dead fish—assaulted his nostrils.

For the rest of the night he was in and out of consciousness. The sun came up, and the dhow was still sailing upstream on a favorable wind. Someone gave him some water. Did the night come again? Was there another day?

Now and then he was conscious enough to understand the words of the soldiers and the boat's crew.

"He is one big fellow."

"Motherless bastard almost broke my nose."

"I think we are nearing the empty lands."

"The gods are kind."

Kaptar slept.

"Help me lift the bastard."

"We must obey the king's orders. Boatman, take the dhow to the shore."

"I will not set foot on that haunted place."

"We have our orders."

The boatman's voice was firm. "If you must dismember him, do it here, for I will not land there and risk the evils of that place."

Another crewman spoke his mind. "You will not soil my dhow with blood."

"Oh, ho! Another country heard from."

"It is *my* boat."

"By all the gods, did you not see the size of the crocodiles that inhabit the river? Help me list him. The king will never know that we did not cut him into pieces, for the crocodiles are large enough to eat him whole in a few bites."

"You're right. Very well . . ."

Rough hands pawed at Kaptar, seizing his arms and legs again. Then came the sensation of flying, the impact of water, and a pleasant coolness. He held his breath and knew that he was sinking down, down. He could feel himself being rolled by the current. He willed his feet to move, and they obeyed—feebly, but enough to bring his head to the surface for a breath of air. He saw the shadowy bulk of the dhow, downstream from him now, before he sank once more beneath the surface.

He sent messages to his arms, to his hands, and made it back to the surface. He wanted to vomit but controlled the urge. He was having enough trouble catching his breath without the heaving spasms that would come if he gave way to the sickness. He felt life coming back to his limbs. The coolness of the water was driving away the mist that obscured his senses. He rolled onto his back and floated, kicking his feet slowly, aiming for the nearest bank of the river. He lost track of time. His head ached fiercely, and more than once he had to cough up water when he momentarily lost consciousness. When he felt his moving feet contact muddy bottom, he tried to stand, fell with a splash, crawled to the edge of the river, and could move no more.

He was awakened by the roar of a bull crocodile. The sound was very near. He forced himself to crawl through the mud, gained dry ground, got to his hands and knees, and at last gave way to the sickness and voided his stomach. Acidity filled his nose and mouth. He coughed feebly and tumbled down, down, down into darkness.

*   *   *

He awoke choking on his own vomit. Fighting for breath, he coughed and spit the vile taste from his mouth. There was light in the east. Two suns peeked upward, and someone was singing. His mother, singing a lullaby of his youth. As the two suns became twin disks, figures danced before his eyes: lovely girls and oddly shaped men bare to the waist, undulating in the heat of the midday sun. Savages from the land beyond the cataracts gibbered at him and made obscene motions. Two carrion crows flew down from the sky to land in a nest in a cloven and cracked and battered and hacked skull. He knew the skull. It was the skull of his mother. The beaks of the birds were heavy with marrow. The gray female spoke to him, urging him to come into the quiet, watery tomb that had enclosed his mother's dismembered body. The siren song tempted him, for he was tired and sick, and death promised release. A cold wind blew and sang an eerie anthem of mortality through the empty eye sockets of the skull.

A great, evil-eyed crocodile moved soundlessly through the water, making only a small ripple. Something told Kaptar that the reptile was real, not a figment of his delirium. The beast, longer than two men lying head to toe, found purchase with its short legs and came lumbering up onto the bank. So it was to be that he would be a meal for the reptiles of the Nile as his mother had been. He could not move. The huge crocodile advanced with caution.

"Damn you, Kaptar, move!"

He looked around, searching for the source of the voice.

"Move, move! Get up and run!"

The voice was hauntingly familiar. He pushed himself to his hands and knees, staggered to his feet. The crocodile halted and eyed him warily.

"Go, go, go!" the voice of his mother urged.

The beast gathered himself for a charge. Kaptar forced his legs to move. He was not far from a rocky ledge. He summoned all of his strength and threw himself up onto the rocks just as the jaws of the reptile snapped on empty air not a handspan from his feet.

Before him stretched an empty, arid plain. In a half circle around that plain, the cliffs of the desert rose high. The barren earth was littered with debris. He forced himself to continue away from the river. If he fell unconscious again, he wanted to be a safe distance from the hungry crocodile. He saw a ruined stela and sat down on a stone by its base. His head ached. The sun was brutally hot. Idly, he read the glyphs carved into the stela. He did not recognize the name enclosed in a royal cartouche.

> *On this day was the king in Akhetaton in a tent of byssus . . . and going toward the mountain to the southeast of the city of Akhetaton the beams of the Sun's disk shining over him with a pure light . . .*

The name in the cartouche was similar to that of the city whose razed ruins littered the ground. In the distance were the remains of a foundation. From the size of it, it was clear a grand structure had once graced that arid plain.

A feeling of deep melancholy brought tears to Kaptar's eyes. When a king could live and die and not be remembered, when a great city could disappear, leaving only its name carved in an isolated stela, what hope was there for Egypt? If such a mighty king could be forgotten by history, what did it matter who wore the twin crowns of the Two Lands? If man could stoop so low that he was willing to deprive another of her right to eternity, was it worthwhile to continue to struggle?

He lay down in the meager shade of the stela and slept, more than willing because of the pain in his head and the malaise engendered by the injury to let his bones bleach in the sun of that empty and desolate place.

When he awoke, the first thing he saw was a dhow sailing down the river. He staggered to his feet and moved to the riverside. No longer did death seem an attractive alternative. His anger at Menkheperre gave him strength. He yelled and waved his arms. The dhow turned toward him, its sail dipping, and grounded near where he stood.

"Are you a spirit?" asked one of the boatmen, staring fearfully at Kaptar.

"Hardly," Kaptar said. "I have been kidnapped and left for dead. The reward will be great if you will take me to On."

He had made up his mind. Menkheperre had to be stopped. He had made a vow to Kemose to look after the boy who, in all probability, would follow Menkheperre to the throne of Lower Egypt.

The boatmen exchanged glances, then nodded.

He climbed aboard. Offered bread by the boatmen, he accepted gratefully, chewing hungrily, unmindful of the grit that was the eventual cause of one of Egypt's worst curses for her people: worn, rotted teeth. Then he drank from the river and rested.

When the dhow came near On, he thanked the boatmen and gave them Musen's name, telling them to return in a day to claim their reward. Then he waded ashore to make his way carefully into the city. He did not want to give Menkheperre a chance to complete the job that his soldiers had bungled.

CHAPTER TEN

When Eri left his family for Mahanaim, he had said good-bye to a boy on the threshold of manhood. Months later, after having traveled from the stronghold of Ish-bosheth back to the armory in Hebron—whose facility was producing well under the supervision of men whom he had trained—Eri returned to find that his son had become a cocky, well-respected young warrior. Indeed, Sunu had so distinguished himself at the Pool of Gibeon that Joab had given him captaincy over a small, hard-riding troop of young firebrands who were as sanguine of mind as Sunu. His assignment from Joab was to bring back to Hebron and the king's court intelligence of the activities of both the Philistines and the Trans-Jordanians under Abner.

With the energy and tirelessness of youth, Sunu's troop traversed all of Judah into Benjamin. Their travels took them past Gibeon, where Sunu examined the battlefield and was surprised that the fight seemed to have happened so long ago.

While on a scout toward the Jordan, the troop had a spirited engagement with a larger number of men loyal to Abner and Ish-bosheth, killing two for one. They lost four men of their number and buried them under a tamarisk tree near the river. Sunu led his remaining men on past Gilgal and into the mountains of the lands of the tribe of Ephraim, where a shepherd told him how to find the ruins of what once had been the sacred sanctuary at Shiloh. He had no way of knowing the exact location of his grandfather's forge in the time when Urnan was known as the smith of Shiloh, but there was an eerie feel to the countryside around the old shrine. It was as if the spirits of those who had died there, including his own grandmother, were in the wind, brushing against his face.

Moving where chance took them, the troop clashed with a Philistine patrol and captured six fine horses before turning south to cross back into Judah near the hill fortress of the Jebusites.

Returning at last to Hebron from the reconnaissance patrol, Sunu reported to the king in the company of Joab. "The Philistine presence in the north is apparently a random thing. They have established blockhouses at important road junctions, and the people say that tax collectors are accompanied by a considerable force. But we had no difficulty evading their scattered patrols—if, indeed, we wanted to evade them. There were times when we encountered them deliberately."

"And the forces of Ish-bosheth?" David asked.

"We met only one organized group."

"How would you assess the mood of the people of Benjamin?" the king queried.

"They are mired in hopelessness," Sunu replied. "The people were not hostile to us, even when we told them that we served David, King of Judah. They long for the security that was afforded them by Saul."

"And do they mention Ish-bosheth?" Joab asked.

"Some are aware that Ish-bosheth claims dominion over Benjamin, but they ask, 'Where is this king who would take Saul's throne? If he is indeed king, why does he not come to us and drive the Philistines back to their place by the sea as Saul did?' "

"And what do they say of David?" the king asked.

"Your deeds are sung beside campfires at night by the shepherds," Sunu said. "It is my opinion, sire, that you would be welcomed by most of the people not only of Benjamin but of the northern tribes, for they are suffering under the heel of the Philistine."

David pondered Sunu's words for a moment, then told his second-in-command, "Treat the people of Israel as if they were members of your own family. I want every man to be an ambassador of goodwill. Let your arm not be lifted against any man of the seed of Abraham who would be a friend of Judah. Tell one and all that David of Judah has sworn to God that all of Israel will once again be independent and free and that David welcomes all who would join him to achieve this cause."

"We hear," Joab said. "We will obey."

More and more responsibility was being delegated by the king to Joab, whose authority, next to David's, was paramount. Joab had developed a fondness for Sunu because of the young armorer's daring and willingness to obey orders. Though there was a difference in their ages, Sunu was maturing quickly, so fondness on Joab's part and admiration on Sunu's had developed into friendship.

After his audience with the king, Sunu returned with Joab to his house, where they took food together. The young scout told his mentor, "I have thought to venture farther to the north on my next reconnaissance."

"Don't put too much strain on your wings, little bird," Joab said with a grin, "lest some Philistine pluck your tail feathers."

Sunu dismissed the notion. "The Philistine is over-confident. He is fat with the tribute he exacts from Israel. It is not the Philistine who concerns me most when we are north of Judah. I fear that our easy victory over Abner at Gibeon will not be repeated."

"Abner ran," Joab said, his eyes hardening at the mention of the name of the man who had killed his brother.

"He will not run again."

"We'll see." Joab changed the subject. "Your grandfather is still in Mahanaim?"

Sunu nodded. "He continues to hope for a negotiated peace between our king and Abner."

"Do you not find it odd that your grandfather hones the blades of our enemies while your father is armorer to David?"

"That is the curse of Cain. We who are marked by the lion are driven to fashion the tools of war without concerning ourselves about the politics of those who wield them."

"How do you explain, then, that you have abandoned your forge for the battlefield?"

Sunu shrugged, then grinned. "It must be the fractious Hebrew blood that I have received from my grandmother."

Joab laughed with him.

Eri and Baalan had been given a fine house near David's. It had three rooms and a stairway to the roof, which was used with great pleasure by Baalan as a place to sit and chat with her neighbors, to dry clothes, and to catch a cooling breeze after the heat of the day. Baalan was pleased to be mistress of her house after all the years when there had been another wife in Eri's home, the childlike Sarah, and content to spend all her time looking after her husband. She loved weaving warm, woolen garments for her Eri and took great pride in searching the markets for the choicest food-stuffs for his meals.

She took pride, too, in her strong, manly son—although if the choice had been hers she would have kept him in the shops with Eri instead of roaming with his band of mounted warriors in the north. For Sunu she made fine linen girdles, seeking out flax and working it into strong, rich cloth.

The sweetest moment of her day was when Eri came home from his work, his hands soiled, his face blackened with the residue of his fires. She had water waiting for him, a cloth to dry himself after his bath, fresh clothing, a meal in preparation. Sometimes, if the day had been very hot, they took the evening repast to the rooftop and ate leisurely in the coolness of evening.

On such an evening Baalan had news. "They have named David's new son Ithream," she said, after she had served Eri and was seated next to him with her own plate.

"I can't keep all the king's wives straight," Eri said, swallowing a mouthful of succulent lamb. "Which one is it this time?"

"The mother is Eglah."

"And how many sons has the king now?"

"This infant is the sixth."

"Hmm," Eri mused, "it must be interesting to be a king and have so many wives."

"Hush," Baalan admonished. "One wife is all you need."

"I don't know. Perhaps I should have something to say about that."

Baalan was moodily silent. Eri hid a grin.

"So. I know David's first son, Amnon, and the second, Daniel," he said.

"Amnon is by Ahinoam and Daniel by Abigail," Baalan said sullenly.

"And the others?"

"The third is Absalom, by Maacah, the daughter of Talmai, King of Geshur—wherever that is."

"By the Sea of Chinnereth in the north."

"That means nothing to me," she said stiffly.

"Then there's Adonijah by Haggith, Shephatiah by Abigail, and this last one."

"He's a busy man, our king." Eri chewed a bite of sweet cake, looking at Baalan's downturned face. "I can't help wondering how it would be, though, all those eager, willing wives."

Baalan made a strangled sound and started to rise. Eri laughed, took hold of her arm, and pulled her into his lap. "I am teasing you," he said, chuckling.

"It is a cruel jest, then."

"Once I had two wives, remember?"

"All too well."

"Perhaps the king is a wiser man than I and has superior knowledge of how to keep more than one woman happy."

"Perhaps," she said, softening as his hand became exceedingly familiar.

"But it is my opinion," he said, as he lifted her and placed her gently down onto a pile of bedding that had been washed and hung to dry earlier in the day, "that if the king had one woman who pleased him as much as you please me, he would have no need for all of those others."

She moaned with pleasure as he quickly denuded her. The parapet around the roof hid them from curious eyes, for their house was the tallest in the quarter.

"Do I truly please you, after all these years?"

"I will show you how much," he said. He took her in his arms and began the sweet ritual that led, after a slow and gradual heating period of playful explorations, to a union so complete that it left them both pleasantly abstracted. They would have slept where they lay, cooled by the breeze of the night under a sky of winking stars, had not the voice of their son come to them up the stairwell.

Baalan pulled on her clothing hurriedly. Eri dressed more slowly. Sunu's head appeared, his face lit by the oil lamps left burning beside the couches.

"Am I disturbing you?" he asked.

"No," Baalan said quickly.

"I am," Sunu said. "You were sleeping."

"No, no," Eri said with some sarcasm. "We were just lying here waiting for you to come up."

"Well," Sunu said, coming over to them and looking embarrassed, "it's done now. I came to tell you that I'm going north in the morning."

Baalan sucked her lower lip between her teeth. "So soon?"

"This time we're going to ride north along the Jordan all the way to Mount Tabor."

"Any particular reason?" Eri asked.

"Joab wants to know if the Trans-Jordanians are penetrating into northern Israel."

"You'll be careful, won't you?" Baalan asked. "You won't deliberately look for a fight?"

"We'll be very careful, Mother," Sunu promised, putting his arm around her and squeezing. He gave her a quick kiss, then retreated back down the staircase.

"I wish he would stay at home," Baalan said. Neither she nor Eri was drowsy any longer.

"Where is home?" Eri was as much surprised by his question as was his wife. He had not until that moment realized that he had been feeling lost, displaced, out of his time. Perhaps it was only that his son was grown up and taking his place in a man's world, leaving the cozy nest to make his own way and his own reputation.

"Where is home?" Baalan echoed. She spread her hands. "Wherever you are."

A wave of melancholy came over Eri. "One should be surrounded by family in his home."

"I agree. That's why I wish Sunu would stay here."

"Well, he is sixteen now, after all. We can't hold him. But he'll be back." He put his hand on Baalan's shoulder. "Do you really consider Hebron our home?"

"Yes, although I do miss Urnan and Jerioth—and especially little Leah." Baalan had always regretted not having children other than Sunu. She looked at Eri.

"Such questions. We have a splendid house. We are safe here in King David's stronghold. God is good. Why are you dissatisfied?"

He shrugged. "It's nothing, really."

"You have been working too hard. Lie down and I'll rub your shoulders."

Her touch quickly dispelled his aberrant sadness. As he sank into sleep, he felt her warmth at his side, her arm over him, both loving and protective.

Sunu and his men skirted the Philistine plain, coming down from the high country occasionally to ride through rich fields of grain. They circled wide around the city of giants at Gath, made a quick raid on a Philistine farmhouse complex west of Gezer, leaving behind smoke, fire, and ruin, then rode northward with their pack animals laden with the choice produce of the plains. A Philistine squadron of mounted light infantry picked up the trail of the small troop of one-score and two. Heavily outnumbered by his pursuers, Sunu took his force into the mountains of the land of Ephraim and continued north. Two weeks later he dismounted atop a hill and looked down over the battlefield where Saul and his sons had perished. On the plain, white bones gleamed in the sun. Central Israel was relatively free of the Philistine presence, for the conquerors had bled the country dry—although shepherds, tending tiny flocks, drove their charges into hiding at the first sound of approaching mounted men.

"The Philistines don't bother to occupy these hills because there's nothing more to steal," Sunu told his men as they rode westward toward the old city of Megiddo. Night was approaching when he smelled woodsmoke. He sent a scout ahead. The man returned quickly.

"One dwelling," he reported. "That's all."

They continued on for about a mile. The sun was touching the top of the western hills when Sunu looked down into a secluded glen, green from the waters of a hidden spring, to see a poor hut with but two tethered goats and several fowl scratching in the yard.

"They must be Hebrew," Sunu said. "No self-respecting Philistine would live in such a hovel."

He rode down the slope slowly. In a hostile land danger could lurk anywhere, even in a crumbling mud-brick hut in the wilderness. Suddenly there was movement in the doorway. A small form emerged, walking with difficulty, swaying jerkily from side to side. Sunu pulled his horse to a halt a few paces away. The cripple was only a boy carrying a shepherd's staff.

"Who are you?" the boy demanded.

"I might ask you the same," Sunu said.

At the cripple's side appeared a girl—wild of hair, with skin the color of honey, big-eyed and defiant as she brandished a rusty, bent sword in front of her.

"The tax collectors have already been here," the girl snapped.

"These are not Philistines," the boy said in a thin, weak voice.

"Who are you, then?" the girl asked, still holding the sword at the ready.

Before Sunu could answer, a buxom older woman ran out of the hovel and fell to her knees. "Spare us, lords!" she begged.

"For the love of God, get to your feet, woman," Sunu muttered, embarrassed.

"We do no harm!" the woman wailed, her eyes streaming tears. "We offer no threat, and we have nothing left worth stealing! I beg you, leave us alone!"

"Stop your groveling," the girl ordered in a voice as hard as iron.

"We will camp by your spring," Sunu said. "You will not be harmed, and your belongings will be safe from us."

The girl looked at him suspiciously. She stood with her back straight, her head high. Even in her tattered clothes there was an elegance about her.

With a whoop, one of Sunu's warriors suddenly

drove his horse toward the insubordinate pair, his sword raised high. The girl drew back her own sword. The boy hobbled forward and, to the surprise of all, landed a solid blow with his staff across the horse's forelegs. The startled animal reared, throwing the soldier off backward to land heavily on his rump. He came to his feet with a roar of anger, his sword at the ready.

"Hold!" Sunu shouted. He leaped from his horse and seized the man's sword arm from behind in time to stop him from a killing blow aimed at the crippled boy.

"It was a jest," the man said angrily, "and now look. The cripple has lamed my horse."

"You heard me say that these people would be safe along with their belongings," Sunu retorted. "Go. See to your animal."

"God bless you!" the older woman cried. "Oh, God bless you, for you have spared the life of those who are the seed of brave Jonathan's loins!"

"Say that again," Sunu demanded, fixing her with a hard stare. He turned to the girl. "You are the daughter of Jonathan?"

"Fool!" the girl snarled at her companion, and her hand landed with a resounding slap on the woman's cheek. "You have delivered us into the hands of our enemies!"

"I am no enemy to a daughter of Jonathan," Sunu said. "We serve David, who was Jonathan's friend."

"Truly?" the boy asked in his reedy voice.

"Truly," Sunu said. "How do you come to be here?"

"It is a story worth the telling," the older woman said.

"I will hear it, then." Sunu turned and pointed at the spring. "We will encamp there," he told his men. "We will share our food with these good people and listen to their tale."

"You are kind, young lord," the woman said, her

eyes leaking tears again. "We have been without proper food—"

"Hush!" the girl ordered.

"We will be grateful for food," the boy said with quiet dignity.

The girl was silent.

"Come, then," Sunu said, handing his mount's reins to one of his men. The boy walked at his side with difficulty, so Sunu slowed his pace. The girl would not meet his eyes but stared ahead proudly.

The men dismounted and unpacked their stores, then hobbled the horses and put them out to graze in the small, green valley. Branches were gathered, and a fire soon moderated the chill of evening. A lamb roasted slowly on a spit, dripping fat into red embers. Sitting by the fire, Sunu listened attentively as the older woman explained their story.

"When word came from Gilboa that Saul was dead, along with Jonathan and two of his brothers, we were alone," the woman said. "Mephibosheth was just five years old." She patted the boy on the head. He pulled away, embarrassed to be treated like a child. "An old woman, a crippled boy, and a girl just entering womanhood."

"How did that come to be? Were you with the king's retainers? And where is the mother of these two?"

"We followed the army," the woman said. "She, the mother, would have nothing but to be close to her Jonathan. Where she is now I do not know, but I fear the worst. When it became known that the Army of Israel had been destroyed in a great slaughter, the others ran. The boy could not move fast. I knew that if we were captured by the Philistines he would be killed, for his infirmity would have made him useless as a slave. Being old, I too, would have been killed. Mara—"

Sunu looked at the girl as he heard her name for the first time. Her almond-shaped eyes were as large and limpid as those of an antelope of the wilderness;

her lashes were as thick and black as her abundant hair. Her nose was one of God's finest sculptings, and her mouth, ah, her mouth . . .

"Mara, of course, would have been used and sold into slavery," the woman continued. "We hid in the hills and traveled as well as we could by night, heading for the River Jordan. More than once we had to avoid the Philistines. When we found this place, so secluded, we felt safe, and, indeed, you are the only ones to have come into this hidden valley since we found it."

"You've not left here since the battle of Gilboa?" Sunu asked.

"No," the girl said. "Twice we set out for the Jordan, and twice we were nearly discovered by Philistines. Then my brother became ill."

Sunu turned to the boy. "So you are Mephibosheth."

"I am, lord."

"My father and your father were friends."

"I pray that we can be friends, as well," the boy said.

"We can," Sunu assured him. "There is no reason for us to be enemies simply because your father's brother Ish-bosheth is at war with David."

The girl's eyes showed her surprise. "So the man from Judah continues his vendetta against the family of my grandfather Saul."

"David yearns to see a free and independent Israel once more. He wants to fight Philistines, not Hebrews."

Mara sneered at Sunu. "Of course you would defend him, since you are his creature. My grandfather knew him for what he was, knew that he coveted the throne that was to be my father's."

Sunu listened to her words, but it was her face that truly compelled him. He was reluctant to admit to himself how much he was affected by the dark beauty of wild-haired Mara. Until he saw the daughter of Jonathan, he had been able to sublimate the urges engendered in a body that had reached manhood, but when he looked at Mara every fiber of his being proclaimed that she was the most beautiful girl he had ever seen.

He had to clear his throat to speak. "My father was a friend to both David and Jonathan. I believe him when he tells me that had Jonathan lived to be king of Israel, his friend David would have served him loyally and joyfully."

"Pah!" Mara said, tossing her long, tangled curls disdainfully.

The older woman gave him a look of supplication as if asking for permission to speak. Sunu nodded.

"What will you do with us, young lord?"

"We have completed our reconnaissance," Sunu replied. "Now we will make our way south to Judah to report what we have seen to our commander and our king. You would do well to come with us."

"I will not go to Judah," Mara said angrily. "We were doing well without you. We shall continue to do so as we make our way to join our uncle over the Jordan."

Sunu felt a surge of exasperation. He spoke not to Mara but to her brother. "If it is important to you that you join your uncle, we will give you safe escort to Mahanaim."

"We ask no favors of you," Mara said.

"Hush, child," the older woman begged. "You will be safe from the Philistines in the company of these brave men."

"Men? Ha!" Mara snorted. "Overgrown boys playing at war is more like it."

"Will I be allowed to ride a horse, Captain Sunu?" Mephibosheth asked politely.

"Of course."

"All by myself?"

"Well, perhaps not at first. We'll have to give you a few lessons before you ride alone."

"Thank you," the boy said, grinning.

"Some of us, at least, have been instructed about

politeness by our parents," Sunu said with a pointed look at Mara. He was immediately sorry for his thrust. Her dark eyes seemed to draw him deep inside them. His pulse skipped a beat. He felt suddenly awkward and gawky—yes, much like an overgrown boy.

Early the following morning Sunu and his men, along with Mephibosheth, Mara, and their companion, departed the hidden valley. They had not traveled far when the woman declared her intent to leave her protectors and make her way alone to her family's village. Sunu tried to convince her to continue on to Mahanaim, but she would have none of that.

"I am old," she said wearily. "I only want to rest these bones among those of my ancestors." Preparing to leave, she added with a spirited smile, "Besides, I am spent and useless. If I encounter any Philistines, they will not consider me worth the bother."

CHAPTER ELEVEN

Kaptar disembarked from the dhow that had carried him downriver to the outskirts of the city of the kings of Lower Egypt. He waited until long after nightfall, then negotiated the deserted streets, always on the alert for the denizens of the night who preyed on the unwary. He did not look to be a worthy subject for a robbery, for he had traded his kilt and tunic for the robes of a common riverman—but he took no chances. He kept to the shadows as he came closer and closer to the royal complex beside the river. The city residence of Musen was nearby.

Skirting all guard posts, Kaptar finally reached Musen's home. He approached it from the rear, circled the high, protective wall to the entrance, and banged on the gate until a watchman, mouthing oaths at having his sleep disturbed, came from his hut. He carried a spear and a torch.

"Go away, scum," the guard growled, "or I will give you a taste of this." He thrust the iron-tipped spear at Kaptar.

"Hear me," Kaptar said. "Tell Lord Musen that Kaptar must see him."

The guard hesitated, for the ragged riverman at the gate spoke with the accents of the highborn and the authority of one accustomed to being obeyed.

"You will be well rewarded for your trust," Kaptar added.

"I'm to awaken Lord Musen on the word of a boatman?" the guard asked, caught in a dire conflict. His instincts told him that the man before him was not scum from the river, but if he disturbed Musen without reason or, worse, if he admitted a would-be assassin, he would not live to see the sun rise.

"On the word of Kaptar, Prince of Upper Egypt."

Inspiration came to the guard. "Kaptar of Upper Egypt is an armorer who bears the mark of the lion, as did his father, who was in slavery with Kemose the King."

"What you say is true." Kaptar was not surprised that the guard knew the legend of the Children of the Lion. It was a tale often told in Egypt. "Bring your torch close." He lifted his robe and showed the purple paw mark on his side.

"Why are you in such rags?" the guard asked, still uneasy. The mark of the lion could be faked.

"That is the business of Lord Musen, not you," Kaptar said haughtily. "The life of Lord Musen's son is in danger. Do you dare delay longer?"

"Wait," the guard said. He ran toward the nearest building. Within minutes he reappeared, accompanied by an officer of Musen's personal guard.

"Hold the torch so that I can see his face," the officer said.

Kaptar squinted his eyes against the glare of the flames.

"Open the gates," the officer ordered. "It is he." He bowed as Kaptar entered the compound. "Great One."

"Have you notified Lord Musen?" Kaptar asked.

"I will do so immediately, Great One. If you will come with me—"

"I want Lord Musen awakened *now*."

"He does not sleep, Great One."

"Take me to him."

"Yes. At once."

To Kaptar's surprise, Musen was fully dressed, as were the others with him in the room where Musen conducted his audiences. The Libyan looked up when the officer entered the room and saluted respectfully. Musen waited for the officer to speak.

"Lord Musen, I bring Kaptar, Prince of Upper Egypt."

Musen's face showed surprise when Kaptar stepped past the officer; then he laughed. "What masquerade is this, Great One?"

"How I came to this state is a tale that can wait," Kaptar said. "I have come to warn you of a plot against the life of your son."

Musen's face darkened. "Speak."

"Menkheperre plans to consolidate his hold on the throne by killing all those who might have a legitimate claim. He tried to begin with me, even though I am no threat to him. Next he will attempt to slay my half-brother, your son, who has the blood of kings through my mother. I beg you, Musen, to mount a strong guard on Namlot's chambers and keep him under watch night and day."

Musen approached his stepson and looked closely at his face. "We have searched for you. We feared that harm had come to you, and we did not know why. You say the king tried to kill you?"

"He did. He will try next to kill—"

Musen put his hand on Kaptar's shoulder. "And you love your half-brother enough to come to me with this warning?"

"He is of my blood," Kaptar said simply. "He is my mother's son."

"Kaptar, I am grateful. As time goes on you will come to know how grateful I am. In the meantime, do not concern yourself about Namlot. He is safe in his bed." He put his arm around Kaptar's shoulder. "Come. We must call two or three pretty little girls to bathe you and get you into some decent clothes." He chuckled. "You smell of dead fish."

"Thank you," Kaptar said wearily. "I will welcome a bath."

Musen turned to the room. "Gentlemen," he said, "you have your orders."

Officers saluted and began to file out of the room. Musen guided Kaptar toward the guest chambers, motioning to attendants along the way. Three sleek and lovely girls, two of them Egyptian and one as dark as a queen of the desert, immersed Kaptar in a perfumed bath and scrubbed the smell of the river off his limbs. Musen sat nearby, watching with amusement.

"You know that by law you are my son," the Libyan said, after a long silence during which the giggling girls washed intimate and instantly responding parts of Kaptar's anatomy.

"That is true," Kaptar said, hiding his revulsion at the idea of being called son by the man who had killed his mother and, not content with that, deprived her of eternity.

"So I have two sons," Musen said. "And I am fond of both of them."

"You touch me," Kaptar said, hoping his words did not sound false.

"I have bad news for you from the south. Your uncle is very ill."

"He was not well when I left Waset."

"His condition has worsened."

Kaptar felt his eyes well up. "I grieve. I must go to him."

"Yes, that is your duty. But is it wise? Thure-Amon has concentrated his support. He has the commander of the army on his side. He will take your uncle's place on the throne."

"So my uncle has suspected all along," Kaptar said.

"Why did you—the two of you—not simply kill Thure-Amon and all those who opposed the first choice of your uncle—you?"

"Shall I speak the truth?"

"I wish you would."

"In my heart, I am an armorer, like my father. Once I dreamed of sitting on the throne at Waset, even of reuniting the Two Lands under one king. I came to realize I was not the man to do that. I am content being armorer to the king, and I pray that Thure-Amon will so name me when my uncle joins the gods."

"He will cut off your head and feed you to the Nile crocodiles."

At the reminder of his mother's fate, Kaptar felt a stab of pain.

"Kaptar, there is one who can reunite the Two Lands," Musen said.

"Give me his name and I will serve him with all my heart and with all my strength."

"He will be called Sheshonk."

"I am not familiar with that name."

"At the moment he is known as Namlot."

The height of the Libyan's arrogance astounded Kaptar. He had already selected a god name for his son.

Kaptar swallowed his ire and was able to say honestly, "It would please me to see my brother on the throne. It would be a fitting tribute to my mother to know that it was her son who joined the divided Black Land as one again, as did the great god Narmer in days of old."

Musen rose. "I will leave you to your pleasures, my son. These lovely young ladies are at your command."

"I will command them to let me sleep," Kaptar said dryly.

"As you will. Come to me in the morning when you have rested. We will speak then of your journey to Waset and your role in the court of the king Sheshonk."

"Lord Musen," Kaptar called.

Musen halted in the doorway of the bathhouse.

"I think, lord, that you know something you have not told me."

Musen smiled slyly. "I know that you will grieve when I tell you that King Menkheperre, may he live, has joined his lamented father in the afterworld."

"The king is dead?"

"Quite dead."

"By the gods, how did it come about?"

Musen now smiled triumphantly. "It was something he ate."

The brief reign of Menkheperre ended in a ceremony that was only a shadow of the rites held for his father, Paynozem. Menkheperre had not had time to order the construction of his tomb; therefore, he was to be placed in a small room in his father' s expansive abode of the dead.

Paid mourners howled as Menkheperre's body was taken to the house of Anubis, god of the underworld. It was as Kemose had once said: The Libyans so admired Egyptian culture and her rich and ancient lore that they adhered to the letter of tradition as laid down by the Amon priests.

"It would be desirable," Musen told Kaptar, "for you to be present at the ceremony of the opening of the mouth and when Menkheperre's body is carried to the tomb. As it is quite necessary for you to be here when your brother is crowned, you must wait no longer to begin your voyage up the river to be at the side of your dying uncle."

"And if my uncle lingers?"

"Would it not be a mercy," Musen asked, looking at Kaptar with his head cocked and his eyes narrowed, "to bring peace to a man in pain?"

Kaptar's urge was to draw his sword and make one quick slash across his stepfather's throat. Only his vow to the memory of his mother and to Kemose saved Musen's life.

Kemose, high priest of Amon at Waset and King of Upper Egypt, opened his eyes with an effort. The old priest who was always with him was standing at his bedside. Two of his priest physicians hovered in the background. The chief adviser was speaking. His words brushed Kemose's ears and were lost until the name Kaptar penetrated the haze of illness and pain.

"Kaptar?" Kemose breathed.

"He comes on the royal barge of Lower Egypt, Great One."

"Quickly. Quickly," Kemose whispered.

The chief adviser turned to the physicians as the king lapsed back into an uneasy sleep. "Will he live until the young one arrives?"

The physician spread his hands. "It is in the hands of the gods."

Kemose's pain filled his mouth and jaws and radiated throughout his body. Great sores had erupted on his face, arms, neck, and torso. It was agony for him to move, but he insisted that the physicians prop him up in a sitting position, for Kaptar was coming.

Suddenly he was at the door—tall, thick of chest, strong of arm, and dressed in the splendor of a prince of Egypt.

"Uncle," Kaptar said, kneeling beside the bed and taking Kemose's hand in his.

"Amon has brought you back to me," Kemose said. He was stimulated by the sight of his nephew. His mind was clear. "The royal barge of the kings of On? That is how you came?"

"Menkheperre is dead. Namlot, son of Musen, sits on the throne."

Kemose nodded, ignoring his pain. "So it is as we thought."

"He will be called Sheshonk."

"That sounds like a name a Libyan would choose," Kemose said disdainfully. He lifted his head. "All of you," he said to his retainers, his voice carrying a hint of his old strength, "leave us. I will speak alone with my nephew."

When the room was empty, Kemose touched Kaptar's hair affectionately. "Since you travel in splendor on the royal barge, you are in favor with this new king and those who have placed him on the throne."

"By chance I learned that Menkheperre planned to kill Musen's son. I warned him and thus earned his trust. I am to be armorer to the king. If I want other titles, they will be mine. Musen suggested Master of the Horse."

"You plan to go back, then."

"Yes. But not before you are with the gods, Uncle —and I pray that will be a long, long time."

"It will be soon." Kemose drew several deep breaths and winced in pain. "Musen sent an honor guard?"

"One hundred Egyptians of a height that does not differ by the width of my smallest finger. Splendidly dressed and well armed."

"Don't challenge Thure-Amon," Kemose advised. "Your one hundred could be easily overwhelmed. However, let them guard you at all times."

"I will."

"And, Kaptar . . ." He abruptly coughed and was unable to speak for a long time. A physician stuck his head in the door. "Go," Kemose gasped, making a violent motion at the man.

"Uncle, you must rest," Kaptar said with concern.

"I will have the rest of eternity soon enough. Hear me. Once I dreamed that you would lead a great army down the Nile and overthrow whatever king held sway in the delta. I know that dream is dead. I know that Thure-Amon is strong enough to take my place, and I wonder why he has not accelerated his ascension. It would take only a pinch of poison or a quick thrust from a dagger and the throne would be his. I would welcome that release."

He paused and brushed his hand over Kaptar's head once more. "But I wander in my thoughts. There will be some internal strife because Thure-Amon has not the blood of kings in his veins. That would be the ideal time for Musen to come up the Nile with his army of Libyan mercenaries."

"He is not ready. He lacks the foresight and the boldness."

"You must leave me and seek the protection of your half-brother," Kemose said.

"That I will not do."

"Hear me. I have produced no heir. Had I done so there would be no question as to who would follow me on the throne. I fear the blows to my seeds when I was kidnapped into slavery on the island of copper deprived me of the ability to sire sons. You are closer to me in blood than any other, but the foreign blood of your father, Urnan, disqualifies you for the throne. We know this, but those whose ambitions are greater than their common sense will see you as a threat. Your life will be in danger from the moment I breathe my last breath. I order you to leave immediately."

"Uncle, I cannot. I must disobey you."

Kemose nodded. "I understand. Keep your guard about you. Will you do this much? Will you leave as soon as you and I have said our last good-byes? Will you promise me that you will not be tempted to stay to honor my ka as I am being prepared for eternity?"

"That I will promise."

"One thing more."

"Anything."

"Ask the physician for the powder of eternity. You and I will have one last glass of new wine. Mine will be sprinkled with mercy from your hands, and I will feel no more pain."

"Ah, Uncle, you ask me to do to you what Musen did to Menkheperre!" Kaptar cried.

"But in the cause of compassion, not greed. By granting me my request to end my misery and let me rest, you will be doing me one final, great service." He squeezed Kaptar's hand. "Do this last thing for me."

Kaptar was weeping. "I pray you, don't ask that of me."

"My hateful pride would not allow the administration of the powder of eternity from the hand of anyone but you. From anyone else it would be regicide. From you, my beloved nephew, it would be blessed mercy." He squeezed Kaptar's hand again. "For me? For the man who loves you as a son?"

Kaptar nodded through his tears.

The chief adviser and the two physicians were called back into the room and came to stand beside the bed.

"This is my wish, and you are all witness to it," Kemose told them. "You, my friend Ahmose, you will provide my nephew with the proper dosage of the powder of eternity. You"—he nodded to his chief adviser—"will bring a container of new wine. The three of you will drink with us. You will be at my side so that the last thing I see in this life will be the faces of friends."

The chief adviser began to weep, then to protest, but Kemose lifted his hand for silence. The physician Ahmose bowed, left the room, and soon returned, carrying a small vial. The chief adviser was back shortly with wine and cups for all. In grim silence Ahmose poured five cups, offering a golden one to the king.

"Good," Kemose said. "Let us drink to all that was and all that will be—and to Egypt." He drained his cup quickly and held it out. "My cup is not full, nephew."

Kaptar poured.

Kemose smiled sadly. "It is not yet full."

Ahmose handed Kaptar the vial of poison. Kaptar fought back his tears. "One more drink, Uncle," he begged.

"All right, then."

"To my mother, your cousin, the princess Tania," Kaptar toasted.

"Tania," Kemose murmured weakly, lifting his cup.

"She came to me," Kaptar said. "When I was wounded and ill, when I could not force myself to move, she came to me and spoke to me. I know, because her voice lives on in my heart. She instilled in me the strength to save myself from the reptiles of the Nile."

"Tania," Kemose whispered, looking into the depths of his cup as if seeing her face reflected there.

"I had a dream, Uncle," Kaptar said, desperately trying to delay the fatal moment. "And after my mother had spoken to me and I moved away from the river's bank, I saw writing on a stela. The name of an unknown king. The name was Akhenaten, and all about were the ruins of his city. A city lost. Forgotten. I don't know why, but it seemed to have some magical significance for me. Somehow that lost city and the unknown king were connected with the loss of my mother and with the knowledge that Musen had, through his vengeful actions, deprived her of her place in eternity."

"He is not unknown to us, this Akhenaten," Kemose said. "Tell him, Ahmose."

"As Musen destroyed your mother and deprived her of her place among the gods, so did King Horemheb the Warrior erase all mention of Akhenaten and a beautiful queen, Nefertiti, and he erased the names and memories of others who followed the Heretic to the throne. It was Horemheb's wish to obliterate a shameful period in the history of the Two Lands."

"You call the lost king 'the Heretic,' " Kaptar said. "What was his crime?"

"He defied the traditional gods of the Two Lands," Ahmose said. "He drove the priests of Amon from their temples and their lands and said that there was but one god, whom he called the Aten."

"Odd," Kaptar said. "Although I never knew my father, my mother told me that he had lived among a strange people who worshiped only one god."

"Yes," said Ahmose, "they, too, were in Egypt. They called themselves the Children of Abraham, but their god was nothing more than the imaginings of a barbaric tribe of nomads. The Heretic elevated the Aten over all others, whose names he ordered erased. In the end it was his own name that suffered that fate. Amon lives."

"I would like to know more about Akhenaten," Kaptar said.

"You are a priest of Amon," Kemose said. "The archives are open to you—but there will be no time, I fear." He held out his cup. "Now, nephew."

"Uncle—"

"I beg you," Kemose said. Suddenly his eyes grew wide. A deadly pallor came over his face as he clutched at his chest. "Ah, gods, it hurts! It hurts!" he moaned.

"It is time, my prince," the chief adviser said.

Kemose's hand shook as he held out his golden cup. Kaptar had difficulty seeing as he sprinkled the powder of eternity into his uncle's wine.

"In eternity," Kemose said, lifting the cup.

"May you live," Kaptar said in a choked voice.

Kemose directed the cup toward his lips. But his hand shuddered, and wine spilled over the brim and dripped red on the linen sheets. He opened his lips and closed his eyes.

"No, not yet!" Kaptar whispered fervently. "Not yet!"

A great tremor ran through the king's body. His arm went limp. The cup spilled its contents on his chest. He gasped once, twice, and was still. The two physicians bent over him. Ahmose put his ear to the king's wine-stained chest and listened.

"Kemose, King of Upper and Lower Egypt, High Priest of Amon and Beloved of All the Gods, may he live, is with the gods."

Kaptar felt as if his own heart had been seized in a strong fist and squeezed mercilessly. He lifted his head and howled out his grief, but even as he mourned, missing his uncle terribly already, there was a small joy in him, relief that the powder of eternity that he had sprinkled into his uncle's cup had not been the cause of death. The gods had simply decided it was time to relieve Kemose of his pain and misery—and, by the gods, how he would be missed.

Kaptar was true to his promise. He left the palace immediately, seeking the protection of his bodyguard of one hundred splendid swordsmen. With four of them in attendance, he paid a visit to Thure-Amon in the temple and gave his pledge of loyalty to the man who would now be high priest and king in Waset.

"I am moved," Thure-Amon said—but his eyes told Kaptar that he was not convinced. Kemose had been right in advising Kaptar to leave immediately. There was, however, one thing more he would do before leaving Waset for an indefinite stay with his half-brother in the north. He found his way with some difficulty to that part of the archives in the great temple where were stored the parchments containing the story of Akhenaten and the Beautiful Woman Who Is Come, Nefertiti.

As he had told his uncle, he was not ignorant of the concept of one god, having heard about the Yahweh of the Hebrews from his mother. He himself was steeped in tradition, but he was touched by the naive attempt of Akhenaten to force his own beliefs on all Egypt. His sadness over his uncle's death blended with a feeling of melancholy as he read of grim Horemheb's determination to erase all recorded knowledge of the Heretic.

It was a terrible time in Egypt. However, as he gained the safety of his half-brother's royal barge with his bodyguard around him, and as the boatmen cast off lines and started the long voyage down the Nile to On, Kaptar was heartened as he thought of the barren, desolate plain where Akhenaten's glorious city had once sprawled.

If the Two Lands were strong enough to survive such a rending period of turmoil and become great again, there had to be hope not only for the present but for the future. There had to be hope for Egypt. In memory of his mother and his uncle, he would bet his life that the future of the Black Land was in the hands of a young boy, his half-brother, who, when Kaptar was back in On and Menkheperre had been placed in the tomb of his father, would be crowned King of the Two Lands. The specially crafted double crown of Upper and Lower Egypt would be heavy on the young boy's head; but at his side would stand two men who would guide his decisions in the coming years, his father and his half-brother. Musen the Libyan, not knowing what Princess Tania had done, would rejoice because he had lived to see his father's dream come true. Kaptar, Prince of Egypt, was the only man alive who knew that the king, Sheshonk, was a true son of Egypt. No Libyan blood flowed in his veins.

CHAPTER TWELVE

The boy Mephibosheth was surprisingly light. Sunu compared him to a bird whose fluffed feathers made it look large although, in the hand, it was of little flesh, hollow bones, and weightless down. He placed Mephibosheth just behind his horse's withers, his crippled legs draped on either side of the great animal's neck. The boy's eyes gleamed with excitement. Another pair of eyes, those of Mara, were on Sunu when he mounted behind the boy in one athletic bound.

"May I hold the reins?" the boy begged.

"Let's get under way; then you can," Sunu said.

He turned the horse to watch Mara mount. He had chosen a splendid animal for her, a mare captured only recently from the Philistines. Mara stood by the horse's head, slender and dignified even in her torn and faded robes, her ebony hair a mass of wild curls, her almond-shaped eyes staring at Sunu unblinkingly.

"We are ready," Sunu told her.

The troop was moving out. The scouts were already out of sight, taking the planned route southward. The hilly terrain would make for slow going, and it would be vital to have riders on the point, well ahead of the main party, lest they blunder into a Philistine patrol.

Mara shifted her feet indecisively.

"You told me you could ride," Sunu said.

She would not meet his penetrating gaze. "I can," she insisted. "It's just that this animal is so huge."

Sunu swung a leg over his horse's flank and slid to the ground. "I'll help you."

"That would be good of you," she said coolly.

He cupped his hands. "Step here."

She put a dainty foot into his palms. Her sandal was worn, the straps cracked and fraying.

"Just put your weight on my hands and swing one leg over," he said when she hesitated.

She made one false start, then managed to step up. But when she tried to lift her leg over the horse's back, her robe prevented extension, and she rebounded from the animal's side. Sunu managed to steady her before she fell.

"You'll have to lift your robe until you're settled on the horse."

Her face grew darker, flushing with a mixture of anger and embarrassment. "Turn your head," she ordered.

"This is no time for modesty. If you expect me to deliver you safely to your uncle, you must listen to me."

"I have listened, *master*," she said, putting nasty emphasis on the word. "Turn your head."

"Yes, *mistress*," he said as he faced away.

He caught a momentary glimpse of inner thigh. She made an involuntary gasp, an explosion of breath, when she landed solidly on the horse's hard back with nothing cushioning her but a thin fleece.

"Well, pick up the reins," Sunu said, for she was clinging to the horse's mane, her eyes wide. She shook her head and would not tear loose.

"You've never been on a horse before," he accused.

"I can do it," she said, but there was no conviction in her voice.

Sunu sighed in resignation, turned, and summoned one of his men. "Take the boy on your horse," he instructed.

Mephibosheth was lifted from one horse to the other. Sunu had to call Mara's name several times to get her attention, for she seemed nearly stupefied, her fingers entangled in the horse's mane and holding fast for dear life.

"I want you to move back."

She looked at him in silence as if she didn't understand.

"Just slide backward. Give me room to sit in front of you. You can hold on to my waist."

"No," she said.

Sunu sighed again. He took hold of the dangling reins from around the horse's neck, then mounted his own animal. "Hold on," he warned her as he signaled his horse to move with a tap of his heel. Mara made a little squeal as her animal followed the other.

"You'll be all right," Sunu said, twisting to look back at her. "Just relax."

"Slow down!" she wailed.

"The animals can't walk any slower. Just hold on and try to feel at ease. You have nothing to fear."

But as if she were top-heavy, she slowly began listing to one side until she was in danger of falling off. Sunu quickly reined his horse to a stop and leaped down. Mara was stuggling to right herself, with no success. He reached her just in time to catch her as she slid off.

"For the love of God," he muttered, "what am I to do with you?"

"I'll walk," she said angrily.

"You wouldn't be able to keep up."

"Then I'll run."

"All day?"

"You're hateful."

"*I'm* hateful?" Sunu shook his head. "Come with me," he said, taking her hand forcefully and dragging her to his horse. Lifting her with ease, he seated her on the animal's back and, before she could slide off, vaulted up behind her. When he put his arms around her to seize the reins she stiffened.

"This is not respectable," she protested.

"I suppose you prefer falling to the ground," Sunu said.

He called to one of his men, who rode back and took the horse intended for Mara; then he kicked his animal into motion, urging it into a trot to catch up with the rest of the troop. Mara squealed as she bounced up and down. Sunu tightened one arm around her to hold her in place; she grasped his arm with both hands and clung tightly. He moved his horse into place at the head of the column.

"Sister, look!" Mephibosheth called out, a huge grin on his face. "I'm doing it!"

The soldier who was riding behind the boy was letting him hold the reins.

"I'll bet you could do it, too, Mara," Mephibosheth said.

"Want to try?" Sunu asked her.

"No, thank you," she said obstinately. She was holding herself rigidly erect, trying to avoid letting her body come into close contact with his.

"We're going to be riding all day," Sunu said. "You'll find it less tiring if you relax and lean back against me."

"I'm all right."

He shrugged. "Suit yourself."

*   *   *

The sun was nearing the zenith when Mara finally gave up and, with an audible sigh of relief, leaned back and rested against him. Sunu's face brushed her hair. It was a tangled mess, but it was shiny and clean. There was a smell about it that he would not have been able to describe. He became aware of the feel of her under his arm, of her warmth and softness against his chest and stomach. He had never held a girl before. Her hands, resting easily on his arm, had a warmth of their own, a heat that began to burn pleasantly as he let his nose brush her great mass of hair. His arm seemed almost to ignite where it came into contact with her stomach as he held her. To his embarrassed horror, his manhood throbbed to life. He shifted his weight so that the hardness would not be pressed against her—although his entire being yearned to do just that.

"I think you can hold me less tightly now," she suddenly said.

He relaxed his arm. Her hands remained in place.

"It's really just a matter of matching yourself to the motion of the horse, isn't it?" she asked.

"Yes," he said, having to clear his throat to voice the word.

"I think I can manage by myself now."

"Good. We'll give you another try when we stop."

"And when will that be?"

"The horses need water. We'll turn eastward and go down to the river soon."

"I am grateful," she said softly.

He wanted to acknowledge her words but couldn't find his own words to do so.

His silence irritated her. "I won't thank you again," she snapped, "since you seem incapable of appreciating such a gesture."

Sunu still said nothing.

They rode on in silence, with Sunu becoming more and more enraptured with the feel of her, letting his imagination caress the wonder that was in his arms. He recalled the peek he had gotten of her thigh and glanced down at the curve of lower leg on display as she gripped the sides of the horse, her robe riding above her knees. Her hair was scented with her own smell, richer than any perfume and more intoxicating than incense. He tried to picture the rest of her, and an uncontrollable shudder convulsed his shoulders. He didn't know what was happening to him. The intensity of his emotions was frightening—and he prayed Mara was unaware of them.

But, in fact, Mara was fully aware of his state. Though yet a virgin, she was not ignorant of the ways of the world, for she had become the object of a few ambitious young men as soon as she had reached puberty. She had felt a man's lips on hers, had known the mysterious warmth and comfort of a man's arms around her. When a particularly severe shudder of need shook Sunu, she couldn't suppress a giggle.

"What?" he managed.

"Nothing," she said.

"Stop. Soon," he grunted.

She giggled again. "I think you had better—before you melt."

Sunu took the remark as a reproach and her laughter as belittlement. All passion fled. He had been riding with his neck bent forward, the better to brush her hair with his nose. He straightened, his face burning.

Turning, he motioned to one of his men to draw close. "Ride forward," he instructed. "Tell the scouts to turn toward the river."

Nodding, the soldier kicked his horse into a run and disappeared.

"Thirsty?" Mara asked teasingly.

In truth, she was not immune to Sunu's manly bearing, his muscular arms and chest, his well-sculpted face. Like Sunu, she was at the stage of her life when inner fires were less deeply banked, ready to burst into flame at the slightest breath of stimulation. She shifted her body, seeking to feel once more the muscular form riding behind her—and the evidence of his desire that had brushed her more than once as the movement of the horse jostled them.

Sunu led his horse over to the stream and dismounted, then helped Mara down. He would not look her in the eye; she did not try to engage him in conversation.

While the horses were being watered, Mara walked upstream with Mephibosheth, removed her sandals, and waded into the cool, clear water of the River Jordan. Kneeling, she scooped water to rinse the dust from her face. Her brother splashed her playfully. She cried out and splashed him back, and then they were engaged in a no-holds-barred water fight. She emerged laughing and soaked.

Watching her from where he sat astride a rock, Sunu felt himself being aroused once again. The wet material of her tattered robe clung to her slim yet rounded figure, outlining her breasts and her shapely legs—and hinting at the mystery of her core.

When it was time to set off again, Mara made no further mention of riding alone. Sunu lifted her to the back of his horse—although this time she rode behind him. Throughout the afternoon, as they rode southward along the Jordan, he fought to keep his mind off her—an impossible task with her arms encircling his waist and, as the day wore on, her cheek resting on his bare back.

By the time the troop reached the crossing that would lead to Jabesh-Gilead and Mahanaim, Sunu had made a decision. He called his second-in-command to his campfire.

"You will continue south with the troop," he said. "Observe the number of Philistines in the blockhouses and take careful note of any patrols. Don't get provoked into a fight unless it is forced upon you. When you reach Hebron, tell Joab that I will report to him as quickly as possible after I have visited my grandfather in Mahanaim."

"Have you considered the possibility that the Benjamites will hold you, once you are in their hands? After all, you were rather conspicuous at the Pool of Gibeon. Some of them will remember."

"There is my safe conduct," Sunu said, pointing to Mara and her brother. "My thinking is this: We cannot ride to Ish-bosheth in troop strength, lest we be attacked before we could explain our mission. I will not risk that. A single man riding with a young woman and a boy will have a chance to identify himself."

The second-in-command nodded. "I hear your orders, and I obey."

At daybreak the troop rode southward, while Sunu and his charges prepared for the ride into Mahanaim. Sunu kept four horses, two of them packed with food and supplies. Since he couldn't very well ride with both Mara and Mephibosheth, he thought Mara would have the best chance of accomplishing the ride alone—a feat she was determined to accomplish. Sunu lifted her to mount. She took the reins confidently—perhaps overconfidently—and immediately kicked the horse in the ribs with her heels. The horse leaped forward, almost dislodging her.

"Hang on!" Sunu called as the horse trotted toward the river.

In the few seconds it took him to lift Mephibosheth onto his own mount and settle himself behind the boy, then gather the leads of the two pack animals, Mara was out of sight in the thick growth at the margin of the river. Sunu was not concerned. He knew that the horse would not go into the water without proper urging. He would find Mara and her mount waiting on the riverbank.

He was wrong in only one respect. Mara was not alone.

As he was about to emerge out of the dense

growth onto the steep bank, his heart leaped. Mara was being pulled roughly off her horse by a mounted Philistine infantryman.

Sunu pulled his mount back within the thicket. "Stay here!" he whispered to Mephibosheth. "Do not move! Do you understand me?"

"Yes, sir."

He dismounted and crept forward. A second Philistine soldier had seized Mara by her other arm. The two of them were having a tug of war over the tasty morsel. Without hesitation, Sunu ran down the slope, sword in hand. He knew he was putting his life in the balance, for it was not likely that two Philistine infantrymen were traveling alone. They were probably on the point for a patrol.

So involved were the Philistines in quarreling over the girl that they were unaware of Sunu's presence until he lashed out at the arm of one of them. His blade sliced cleanly through flesh, and the force of the blow broke bone. The Philistine screamed in surprise and pain. A backstroke to the neck silenced him as Sunu's blade cut artery, sinew, and tissue. The man fell with his head lolling loosely.

The second Philistine managed to draw his sword, but he was facing a man frenzied by a threat to a girl who had, in virtually a moment's time, become the most important thing in his life. The fury of Sunu's attack, the strength of his forge-strengthened arm, sent the enemy reeling backward. It was over so quickly that Mara had time only to lift one hand to her mouth and gasp in horror as Sunu's blade opened the Philistine's stomach and spilled out bloody coils of entrails.

Sunu lifted Mara quickly and threw her onto her horse.

"You're bleeding," she gasped, for his arms had been sprayed with gore.

"Go, go!" Sunu said, slapping the horse on the flank to force the animal into the river.

Waiting within the dense growth, Mephibosheth,

hearing Sunu's shouted urging, decided it was time to
see what was happening. Gathering up the reins of
Sunu's horse and those of the pack animals, he kicked
his mount, echoing, "Go, go!" and broke through to
the riverbank. Sunu ran to meet him, vaulted up behind the boy, and kicked the horse into faster movement. Water splashed up, cooling and pleasant, as they
forded the river. Mara was waiting on the other side.

"Quickly, quickly!" Sunu said, hearing the blast of
a Philistine signal trumpet. The sound was far too close
for comfort. He urged his mount into a jarring climb
up the bank. Mara clung to her horse's mane for dear
life as it followed suit. When they were safely hidden
among the thick brush, Sunu turned and looked back.
He caught a glimpse of several horsemen coming down
the far bank.

"We must put some distance behind us before
they discover their compatriots and decide to pursue,"
he said. "Your horse will follow mine. Just hold the
reins firmly and move with the motion. Don't fight it."

He prodded his horse into a lope, then looked
back. Mara was being quite brave, although her face
was pale. She gripped the reins with one hand and the
horse's mane with the other.

They left the riverside thickets and entered groves
of olives and fruit trees that showed signs of neglect. A
ruined farmhouse bespoke raids made by the Philistines over the Jordan. Sunu did not feel safe until they
had climbed a ridge into barren countryside and were
down the other side, out of sight of anyone coming
from the river. He called a halt when the sun was a
quarter high, to allow the horses to drink from a
spring.

Mara accepted his help in dismounting. "Your
arms. They're all bloody," she said as he lowered her to
the ground.

"It isn't my blood." He indicated her robe, which
was stained with splotches of reddish brown. "Neither

is that. It must have rubbed off my arms when I put you on the horse."

She stood very close, her face two handspans from his. The top of her head came to his chin. "You were very brave," she said softly.

"Well . . ."

"And savage," she added. "So feral and frightening that I didn't recognize you."

He stiffened, feeling he had been criticized. "Would you have preferred that I enter into negotiations with the Philistines?"

"I didn't mean—"

"We could have talked about which of them was to have you first while their companions rode down upon us, making the competition for you even more intense after they had killed me and your brother."

She put her hands on his arms. Her eyes burned into his. "You misunderstand. I wasn't condemning you in any way."

"Oh."

"You saved me," she said simply.

It was as if there were invisible bands drawing his face down toward hers—and as if she were frozen in place. The distance closed gradually until, with a sigh, his mouth met hers, finding a moist warmth, a yielding firmness.

The sun stood still. Joshua was not the only one who could command miracles, Sunu thought with the one part of his mind unaffected by the intoxication of young love.

The sun moved again when Mephibosheth's voice intruded on paradise.

"Someone comes!"

The "someone" was in fact a group of armed men who surrounded the spring, advancing with weapons at the ready. Their leader demanded Sunu's identity.

"I am Sunu, son of Eri and grandson of the smith of Shiloh, who is with Abner and Ish-bosheth in Mahanaim. And here are the son and daughter of Jonathan, niece and nephew of the king who reigns east of the Jordan."

There was clear disappointment among the men of Manasseh, some of whom had their eyes on the fine Philistine horses and others on something of more ephemeral value, the girl.

The leader studied the threesome carefully before acquiescing. "We will escort you to Mahanaim. The king knows not that he has living relatives. He will surely be most pleased to learn of you." He sent one of his group on ahead to announce their arrival.

Sunu's lips still burned with Mara's kiss, but there was no opportunity to speak with her as they rode the short distance to Ish-bosheth's capital. Once there, they were immediately taken into the king's domicile, where their arrival caused a stir. Mara and her brother were embraced by the king and whisked away, while Sunu found himself being clasped hard against the muscular chest of his grandfather, who then took him under his wing.

"Just look at the boy," Urnan said proudly as he escorted Sunu into his house, where Jerioth greeted them. "He has outgrown not only his father, but me as well."

"I'm sure he did not do it deliberately to give you shame," Jerioth quipped. She kissed Sunu fondly, then squeezed his shoulder. "And you are far more handsome than either your father or this old jackal."

"It is good to see you, Grandmother," Sunu said.

Leah, who had been overlooked in the moment of greeting, tugged on Sunu's kilt. "You my bro-ver," she said.

Sunu looked down on a smiling little girl of two years, saw in her face the cheekbones and nose of his father. He knelt. "You're Leah?"

" 'Eah," she said, nodding.

"You are by far my prettiest little sister."

"You pretty, too," Leah said, to Sunu's amusement.

Sunu's stomach suddenly rumbled. He realized he couldn't remember when he had last eaten.

"Food, woman!" Urnan commanded Jerioth with exaggerated vehemence. "The boy's gut is crying out from hunger! Give the boy food!"

"Me hungry, too," Leah said.

"Ah, I am nothing but a slave in your grandfather's house," Jerioth said with a grin. She kissed Sunu again as he stood up with Leah perched on one arm. "It's so good to see you—so good, in fact, that I won't ask how it happens that you are here. We have been told that you have become one of David's mighty men."

Sunu laughed. "Hardly that."

"Your courage and skill were noted at the Pool of Gibeon," Urnan said.

"I will consider myself a mighty man when, like Benaiah ben Jehoiada, I go down into a pit and slay a lion with nothing more than a spear," Sunu said.

"Hear our hero talk," Urnan teased. "My beloved witch is too polite to ask how you come to be here in the camp of people who, unfortunately, must be considered your enemies, but I will."

"I came with the son and daughter of Jonathan. I found them stranded and alone in the north. They had been surviving in the care of an old woman since the battle of the Gilboan hills."

"You have earned the gratitude of Ish-bosheth for uniting him with his kin," Urnan said.

Jerioth thrust a cup at Sunu. "New wine," she said.

"My grandmother is an angel," Sunu said.

"My grandson is a flatterer," Jerioth said affectionately.

He drank deeply. "All the dust of Israel was in my throat."

"I will have food for you soon," Jerioth said. "And unless you wish to repeat the entire story, don't start telling Urnan of your adventures until I, too, can hear."

"Me, too," Leah said.

"You, too, little one," Sunu said. And as he looked upon his half-sister he couldn't help but wonder if a child of his by Mara would be as pretty.

There was nothing palatial about the residence of the man whom Abner had proclaimed to be king of all Israel. Ish-bosheth and his family occupied two ordinary houses constructed of white limestone, each of two stories with a small courtyard and an external staircase leading to the roof. They were no grander than the house of Urnan the armorer, although they were separated from the other, closely packed dwellings of the village. In the open areas near the king's houses, orderly rows of tents had been set up to shelter Abner's army.

Early the next morning Sunu found himself walking past the king's dwelling. He saw movement on a rooftop and felt a surge of delight when he recognized the face of Mara. Had her features not been burned on his heart like a brand, he might well have mistaken her, for her wild, curly hair was covered by a colorful scarf.

She waved at him. He lifted his hand to her, his heart pounding. She motioned for him to stay where he was, looked behind her, waved again, and disappeared for a moment before coming down the outside stairway and running across the yard toward him. She was dressed like the royal princess she was. Her undergown was of white linen striped vertically in brown, her tunic was royal blue trimmed in red, a fringed sash cinched her narrow waist, new sandals adorned her dainty feet, peeking out from under the hem of her gown, and a band of gold encircled her forehead.

She halted a few feet away, her face showing confusion for a moment. She recovered quickly and smiled. "Did you find your grandfather well?"

Sunu grinned. "Urnan is indestructible. Strong as a bull and twice as cantankerous when aroused."

"Then I shall always remember to walk softly around him," Mara said. She seemed oddly shy.

"You—" He couldn't speak his thoughts.

"Yes?" she coaxed.

"You are beautiful."

She blushed with pleasure. "My uncle will thank you in person for helping me and my brother."

"That isn't necessary. Although I do have reason to see the king."

"And what reason is that?"

He hesitated a moment. "It has to do with you."

"Have I not a right to know, then?"

"I will ask your uncle for your hand in marriage."

"Perhaps," she said flippantly, "you should ask *my* opinion of that possibility before you approach the king."

He cleared his throat. "I had assumed—because—"

She laughed. "Because I kissed you? For one kiss you assumed that I would rush into your arms to be your wife?"

Hurt flooded Sunu's being. He felt his face swell.

"Oh, don't puff up like a toad," she said sharply.

"If I have overstepped myself, I apologize humbly, princess." He turned, walking with his head high and his back straight until he felt her hand on his arm. He halted and looked down into her face.

"Are you so young and inexperienced that you don't know a woman wants to be wooed?" she asked.

"I know little of these things," he admitted, still smarting from what he thought was rejection.

"A woman likes to be serenaded," she said.

His hopes soared. He laughed. "Were I to sing to you, my chances of gaining your approval would be destroyed forever. I bray like a donkey."

"There are other ways of wooing a woman."

Sunu looked at her thoughtfully. He stared at her

shapely earlobes, adorned with earrings of silver. "Would you come to my grandfather's shop this afternoon?"

"Why should I?" she asked, but her smile was encouraging.

"If for nothing else, to see why I want you to come there."

"My, my, aren't we enigmatic."

"Well? Would you?"

"Yes," she agreed. "But only to see what silly reason you have."

She arrived at Urnan's forges earlier than the appointed time. Sunu, his back to her, was unaware of her presence at first. He was stripped to the waist. His hair, which had grown quite long since he took up being a warrior, hung heavy with perspiration to the shoulders. His arms, developed by his work at the forge, bulged with muscle. His body gleamed with moisture. The sight of him made Mara quite breathless. She watched for a long time, wondering what delicate work he was doing as he tapped lightly with a small tool.

For his part, Sunu became aware of an odd warmth, and when he looked around and saw Mara, he knew the sensation was caused by her eyes on him. Pleased, he smiled, his white teeth a contrast to his smoke-darkened face.

"You're early," he said.

"Would you like me to leave?"

"No!" he said in quick panic. "It's fine that you're early." He motioned her to come forward. With a pair of tongs he picked up the object he had been working on the anvil. "As a matter of fact, I've just finished." He smiled shyly. "It's for you."

He displayed a delicately wrought gold earring, joined in three sections. It was so long, it would dangle to the base of her jaw.

"Ooh," she cooed in admiration. She reached out to touch it, but he snatched it out of reach.

"It's hot," he warned. "Wait." He doused the earring in water. "It needs just a bit of polishing."

"It's beautiful," she said.

He buffed the gold quickly and expertly while she watched.

"I thought armorers made swords and spearheads and the tools of war."

"We do."

"How did you learn to make jewelry of such exquisite beauty?"

"From my father and his father and their fathers before them."

He took a matching earring from a shelf and held the pair out to her. "Is this a form of wooing?" he asked.

She nodded. Quickly she removed the silver earrings she had been wearing. "Put them on for me."

"My hands," he said, holding them out. "They're filthy."

"Put them on, please," she said, looking up into his eyes with a radiance that dazzled him.

He did his best to touch only her earlobes, but in spite of himself he left a dark smear on her left cheek. She felt the earrings with her fingers.

"They're deliciously heavy," she said.

"Do you like them?"

"Oh, yes. Very much."

"There's this, too," he said, taking a golden bracelet from the shelf.

"It's too much, Sunu," she protested.

"No. Nothing could ever be too much for you." He lifted her hand. He placed the cuff around her wrist and closed it tighter.

"There's no one else here," she remarked, looking around the shop.

"No, there isn't. My grandfather is resting. The others are working in the other shops."

"We're all alone."

"Yes," he agreed.

"Silly," she said, lifting her face, "do I have to beg you to kiss me?"

"Not more than once." His embrace left her slightly soiled, but she didn't care.

CHAPTER THIRTEEN

The sun shone brilliantly in a cloudless sky, although winter had sent a scout of cool air ahead of itself, giving a preview of what awaited. Jerioth and Leah were on the rooftop of their stone dwelling, where the sun's warmth was captured behind the parapet walls. Jerioth was cracking almonds to extract the sweet nutmeat—and having difficulty keeping up with demands of Leah's appetite.

"Goodness, child, there'll be none left for your grandfather if you eat them all," she admonished as Leah plunged her hand into the bowl of shelled nuts for yet another helping.

Leah's response was muffled by a mouthful of almonds, but she didn't reach for the bowl again. "Those Urnan's," she said after swallowing a couple of times.

"That's generous of you," Jerioth said dryly.

"Urnan come soon?"

Jerioth looked at the sun. It was still early; Urnan would be at the armory for some time yet. "No, I'm afraid not."

As if to prove her wrong, Urnan's voice sounded from below. "Where are my two girls?"

Leah ran to the stairway and called out, "Here, Urnan! Here!"

Jerioth put aside the bowls of shelled and un-shelled nuts and rose to meet her husband as his head —with its curls now more gray than dark—appeared at the head of the stairs. Although he wore his work clothes, the garments were unsoiled. By looking at his hands and face, Jerioth could tell that he had not worked a forge that day.

"You're early," she said, giving herself into his embrace.

"Me, too," Leah said, tugging on Urnan's kilt.

He lifted her, and she was hugged between the two adults.

"You early," Leah accused.

"Is an old armorer to kings not permitted to take some time off?" Urnan asked.

"If it were left to me you'd take *more* time off," Jerioth said.

"Well, I might say that I will be doing so, but one cannot foresee the future." Urnan smiled at his wife, adding, "Most of us can't, anyway."

He sat down on a bench and indulgently bounced Leah on his knee, the look on his face declaring, *Well, old man, here you are with a two-year-old you've taken as your own, and who knows what's to become of the lot of us.*

Jerioth went back to shelling almonds. "There's an excellent nut crop this year," she said.

"Good, good."

"It seems almost sinful," Jerioth went on, "what with people west of the Jordan going hungry, their fields ruined by the Philistines, while here we are in plenty."

"You hungry, Urnan?" Leah asked.

"Not just now."

"We're having a lentil stew," Jerioth said.

"A bowl of pottage," Urnan said, "such as Jacob gave to Esau."

"I suppose." Unlike her husband, Jerioth took little interest in the old tales told by the Hebrews. "And a nice roast of lamb."

"Good," Urnan said.

"You have something on your mind, don't you?"

"You have come to know me too well, wife."

"How else can I anticipate your needs and attend to them?"

Urnan put Leah down, patted her playfully on the rear, and went to sit beside his wife on her bench. He put his hand tenderly on the nape of her neck.

"What's bothering you, my love?" she asked.

"Perhaps it's nothing. Perhaps I'm imagining that I see things coming that are not going to happen."

She laughed. "Remember? It is I who am called a witch."

"Tell me this, then: Is Ish-bosheth possessed by the same devils that afflicted his father?"

"Ah."

He smiled at her. "A brilliant answer."

"I cannot answer. Tell me why you're concerned."

"Small things. I wouldn't notice had I not known Saul, had I not been close to him so that I saw him in his rages. Ish-bosheth has not yet reached the point of losing his presence entirely, of course. And perhaps it's only his nature to use words like arrows against those who are his strength."

"All is not well between Ish-bosheth and Abner?"

He sighed. "At first all went quite well. Ish-bosheth seemed to be very aware that he doesn't have the leadership qualities of his father or his brother Jonathan. He was grateful to Abner for in effect giving him the throne of Israel and protecting his right to sit on it with a strong sword arm and the loyalty of what was left of Saul's army."

"But now . . . what actions of Ish-bosheth disturb you?" Jerioth asked.

"I first noticed a poison was creeping into their relationship when Abner came back from the defeat at the Pool of Gibeon," Urnan replied. "Ish-bosheth didn't openly accuse Abner of cowardice, but he implied as much."

"Have you talked with Ish-bosheth about this? He values you, for he knows that his father trusted you and relied on your advice."

"I limit my words of dubious wisdom to times when they are solicited." Urnan shrugged. "I have no reason to depart from that practice."

"You have not yet said exactly what is bothering you."

"A woman," he said with another shrug.

"Rizpah," she said.

He looked at her quickly. "You *are* a witch."

She laughed. "I am a woman. In God's name, are you men so blind as to think the king's general can creep into the bed of Saul's favorite concubine without being observed?"

"A slave or a servant spread the word?"

It was Jerioth's turn to shrug. "It is common knowledge among the women of the royal compound."

"Does the king know?"

"You can judge better than I whether or not Ish-bosheth would keep his silence if he knew that Abner has defied the laws and established an alliance with the king's concubine."

"No," Urnan said. "He could not know. If he knew, he would have confronted Abner." He shook his head. "My dear little witch, I am unwilling to waste what could very well be the last good years of my life in giving loyalty to another madman."

"What would you do?"

"There's the armory in the Wilderness of Judah."

"Or Hebron, with Eri and Sunu?"

"Or Hebron," he agreed, nodding.

"I am sure you know that whatever your decision, it is my wish as well."

He kissed her forehead. "Don't start packing just yet. I think the time may have come for me to have a talk with Ish-bosheth."

"Husband," she whispered urgently, "be very, very careful. If he is indeed possessed by Saul's devils, he could be dangerous to you. Saul was your friend, even when he was in his rages. You hardly know this son of his."

"Your caution is well taken." He hugged her. "Don't worry. You are the main reason I intend to make the best of the years I have remaining."

"Urnan," Leah piped up, holding out her arms to him.

"Would you like to try calling me 'Grandfather'?" Urnan asked as he picked the child up and put her back on his knee.

"No," she said.

"Why?"

"Can't say gran-fadder."

"Actually, I think you just did." He hugged her close. He was tempted to tell Jerioth to make preparations to join Leah's father in Hebron. There, at least, was a king who was not likely to be possessed by anything other than his strong belief in the God of Abraham. Urnan had too much to live for to become dangerously involved in the affairs of Ish-bosheth and Abner. He would not be in any hurry to talk with the king.

But another Child of the Lion was consumed with urgency. With the kisses of the beautiful Mara still impressed on his lips, Sunu, son of Eri—with polished gear, neatly combed hair, and garbed in fresh tunic and kilt—presented himself at the house of Ish-bosheth,

King of Benjamin, Ephraim, and all Israel. He was met at the door by the object of his passion, and he was achingly aware of her at his side as he entered the palace. She touched his hand before leaving him to observe the audience from a balcony, hidden from her uncle's view.

The king was dressed in royal purple finery. Well-equipped soldiers lined the walls of the makeshift throne room. Abner stood a pace behind Ish-bosheth to his right.

"You may speak," Ish-bosheth said as Sunu approached and gave the king a respectful bow.

"I am grateful to you for giving me welcome," Sunu said formally.

"As we are grateful to you for your services to us in regard to my brother's daughter and son," the king said magnanimously.

"It is his daughter, Mara, who brings me before you," Sunu said. His mouth was suddenly as dry as the desert. He swallowed.

"How so?" Ish-bosheth asked with a frown.

"Ish-bosheth, King of Israel," Sunu said, observing protocol, "I have come before you to humbly ask the hand of your niece Mara in marriage." Stunned by his own daring, Sunu fell silent.

Ish-bosheth jerked forward to the edge of his throne, his face clouded. Abner leaned closer, and the king turned his head to glare at him.

Abner spoke quietly, his words for the king's ears alone. "I ask you not to answer hastily," he whispered. "I beg you to consider all aspects of this proposal."

Ish-bosheth made a dismissive motion toward Abner. He turned to Sunu, opened his mouth as if to speak, then looked back at Abner uncertainly. When he did finally speak, his words were slow and measured.

"Your request takes us by surprise. Leave us now and we will consider your proposal."

"I am grateful," Sunu said. "As you may well

know, I have no store of riches, but I have my craft, and as long as I have that, I am not a poor man."

"Leave us," Ish-bosheth commanded.

Mara was waiting for Sunu at the entrance. "You heard?" he asked.

"I heard." Her face was solemn.

"How do you think he took it?"

"How can he say no?" she asked. "You saved my life. And I love you."

He took her hand in his. "You think, then, that he will say yes?"

"He *must*!"

Ish-bosheth waited until Sunu was gone, then turned to Abner angrily. "I don't know what it is you're thinking, but I remind you that my brother's daughter is a royal princess of Israel, and she will *not* be wife to a common tradesman."

"The armorer is hardly that," Abner countered. "Think, my friend. Sunu is more than one of David's mighty men. He is the son of Eri, who is at present the royal armorer to David. He is the grandson of Urnan, your own royal armorer. You know the value of Urnan to our cause. You know the worth of his wisdom, for you have wisely listened to and weighed his counsel, just as your father did when he was king. An alliance between such an influential family and the family of Saul could be of immense value to us."

Ish-bosheth frowned. "David will not bow down to me simply because the son of his armorer is married to my niece."

"No, but will a father fight against both his own father and his own son? Will Eri continue to manufacture arms for David if both his son and his father are in our camp? Without Eri in Hebron, David would have to depend on armorers with far less skill to provide his army with weapons."

Ish-bosheth shook his head. "But Mara is a royal princess," he said stubbornly.

"How much gold is in your treasury?" Abner asked.

"You know the answer to that as well as I. The gold of Israel is in the hands of the Lords of the Five Cities."

"Not all of it," Abner said. "Urnan the smith is a rich man."

"Not because of what *I* have paid him."

"No, because of his skill with things other than swords. He sells bracelets and necklaces and earrings of his own crafting, and his trade reaches far—into the towns of the south all the way to Zoan. What I'm saying to you is this: As the boy told you, he is not a poor tiller of the land. He is the heir of a rich family, a family with the means of living well. When this dispute between us and David is settled and we have driven the Philistines from the land once more, Mara would be a wealthy and honored woman as the wife of this Sunu. You could make a far worse alliance, for example, by marrying her to some ragtag so-called prince of some insignificant kingdom."

"We will consider," Ish-bosheth said regally. "We would know more of this family of armorers. Call the smith Urnan to me."

Urnan's dwelling was cozy—a fire on the hearth was keeping the chill at bay, he had just finished a splendid meal, and he was looking forward to spending the evening with the two females in his life. Therefore, when one of Abner's officers, a man Urnan knew well, knocked on the door and announced that Urnan's presence was wanted urgently in the king's chambers, Urnan groaned.

"What is it that can't wait until morning?" he asked the soldier.

"I was not taken into the king's confidence, Urnan."

Sighing, Urnan told Jerioth he would return as quickly as possible—but perhaps she had better not wait up for him. Giving her a quick kiss on the forehead, he grabbed a cloak against the cool of the evening and headed out the door.

As he and the officer walked together toward the palace, Urnan asked, "Is anything unusual going on?"

"Not to my knowledge. I will tell you all I know. I was officer of the guard when your grandson—"

"Sunu?"

"Yes. When he asked to see the king. He'd been gone only a short while when Abner told me to fetch you."

I wonder what Sunu is up to, Urnan asked himself. He would know soon enough.

He entered the throne room and bowed before Ish-bosheth. Nodding to Abner, he greeted him by name.

"My friend," Ish-bosheth began, "we have just had an interesting audience with your grandson."

"So I am given to understand," Urnan said.

"To get directly to the point," Ish-bosheth continued, "your grandson has proposed an alliance by way of marriage between my family and yours."

Aha! So the fetching Mara has captured Sunu's heart as well as pleased his eye, Urnan thought to himself. "I'll be damned," he murmured.

Ish-bosheth frowned. "I do not like to hear curses," he said.

"No, you weren't around your father too much, were you?" Urnan said with a grin. "Forgive me. Tell me more about what my grandson has in mind."

"You are, of course, well aware that he spent considerable time with my niece during their journey from the Gilboan hills to my city."

"So I understand," Urnan said. "But it was a matter of necessity, and they *were* chaperoned by the girl's brother."

"A mere boy," Ish-bosheth said.

"Is my grandson being accused of impropriety?" Urnan asked, bristling.

"Not at all, my friend," Abner said quickly. "In fact, we are looking upon Sunu's proposal of marriage with Mara with great interest."

Urnan relaxed but did not lose his edge of wariness.

"Abner has advanced the possibility that your son, Eri, might join us if both you and *his* son were serving the King of All Israel."

"I cannot speak for my son," Urnan said tightly.

"Surely a man would not fight against both his father and his son," Ish-bosheth said.

"Although my grandson is a notable exception to the rule, armorers usually do not fight."

"It is the same, nonetheless," Ish-bosheth said angrily. "Eri fights by providing David with weaponry."

Urnan was silent. He was not at all pleased with the direction the conversation had taken.

"If we should see fit to give my niece in marriage to your grandson, there would, of course, be a respectable bride-price," Ish-bosheth added.

"That would be between you and Sunu," Urnan said.

Ish-bosheth raised his eyebrows. "No help from his grandfather?"

"The responsibility is his and that of his father."

"The bride-price I would be most interested in would be the presence of the armorer Eri in my city," Ish-bosheth said.

"Again, I cannot speak for my son."

"You sorely tax my patience!" the king shouted.

Urnan drew back his shoulders. "Sire, as you may remember, I was a friend of your father's and of your brothers'. I consider myself to be a friend to you, as well."

Ish-bosheth was somewhat contrite. "Yes, of course—but you vex me, Urnan, with your avoidance of the issue."

"Since you have summoned me away from my evening meal and my family," Urnan said, "perhaps it is the appropriate time for me to broach a different subject. I would speak of this civil war between you and David."

"I prefer to call it a rebellion against God's anointed king," Ish-bosheth countered.

"Be that as it may, what kind of people are you that one powerful enemy is not enough? Why must you fight among yourselves?"

"A heathen would not understand."

Urnan took a step forward. "Ish-bosheth, once your father valued my counsel. May I speak freely?"

"I'm sure you will whether or not I agree to it," the king said sullenly.

Urnan silently concurred. "Ish-bosheth, it is madness to continue to war against Judah. My advice to you is this: Send an emissary to Hebron. Tell David that you want to end this internecine war between the tribes of the Children of Abraham."

Ish-bosheth scowled. "And be prepared to bow down to the usurper, to the man who conspired with Samuel to take the throne from my brother Jonathan?"

"David is a reasonable man, a man of God," Urnan said. "Let me go to him. Let me propose a coregency, a cooperation between Judah and Israel. A united country could drive the Philistine back to his coastal cities."

"I will *not* recognize the usurper!" Ish-bosheth fumed.

"The future of the Hebrew nation, if it is to have any, lies in unity, not in bitter discord among the various tribes."

"My father was the anointed of God," the king said stubbornly.

"He was anointed by Samuel," Urnan amended. "As was David."

Ish-bosheth's face became engorged with blood. Urnan was reminded of the way Saul looked just before giving vent to one of his rages.

"Leave us, smith," the king said, fighting for control. "Leave us quickly!"

"As you wish," Urnan said. He backed away from the king's chair for a few steps, then turned and left the throne room.

Ish-bosheth waited a few moments until the armorer had gone, then ordered, "Bring the pup of that old jackal to me."

"Have a care," Abner cautioned.

"Don't defy me, Abner!" the king warned in a high, shrill voice.

"I beg you to consider your actions and your words carefully."

"Find Sunu!" the king screamed.

In the length of time that it took to locate Sunu, Abner was unable to cool the king's temper. He was shaking his head in frustration when Sunu entered the room with Mara at his side.

"Hear me," Ish-bosheth intoned.

Mara reached for Sunu's hand. Her uncle's face purpled with rage as he noted the gesture.

"We have decided, Sunu the armorer, that your request to be united in marriage with my niece, the royal princess Mara, is both impertinent and disrespectful. In making such a request, you have shown us your lack of breeding and your heathen disregard for the traditions of Israel."

"Uncle, please!" Mara begged, her face contorted with pain.

"Silence! No daughter of a son of Saul will marry a common craftsman!"

"Please," Mara whispered.

"And you, shameless wench, cease your touch of the one who stands at your side. Leave me now, both of you. You, Mara, go to your quarters. You, smith, go wherever fancy takes you. If you care to work with your grandfather, that is your concern. If you care to rejoin those who defy the anointed King of Israel and the will of God, a curse be on you!"

"Uncle!" Mara wailed.

"This audience is over," Ish-bosheth said.

Mara led the way from the chamber, her posture regal, her head high, her sandaled feet slapping the tiles angrily. In the hallway outside she exploded.

"How dare he!" she flared. "How dare he call you common!"

Sunu's hand was on his sword hilt. The hot blood of youth was reluctant to accept an insult, even from a king.

"What will you do?" Mara asked. "I know you are a man, and a man will not take such affront without redress."

Sunu's tension suddenly drained from him. Despite himself, he laughed. He placed one palm on either side of Mara's face, framing her mouth, and kissed her lightly. "Will you forgive me if I don't draw my sword and challenge the king, Abner, and all the members of the king's guard?"

She flushed with contriteness. "Forgive *me* for—"

"For loving me?" He kissed her again, heedless of the glare of the royal guards in the corridor. "That I will never forgive, if by that you mean you wish to be released from loving me."

"Never," she promised.

"Obey your uncle," he said.

"I will not," she said quickly.

"Obey your husband-to-be, then," he said, the words audible only to them.

She nodded. Her eyes filled.

He bent to her ear. "Go to your room. Dress for travel, and make a small pack of necessities only."

Her eyes gleamed.

"Oh, yes," she whispered.

"Watch for me when the stars are well out, from the window that overlooks the courtyard."

She nodded vigorously.

He looked into her eyes. "Be absolutely sure this is what you want."

"I am sure."

In the still hours of the night, Sunu made his way through the royal complex, keeping to the shadows. When he arrived under the courtyard window, he thought perhaps Mara had fallen asleep because he threw several small pebbles into the opening before she appeared, a darker form against darkness. She leaned out, and he caught a large woolen bag that she dropped down to him. And then she was coming out of the window backward, her toes searching for purchase in the masonry. He heard her grunt, as if pained. Perhaps she had stubbed her toe or scraped her shin. She dangled from the windowsill by her hands, her feet beyond his reach.

"Turn loose," he whispered. "I'll catch you."

"I—I don't know . . ." she whispered back.

"You can trust me. I promise."

He caught her as she dropped. His arms went around her waist, and they tumbled to the earth, she atop, her back to him. As agile as a cat, she turned in his arms, her body pressed to his. He felt the thrust of her pelvic bone against him, the softness of her breasts. Her mouth found his and lightning flashed through his body. He held her face from his.

"Are you hurt?"

"No. Oh, no."

"Come, then."

They scurried to their feet and left the royal compound without incident. The guards were lax, it seemed, because there had never been a raid over the Jordan by David's men. Wending their way through the sleeping city, they arrived at the small eastern gate, whose guard was sleeping as peacefully as he had been earlier in the night when Sunu took two horses outside the walls and tethered them behind a thicket.

Soon the young lovers were mounted and traveling slowly and cautiously away from Mahanaim. Sunu followed a well-traveled road heading south, which would eventually lead to the town of Succoth. A moon helped them see their way. The road was wide enough to ride side by side. After her initial excitement, Mara was subdued.

"If you regret your decision," Sunu said, "it isn't too late to turn back."

"I am with you," she said. "I have no regrets save that of wondering when I will see my brother again."

"One day the men of all the tribes will be fighting the right enemy. Then we can all be together."

"Where do we go?"

"To Hebron."

"I am of the blood of Saul. Will David hate me?"

"He will love you as the daughter of his friend."

Mara accepted his statement. Had he told her that the moon was made of goat cheese she would have believed him.

It was not too long before dawn when, feeling safe from pursuit, Sunu led Mara from the road to find a sheltered spot among tamarisk trees, where he spread bedding.

"Rest," he said.

"Oh, yes." She fell down on the fleeces gratefully. "But aren't you . . . aren't you going to . . . rest?"

"I'll keep watch."

"Oh. All right." She closed her eyes, but then her lids immediately popped back open. She recalled the feel of him against her as she rode in front of him, the feel of his hard body when she lay atop him after dropping from the window. "Sunu?"

"Go to sleep."

"Sunu, come here," she said, her voice husky.

Her obvious desire produced an explosion within him. He went to her and knelt beside her. Her arms came up and encircled his neck, pulling him down on her, torso to torso. Her mouth was paradise to him; her passion matched his. They were heedless of the coolness of the night on their bare limbs as they explored each other unceasingly, the thrilling exploration of the inexperienced. Several false starts delayed their union —but only until nature helped the inevitable. They clung to each other tightly. Mara grasped his hips with her thighs to pull him into her deeper and deeper until, in haste and mutual surprise, their efforts gained the age-old reward. She gasped as her contractions matched his eruptions. The fading stars looked down with a thousand eyes, and as Mara looked up, she fancied she could see envy in each of them.

They reached Succoth, where Sunu traded gold for a small nomad's tent. He was in no hurry to reach the point opposite Jericho and Gilgal where they would have to cross the river into Benjamin, there to travel south to the border of Judah. Mara made no objection to spending three days camped in a little glade near the river with the horses hobbled and grazing happily on browning grass. She was content. She was with the man she loved, and he could not get enough of her body. His lust flattered her while satisfying her own desires, for she had fast developed a need for the mighty instrument that lay hidden under his robes. Summer was paying one last return visit, making it warm enough for them to swim in the river to wash away perspiration and the leavings of lovemaking—only to come out of the water, dripping and cooled, to embrace and feel the allure of wet skin and the beginnings of renewed desire.

It was only when the weather finally turned and a cold rain dripped through the tent that Sunu took them across the river into territory controlled by the Philistines, which necessitated rapid and careful travel to Benjamin. Several days later they reached their final destination and rode through the gates of Hebron. Word quickly spread that Sunu, who had left his troop to go to Ish-bosheth's court, was back. Joab, arms crossed over his chest, eyebrows raised quizzically, was waiting at Eri's house when Sunu and Mara rode up.

Sunu dismounted and saluted.

"How nice of you to rejoin us," Joab said.

Baalan came rushing out of the house to throw herself into her son's arms. "Where have you been?" she demanded.

"Please, if you all will give me a chance to explain—"

"I'm certainly willing to do that," Joab said wryly, glancing at the beautiful Mara.

"And I," Baalan said, "although I am only your mother and, therefore, have no real right to know where my son wanders all alone."

Sunu reached up to help Mara dismount. "May I present Mara, daughter of Jonathan, Princess of Israel."

Joab now studied Mara intently. "Indeed," he murmured. "Jonathan's daughter, you say."

"Mara, this is my commander, Joab," Sunu said. "And this lady who is so concerned for my fate is, of course, my mother."

Mara nodded to Joab, then smiled at Baalan.

"As soon as it can be arranged, Mother, Mara will become my wife," Sunu added.

Without warning, Baalan burst into tears. Mara looked stricken. Joab simply shrugged. Sunu was mortified.

Baalan was quick to reassure Mara. "Forgive me. These tears of mine are not your fault—and they are not from sadness. I am delighted that my son has found someone he wishes to spend his life with. It's just that I haven't yet gotten used to the fact that Sunu is now a man. It seems only weeks ago that he was yet a boy." Smiling now, she took Mara's hand. "I have prayed so for a daughter, and I've been brought such a beautiful one." She took Mara into her arms. Mara hugged her back, and her eyes filled with tears as well.

"In the name of the gods," Sunu said, rolling his eyes.

"Men can't possibly understand," Baalan said, sniffing and wiping her eyes with the back of one hand. "Isn't that so, Mara? Go away, both of you. My daughter and I have plans to make. There is much to be prepared before a proper marriage celebration can take place."

To Baalan's dismay, Mara joined with Sunu in protesting any delay in the marriage.

"But there are so many things to be done," Baalan insisted.

"All you have to do, Mother," Sunu said, "is find the priest Abiathar or one of his Levite brothers and tell him that we want a simple ceremony."

"But I must have time to plan the feast," Baalan wailed.

"I'll roast a calf," Joab said.

"I'll help you, Mother," Mara said.

"Oh, well," Baalan said, "if you *must* do this beautiful thing in haste."

The marriage ritual was conducted by Abiathar, David's personal religious adviser, and although prepared in haste, it was a pleasant ceremony. David and all his wives were in attendance—the king singing while accompanying himself on his lyre—as was virtually every resident of Hebron. Then it was done, and a Child of the Lion and a princess of Israel retired to their house, a gift from the king. Temporarily, at least, peace prevailed in Hebron.

CHAPTER FOURTEEN

Ish-bosheth was sitting alone in his throne room when a weeping kinswoman brought him the news that Princess Mara's room had been empty when it was time for her to be awakened.

"Stop wailing, woman," Ish-bosheth said angrily. "Has the royal household been searched?"

"Oh, yes," his cousin assured him. "I fear, lord, that she has been abducted."

"Are there signs of force in her room?"

"No, but . . ." She hesitated.

"But what, woman?" Ish-bosheth thundered.

"Her favorite things are missing. Pieces of jewelry, several garments, her purple tunic, her heavy cloak—"

"But no signs of a struggle?"

"No, lord."

Ish-bosheth's face darkened. "It would seem that

the little fool has not been snatched but went willingly —and I need only one guess as to her companion." He motioned his cousin to leave him, then called one of the officers to his side. "Find out if the armorer Sunu is in the city. Quickly!"

Urnan awoke early. The days when he could sleep beyond the rising of the sun were long past, and invariably his eyes opened with first light. With winter coming, a crispness was in the air, a chill that made it delicious and sensuous to turn over; feel the smooth, soft, womanly wonder of Jerioth's body; and lie there listening as a cock proclaimed the start of another of God's days.

"Urnnn," Jerioth murmured, half asleep. She pushed her rump against him and sighed.

"My little furnace," he said, for she was so warm, so delightfully warm.

He momentarily closed his eyes and reviewed the events of the day before. After being ordered out of the king's chamber, he had gone directly to his shops— for work went on regardless of the vagaries of kings. He had done what he felt was his duty: He had warned Ish-bosheth of the folly of civil war. The king's rage had not been unexpected, since he was, after all, Saul's son. However, Urnan was more and more persuaded by the belief that the years were too precious to be spent in service to a madman. He would make a decision soon. Meanwhile, there was the matter of Sunu's romance to be considered—as if there wasn't trouble enough in a careworn world without his grandson falling in love with a princess of Israel.

Sunu had not come back to the house until late, long after dark. He had eaten alone, picking at the food Jerioth had put aside for him from the family's evening meal. It was obvious that he had a weight on his mind, but he was evasive when Urnan asked questions. Urnan had assumed the lad did not yet know Ish-bosheth's decision and was feeling uncertain. Sunu had gone to his bed early, leaving Urnan and Jerioth under the impression that the king was still weighing the merits of having Sunu as a son-in-law.

Now it was morning—and the king would most certainly have reached a decision.

Well, Urnan thought as he ran his hand over Jerioth's smooth flank, *it will all work out one way or the other.*

An alliance by marriage between his family and that of the king presented certain advantages both personally and for the good of all. Perhaps Ish-bosheth would be more inclined to listen to reason when Urnan was bound to the royal family by his nephew's marriage.

Urnan and Jerioth broke their fast with bread and fruit. Leah joined them halfway through the meal. She, too, was a warm little bundle as she crawled sleepily into Urnan's lap. He sat cross-legged on a mat with Jerioth on his right. Jerioth asked him if she should awaken Sunu.

"No. Let the lad have his sleep," he replied.

Urnan finished his food and got on his way. He stepped out of the house into the bright morning, paused and stretched lazily, then walked leisurely to his shops, where his smiths and apprentices were stoking banked fires in preparation for the day's work. Hammers were singing metallically when one of Ish-bosheth's officers approached. Urnan gave the officer a friendly greeting.

"I seek your grandson," the officer said.

"Ah, you know these young ones," Urnan said, shrugging. "They're often difficult to stir in the mornings."

"Then he is in his bed in your home?"

"I didn't wake him, so he no doubt slumbers still." Urnan smiled, remembering how agreeable it was to a young man to sleep until sated with rest. Unaware of the scene that had taken place in the king's chamber after he had left, he asked, "Do I take your inquiring after my grandson's whereabouts to mean the king has reached a decision about Sunu's petition?"

"Of that I have no knowledge," the officer said. He saluted and turned away, heading for Urnan's house.

A sudden feeling of unease assailed Urnan. "Hold," he called. The officer waited for Urnan to catch up to him, and together they walked to the armorer's house. Jerioth met them at the door, a puzzled look on her face.

"Is Sunu awake yet?" Urnan asked.

"He isn't in his room," Jerioth said. "His bed hasn't been slept in."

"I must report this to the king," the officer said.

"Why are you seeking my grandson?" Urnan asked.

"The princess Mara is missing."

Jerioth grabbed Urnan's arm and looked up at him with concern.

"Don't worry," Urnan said, although his words lacked conviction.

The officer went toward the royal quarters at a trot while Urnan went to the stables. He was not at all surprised to discover that the Philistine horses Sunu, Mara, and the boy Mephibosheth had ridden into Mahanaim were gone. "Those young idiots!" Urnan muttered.

He then hurried off to Ish-bosheth's residence. Before he reached his destination, he encountered Abner as the commander of the army emerged from a side street.

After an exchange of greetings Abner said, "I take it you're going to see the king."

"Yes."

"Be warned, Urnan. He is being very much like his father this morning."

Urnan nodded. "I thank you for alerting me. Abner, what happened here yesterday regarding my grandson?"

"The king rebuffed Sunu's proposal in an insulting manner." Abner put his hand on Urnan's right arm. A man of war himself, he knew that the arm he touched could do more than form a sword blade on the anvil. "Am I right in assuming that the boy has fled with the king's niece?"

"His horses are gone."

"I've been ordered to find him, to bring her back."

"And what are your orders regarding Sunu?" Urnan asked.

"My friend, neither I nor any of my men will obey those orders," Abner said.

"So he has told you to kill my grandson."

Abner nodded grimly. "But I assure you the search parties will ride slowly, and they will not find them."

"I am in your debt, Abner."

"Not as much as I am in yours, my friend." He patted the hilt of his sword. "I, at least, know your value."

They entered the king's chamber together. Ish-bosheth was pacing in front of his throne. "Well," he demanded, "where are they?"

"I have detailed four companies of soldiers to follow all roads leading out of the city," Abner said.

"And why are *you* here?" the king demanded of Urnan, stopping in his tracks to glare at the smith.

"To plead for your understanding," Urnan replied. "We must remember that they are young; the fires burn hotly, and impatiently, in the young."

Ish-bosheth turned to Abner. "I want the head of the thief on a stake in the courtyard before the sun sets."

"Ish-bosheth, you are speaking of my grandson," Urnan said sharply.

The king had to look up into Urnan's face. "I am speaking of the dead thief who has taken my niece by force."

"My king—" Abner began.

"Why are you still here?" Ish-bosheth demanded. "Why are you not with your men pursuing the abductor?"

"I repeat, Ish-bosheth, you are speaking of my grandson," Urnan said. There was a dangerous edge to his voice that made the king's face go pale for a moment.

"Yesterday I ordered you out of this room," Ish-bosheth said, his own voice shaking. "I have not, to my knowledge, given you permission to reenter."

"So be it," Urnan said with a curt nod. He turned on his heel and stalked out of the room.

"You're a fool," Abner told the king.

Ish-bosheth's face contorted with rage. *"How dare you!"* he screamed. *"How dare you!"*

Abner was uncowed. "Do you realize what you're doing? You're driving away a valuable ally—and, not incidentally, the most valuable armorer in all of Israel."

"We don't need him."

"Tell me that when your sword is shattered by a better-crafted blade wielded by one of David's mighty men," Abner countered. "My advice is to go after Urnan. Don't send for him, because he won't come. Go to him and assure him that you hold no enmity toward his grandson, that you value his services and welcome him and his to your family."

Ish-bosheth hung his head. "So it has come to this. Even you have turned traitor."

"Don't question my loyalty," Abner said heatedly. "As I was bound to Saul, so am I bound to you in kinship and in service. I was with my cousin Saul even when he was possessed by devils. I told him when he was wrong, and he listened. It seems the curse that drove your father to the Gilboan hills and his death has fallen upon your head as well, my king. Don't question my loyalty."

"Then give me the head of the common laborer who has taken my niece."

"That I will not do, Ish-bosheth."

"You would defy me?"

"In that matter, yes."

"First you break the laws of God, and now you obstruct my will in a matter of my own family."

Abner was taken aback. He stared at the king in silence.

"Do you think I am blind?" Ish-bosheth asked. "Do you think I am not aware that you sneak into Rizpah's bed in the dead of night like a whoremonger?"

Abner was a proud man, a man who feared God. The king's accusation touched a growing reservoir of guilt, for he knew better than anyone that he was doing a great sin by having congress with the woman who had been Saul's concubine. He had no defense save silence.

"Shall I tell the priests?" Ish-bosheth asked with a smirk. "Shall I tell them that the commander of the Army of God is a common adulterer? What would the people say, Abner? Do you think they would demand —with their protests heated by the piety of the priests —that I find myself a new general?"

Abner lifted his head, his eyes blazing. "If that is your wish, do so." He turned and stalked away.

"Abner, wait!" Ish-bosheth called after him after a momentary pause.

But Abner merely stiffened his back and quickened his pace. He had known from the beginning that Ish-bosheth lacked the leadership qualities possessed by Saul and Jonathan, but he had felt that with his help, Ish-bosheth could rally a defeated Israel. He had regretted the war with David from its onset. Now, like Urnan, he made a decision: He was not willing to waste his loyalty or his vigor on another madman.

Ish-bosheth took several quick steps after Abner, wanting, longing, to catch the general, to tell him that he appreciated what Abner had done, that he valued Abner's affection and his loyalty. But he was the king. He stopped and held his head high, his mouth set stubbornly. He had his pride.

*   *   *

Throughout the day, Ish-bosheth waited for Abner to return. When he did not, anger took over. In the early evening he called the commander of his personal guard and gave him orders.

"My king," the officer said, hearing the unthinkable, "I beg you to reconsider!"

"Will you, too, challenge me?" Ish-bosheth asked in a sad voice.

"No, sir, I will not," the officer said. He bowed, backed away, and spent the next few minutes going over the roster of his men in his head until he came up with three who would not flinch from the job assigned to them by the king.

Jerioth came in from putting Leah to bed and stopped in the doorway, watching her husband. Urnan was reclining on a couch, his face lit by a flickering oil lamp and a dying fire on the hearth. She was concerned. She had never seen him so consumed by an inner struggle. Often, when there was a decision to be made or when he was mulling over some problem involving his work, he would become moodily silent and withdraw into himself until he had resolved the issue. This time he seemed unable—or unwilling—to make a decision.

"It's getting late," Jerioth said.

A cold wind mourned around the corners of the house. She put more wood on the fire. It blazed up nicely but was not adequate to dispel the chill. She wrapped herself in a shawl and curled up on the couch beside Urnan.

"Go on to bed," he said.

"I'll wait."

He nodded, accepting her offer of companionship. She closed her eyes and soon dozed off.

She was startled awake by the clash of metal on metal. Crying out, she leaped to her feet, horrified by the scene of violence illuminated by the light of the flickering fire and the oil lamps. Urnan was backed into a corner, sword in hand, facing three men. One vaulted forward, and again there was the ring of iron on iron. Urnan made a ferocious, animallike sound and lunged forward. His sword seemed to barely touch the throat of one of his attackers, but blood fountained forth. The man fell and clawed at his throat, making horrible choking sounds for several seconds before he was still. His death held Jerioth's attention, the gruesome sight strangely compelling, even though Urnan was fighting for his life against the two surviving invaders.

They were Ish-bosheth's men, royal guardsmen—and skilled swordsmen. Urnan was being slowly overwhelmed, Jerioth realized. Coming out of her horrified paralysis, she bent down, seized a burning brand from the hearth, and brandished it like a club to slash one of the guardsmen across the cheek from the side. He screamed in pain and surprise and whirled. His sword made a hissing sound as he slashed at her, but she danced away.

Urnan sidestepped his attacker and sliced his blade against the neck of the man whose face had been burned. The blade severed tendons and bone, opening the man's voice box so that he made terrible croaking sounds as he fell. Then it was one on one and quickly over, for the smith of Shiloh was a master swordsman. He had fought at the side of Saul and Jonathan; now he was fighting for not only his life but that of his wife and his granddaughter, who, awakened by the clangs of sword on sword and the screams of the dying, ran to be gathered in Jerioth's arms.

Urnan stood over the third man, who was bleeding from a wound in his side. "Was it Ish-bosheth who sent you?" he demanded.

"Help me!" the man begged.

"Answer me! Did the king send you to kill me?"

"Yes, it was Ish-bosheth. Help me."

"Pray for your soul," Urnan said coldly, "because you are beyond human help."

The would-be assassin died with his legs kicking out a futile protest.

Urnan was breathing hard. "Ish-bosheth has made my decision for me," he told his wife.

"Do I have time to pack a few things?" Jerioth asked.

"We will take the time. We will not allow this mad-man who fancies himself a king to drive us away with nothing but the clothes on our backs."

Urnan angrily wiped the blood from his sword, then set out for the stables. When he returned with four horses, he found Jerioth working fast, gathering the necessities of life along with a few small treasures she had acquired in Mahanaim. Urnan walked over to the hearth, removed a stone, and took out the bags of gold he had accumulated through his trade.

"Why did this happen?" Jerioth asked as they positioned the packs of belongings on the backs of two of the horses.

"Like father, like son," Urnan replied. "Saul sent assassins to kill David in the dead of night." He kissed Jerioth quickly. "David was saved by a warning from Michal. Urnan the smith was saved by Jerioth wielding a stick of firewood."

She shook her head in negation.

"Don't deny it. You did well, my love, very well. You were brave, and I'm very proud of you," Urnan said softly.

"Well, you're the only husband I have," she said lightly. "And I'm getting too old to break in another one, were I to lose you."

"Then I will have to make sure that you don't," Urnan said.

He boosted her up onto her horse and handed Leah to her. They left the town at a slow walk, taking the same road, the way leading to Succoth, that Sunu and Mara had taken before them.

*   *   *

Ish-bosheth's pursuers overtook them before dawn. Fortunately they were warned by the sound of galloping hooves. Urnan led them to concealment in thick brush growing alongside the river and let the king's guardsmen thunder past. He had planned to stay on the eastern side of the River Jordan almost to the northern end of the great Salt Sea, but Ish-bosheth's apparent determination to find him convinced him it would be safer to cross over, even though it meant riding through territory occupied by the Philistine all the way through the lands of Manasseh, Ephraim, and Benjamin.

They found a place to ford in the light of false dawn and were across the river when another party of Ish-bosheth's guardsmen rode south on the Succoth road. After riding half the morning into Israel, Urnan selected a sheltered spot where they rested until midafternoon. The countryside was mainly deserted. There was grim evidence in the form of destroyed houses and sacked villages that Philistines had been there, but for three days they traveled steadily southward uneventfully.

On a markedly chilly night, Urnan made camp in the shelter of one standing wall at a site that initially meant nothing to him. It was only when he made a quick scout around the place that he realized where it was that they would be sleeping: the ruins of the ancient shrine at Shiloh—no more than an arrow's flight away from the spot where he had been forced to watch as Philistines, under the command of Galar of Ashdod, repeatedly raped his wife and then killed her. He found himself telling Jerioth about those long-past moments of horror. She held him close while he cried, murmuring as if to a child, "Hush. Hush now, my love."

He slept fitfully. A cold wind swirled around the tent, and the wind was the voice of the dead—mourning, keening out the melancholy protests of a woman who had died too young. Urnan was more than willing

to leave the place with the feeble glow of a weak sun
lighting a grim, glowering day.

More than once they had to make a wide detour
around one of the Philistine blockhouses that guarded
every road junction. When they finally rode past Jerusalem, sitting in walled defiance on its hills, Urnan began to breathe easier. The ride through Judah was
blessed by sun, although the nights were nippy. They
saw a prosperous land, a peaceful land. David's alliance with the Philistine protected his kingdom against
invasion from the dwellers of the plains to the west.
Only sporadic clashes with those who paid allegiance to
Ish-bosheth brought about the wailing of widows and
the sobs of children left fatherless.

But as they drew near Hebron, it was evident to
Urnan that the peaceful countryside was not at all illus-
trative of the mood of Judah's king and those who bore
arms for him. From far off he saw the smoke rising
from Eri's forges. Charioteers were training horses in
the fields below walled Hebron, and the city itself echoed with the tread of armed men.

But nothing, not even the telltale signs of ongoing
conflict, could place a weight on Urnan's spirits. With a
fullness of heart, he led his wife and daughter through
the city to Eri's spacious house.

Reunion. Three generations of the Children of the
Lion were gathered. Jerioth noted that Mara looked
more mature, although she had been a married woman
for only a short time. Sunu was the ideal image of a
warrior. Eri, strong and handsome and very much like
his father, seemed to have mellowed. He took his
daughter, Leah, in his arms and whispered to her. She
giggled and kissed him on the cheek. Baalan was more
beautiful than ever.

David and Joab arrived soon after to greet Urnan.
"I give thanks to God that you are once more with us,
old friend," David said.

"There are things you will want to hear," Urnan

said, "but if I may, I will let them wait until we have selfishly enjoyed being a family together once more."

"Of course. Come to me at your convenience," David said. "For there are things you will want to hear as well, now that you are one of us again."

Joab clasped Urnan's strong right arm. "Is it to make weapons or wield them that you have come?" he asked. "If it is the latter, fight at my side."

Urnan laughed. "I will leave the fighting to the fierce young ones, like my grandson, Sunu."

"So he says," David commented with a chuckle. "But never fear. When he is called upon, he will be like an old warhorse that has been put out to pasture in the valley, yet paws the ground fiercely at the sound of the trumpets. All it will take is one smell of battle from far off, the thunder of the captains, and the shouting. He'll say, 'Aha!' and be off. This is not a man to turn his back to the sword."

Urnan smiled. "David, you always did have a way with words." But he was flattered. For the first time since going over the Jordan to Mahanaim he did not have a vague, undefined feeling of displacement. He was a man among men, and, by God, they had a true leader.

CHAPTER FIFTEEN

Sunu considered his discovery of the pleasures of the flesh one of the supreme revelations of life. He and Mara celebrated a continuous love feast so intensely that others in the family couldn't help but notice. One evening when the young lovers retired long before the others were ready to call it a night, Jerioth remarked to Baalan, "Their passion shines out from them like the flames of a torch."

Baalan laughed. "I know. The emanation is thick enough to slice with a knife, bottle up, and keep forever, to remind us when we are old and sere that there was indeed a time of unquenchable youth and ardor."

"Only one thing can separate those two," Jerioth said.

Baalan nodded sadly. "The call to glory. I pray that there will be peace."

But there was no peace, even though the Philistines, having sucked Israel dry, were content to fortify their strong points and withdraw the main body of the Army of the Five Cities back to the coastal plains, where the kilted soldiers scattered to their homes for the winter. Two patrols, one from Mahanaim and the other from Hebron, clashed near Bethel, and the men of Judah suffered casualties. When the survivors staggered back to David's stronghold, Joab sent word to Sunu to join him.

"I am going to take three hundred men into the north and avenge our dead," Joab said. "I will need eyes ahead of me, Sunu. I will need your mounted troop to act as my point."

Hearing the news, Mara wept, although being young and adventurous herself, she was secretly proud to be married to a man who was on familiar terms with the foremost among David's mighty men. On the day Sunu rode off, she managed to hold her tears until he was gone. She spent one night alone in the house that had been their home, and then she was on Jerioth's doorstep, asking if she could stay with Jerioth and Urnan until Sunu returned. Jerioth, welcoming her, sent men to bring her things and installed her in a bright and airy room overlooking a small garden. There was nothing for Mara to do except wait and pray.

On a barren hillside outside the town, David and Eri walked, old friends whose lives had been entwined for decades. In the valley below them, chariots wheeled and darted and charged and turned, the iron-rimmed wheels plowing into the arid earth. Horses neighed in excitement and fear. The shouts of the men involved in the exercise rang out over the rumble of their vehicles' wheels and their animals' hooves.

"They are almost ready," Eri remarked, watching the drill.

"They will be ready when they are not only a match for Galar's chariots but superior to them."

"May you have patience," Eri chuckled.

David's voice was filled with grim determination. "They will be better."

"Because you order it?"

David looked at him, and a boyish smile sweetened his stern countenance. "Because God orders it," he said.

Eri sat down on a rock. "In truth, they are getting better."

"Yes," David agreed.

"Who's that?" Eri asked, pointing.

Among the dust clouds raised by the churning wheels of the maneuvering chariots flew a rider at full gallop. He didn't draw his bridle until he reached the slope where David stood, at which point he flung himself off his horse to land erect.

"By God's grace, David," the courier said, "a messenger awaits you in town—a man I think you will want to see as quickly as possible."

"And what is the urgency?"

"He is from Abner. He said for me to tell my king that Abner, his commander, offers alliance."

David smiled broadly. He put out a hand and pulled Eri to his feet. "Come along, old friend. This is one messenger I will not keep waiting."

They hied down the hillside and through the town to the palace. In an anteroom, guarded by two soldiers leaning on their spears, stood the Trans-Jordanian, looking worn and drawn.

"You have traveled far," David said.

"And fast, my king."

"Bring food and drink for this worthy man," David ordered.

Servants scurried off to obey. David motioned to Eri to follow him as he led the messenger to an inner chamber where bread, wine, fruit, and meat were quickly laid out.

"Your name?" David asked.

"I am Shobal, son of Malloch and a kinsman of Abner."

"You are welcome in Hebron, Shobal. Refresh yourself. We will hear your communication from your commander as you eat."

"You are kind, lord." Shobal drank deeply from a silver chalice, then picked up a joint of mutton and gnawed hungrily at it. After several bites he put it down and wiped his mouth with the back of his hand, then stood erect. "The word from Abner to the king of Judah is this," he said. The singsong recitation that followed had clearly been memorized word for word.

" 'My friend and lord, David, King of Judah, hear me, Abner, once chief over the Army of Israel under Saul, may God rest his soul, commander of the Army of Israel at Mahanaim. Hear me: In the sight and hearing of God I declare that I have had my fill of fighting against my brothers. Hereby, and with the words delivered to you by my messenger, my kinsman, I offer you my wholehearted services with a promise that my hand shall be with my lord David until David is King of All Israel.' "

David smiled and nodded. "Shobal, you have done well. I receive your kinsman's words with rejoicing. Eat. Drink. Refresh yourself. When you are finished, you will be shown to a room where you may rest."

"Lord, I would hasten back to Abner."

"In time. In time," David said soothingly. "Matters of such import require more than a moment's consideration."

He motioned to Eri, who followed him from the room. David turned to him, his face all asmile. "If that fellow couldn't hear me, I'd whoop with joy." He clasped Eri's shoulders. "This means an end to the shedding of the blood of brothers. This means that soon we can get on with the work that God has given us." He led Eri down a long corridor.

"You will, of course, accept Abner's offer," Eri

said. "I will be pleased to act as your emissary to arrange this alliance."

"In time, my friend," David said, still smiling. They were now out of earshot of the chamber where Shobal was eating. David glanced around, then danced a jig, slapped his thighs, and whooped.

Shobal was kept waiting for three days. When he was finally recalled to the king's presence, he was rested and refreshed but obviously concerned by David's delay in accepting Abner's offer.

"You look well, Shobal," David said.

"Your hospitality is responsible for that."

David studied the man for a few moments, then said, "If you will, commit these—*my* words—to memory."

Shobal straightened, holding himself stiffly, and a look of intensity came over his face.

"From David, King of Judah, to his friend, Abner, Commander of the Army of Israel, greetings and the blessings of God. David accepts your offer of alliance with rejoicing and looks forward to clasping his friend to his breast in friendship. David is sure that his one reasonable condition to this alliance will be met by his friend Abner. The condition is this: that Abner bring with him to Hebron David's wife, the princess Michal, daughter of Saul, who was given in marriage to David in reward for having slain the giant, Goliath."

Dutifully, his brow furrowed in concentration, Shobal repeated the message word for word.

"Good, good," David said. "Go now, and we will await with impatience the arrival of Abner and my first wife."

The Trans-Jordanian saluted, bowed, wheeled, and marched out of the room.

"See to it that he has a fine horse," David told his captain of the guard, who then hurried to catch up with the messenger. He held up a restraining finger to Eri,

who was obviously anxious to speak, and said to his
guards and courtiers, "All of you, leave us."

When he was alone with Eri, David chuckled. "I
saw your face when I gave Shobal my demand."

"It came as a surprise to me," Eri admitted. He,
too, chuckled. "It should not have, knowing you as I
do."

"Oh?" David inquired, one eyebrow cocked.

"Of course, your love for the woman who was your
first wife is still strong. . . ." Eri said with a wry smile.

"Truly," David said.

"I suspect, however, that there are considerations
other than that of love."

David nodded. "Go on."

"Michal is Saul's daughter. Having the daughter of
Saul standing beside you as your wife gives you a
stronger claim to the throne of all Israel. A son born of
Saul's daughter, having the blood of two kings, would
unite the blood of Israel and Judah and give that son
an even more legitimate claim to the throne."

"There is that," David said. "A man must be practical when God gives him great responsibility—but I
never forget, Eri, that she saved my life by warning me
of Saul's intentions to kill me in my bed." He walked
over to pick up his lyre and strummed it while standing,
humming abstractedly. When at last words came, they
were from a traditional Hebrew love poem.

Eri sprawled on a couch. He never tired of hearing
David's music. The old words caressed his ears and
made him think of Baalan as she had been when he
first took notice of the new slave in his household. He
closed his eyes in reverie and did not open them until
David's song ended.

David smiled. As if his thoughts had joined with
Eri's in looking back to the past and recalling his youth
—and recalling, too, the thrill of young love—he
mused, "Ah, but, my friend, when Michal first came to
me she was as fresh as the dew on newly grown

grass . . . and her womanly juices sweeter than a sun-ripened date."

Sunu led his mounted troop through a verdant valley and into the hills to the west of Bethel. They had been riding for days in a countryside slowly recovering from the Philistines' greedy depravations. Sheep grazed the hills once more, and there was evidence in dried stalks that the harvest had been good. Wherever they rode, people questioned them about the man who was king in Judah.

By David's strict orders, neither Sunu's troop nor Joab's main body of infantry took foodstuffs from the populace without proper payment. The fight was not against the people of Benjamin and Ephraim but against ambitious men over the River Jordan who claimed power that was obviously not within their reach. To Sunu's bemusement, most of the people with whom he talked did not even know the name Ish-bosheth.

"King of Israel?" an old man said contemptuously. "There has been only one king of Israel, and his name was Saul—he who was anointed of God by Samuel."

"David, too, is anointed of God by Samuel," Sunu pointed out.

The old man reflected on the notion, making chewing motions with his toothless gums. "Send us this David, and let us look upon his face."

Several days later the small company of soldiers crested a hill and came upon a foot patrol in force from east of the Jordan near Ai. The Trans-Jordanians, superior in number, ignored Sunu's attempt to initiate talks. Spears lanced through the air. An arrow found its mark in the fetlock of a horse, and the animal reared and screamed in pain.

"For God and David!" Sunu bellowed, pointing the way with his sword as he led the charge. The troop formed a front and thundered down, heedless of spears and arrows. The Trans-Jordanian infantrymen fell un-

der the hooves of the warhorses. There were screams
of mortal agony, howled war cries, shouted orders as
the Trans-Jordanian captains tried to rally their shattered formation.

Sunu wheeled his horse and, followed by his men,
all of them screaming bloodthirsty challenges, swept
back through the confused mass of infantry, leaving
dead and wounded behind them. Sunu's blade dripped
red. Sticky blood saturated the hilt of his sword and
made it slick, soiling his muscular forearm.

When the skirmish was over, the silence of death
lay over the battlefield, broken only by the moans of
the wounded and the prayers of men for their dying
comrades. Only a few of the men loyal to Ish-bosheth
had escaped the terrible, swift swords of Sunu's warriors—but they soon returned with others of their number to retaliate.

Joab's main force appeared just in time to counter
the attack by another, sizable army of Ish-bosheth's infantry. All day the noise of battle rolled across the valley and into the ancient hills of the land promised by
God to Abraham—and the blood that flowed was the
blood of brothers, Hebrews all. The losses were great,
but greater on the side of Ish-bosheth's legions.

"My God, my God!" a priest moaned when at last
the battle was over and the wounded were being gathered for treatment or for comfort in their last minutes
on earth. "Why must this dreadful slaughter be inflicted on brother by brother? Give wisdom to our
leaders, O Lord, and deliver us from this carnage. Let
our swords be directed against the enemy, not against
ourselves."

"Amen," Joab said fervently.

With the morning, oxcarts were loaded with the
wounded, who were sent south to their homes in Judah
to nurse their injuries and heal. Sunu led his troop in a
scout toward the Jordan to find that the remnants of

Ish-bosheth's army had crossed back over, leaving the field to the victors. He made his report to Joab.

"They can't survive such losses indefinitely," Joab said. "With each encounter they are weakened."

"What are your orders?" Sunu asked.

"Northward. I know of a Philistine blockhouse that is vulnerable to attack. We will kill the real enemy for a change."

. Sunu smiled. Nothing would suit him better. Although their attacks on Philistines were infrequent, lest the alliance between Judah and the Lords of the Five Cities be broken prematurely, it was possible to destroy a blockhouse now and then while pretending to be Benjamites under the orders of Ish-bosheth. Sunu rode northward gladly and was in the forefront of the attack. Leaving his horse at the walls, he vaulted over and closed with two Philistine heavy infantrymen who had been surprised from their early morning sleep by the assault and were not fully dressed. He killed swiftly in the name of Yahweh, God of the grandmother he had never known.

Shobal ben Malloch, who had arrived in Mahanaim after dark so that his coming was not noted, found his way to his commander's home and knocked. Responding to the summons, Abner came to the front door with an oil lamp in his hand, saw his emissary's face, and said, "Enter, quickly."

"I have ridden fast," Shobal said.

"I feared for you," Abner remarked.

"I was delayed in Hebron by David."

"Surely he did not have to take time to consider my offer."

"Yet he did," Shobal said. "For some days."

Abner stroked his beard thoughtfully. "Tell me, then."

Shobal stood at attention, for that seemed to help his memory, and recited David's message verbatim.

"Almighty God!" Abner whispered fervently when the message had been delivered. "Michal!"

"Those are his words," Shobal said.

"You have done well. You will be with me when we join David for the glory of all Israel."

"My loyalty is yours," Shobal promised.

"Go to your bed. Rest."

Abner returned to his own bed, though he himself had little rest the remainder of that night. Ish-bosheth had given his sister, Michal, to Phaltiel, son of Laish, to strike an alliance with a minor sheikhdom. As he tossed and turned, Abner cursed the situation. He was a soldier, not a politician. He did not understand why David, who was also a man of war, felt it necessary to complicate things by demanding the return of Michal. Just before sleep finally came to him, Abner resolved to meet the challenge head on. Direct action was the only thing he knew.

So it was that he stood before Ish-bosheth early the next morning. "We have suffered another slaughter at the hands of David," Abner informed him. "Meanwhile, our men fade away, unwilling to fight against their brothers. Thus, I have made a decision."

"Without, of course, consulting your king," Ish-bosheth said sarcastically.

"I have been in communication with David."

The king's eyes narrowed, his face flushed. "Go on."

"I have decided it is time to end this internecine war," Abner said firmly.

"Are you a traitor to me, then?" the king asked, getting to his feet.

"I will not abandon you—but neither can I abandon Israel."

"You fool!" Ish-bosheth spat. In a fury he fairly leaped to one of his guards, jerking the ceremonial spear from the man's hands. He had not yet drawn back his arm to throw the weapon when Abner's iron hand closed over his wrist.

"Too often you have emulated your father's madness," Abner said, remembering how Saul had twice cast spears at David. "Hear me. Sit down. Control your emotions, and hear me."

Ish-bosheth was shaking as if with fever, but he allowed Abner to lead him back to his throne.

"I have given my pledge to David to make a league with him and to bring all Israel unto him."

"I am to die," Ish-bosheth lamented softly.

"Nonsense. David has never raised his hand against the blood of Saul—although at least twice he could have slain your father during the time when Saul hunted him like an animal. He will not lift his hand against you. You will be a part of this league."

Ish-bosheth sneered. "As a subject of the great King David?"

"I would rather be a citizen of a united and strong Israel than king of a dunghill," Abner said, regretting the sting but finding it necessary.

"Go to him," Ish-bosheth said. "I will rally my army and fight both of you."

"When I go, my friend, there will be no army," Abner said, feeling great pity for Ish-bosheth. "Come with me. Join us in freeing Israel of Philistine domination."

"No."

"So be it. There is one thing more."

"One thing more to humiliate me, no doubt."

"David is to have delivered to him his wife Michal, for whom he paid Saul one hundred dead Philistines, proving their number by their foreskins."

"Take her. I don't care. She, too, has turned against me."

"It is your duty, since you gave her to Phaltiel, to send for her."

Ish-bosheth shook his head slowly in defeat. "You

have taken everything else from me. Take my name. Send the order in my name."

Abner nodded curtly. "As you wish."

The order went out. Ish-bosheth secluded himself in his rooms and was not present when Abner's men returned to Mahanaim with Michal and delivered her to Abner.

"Why am I taken from my home, Abner?" Michal asked in quiet dignity when he greeted her.

"To be with your husband."

Michal's face was set as if carved in stone, for shame was strong in her. She turned and pointed to a man with a tear-stained face who cowered behind the soldiers. "There is my husband. He has followed me, weeping, all the way from Bahurim."

"I speak of David."

She was silent for a moment, her face showing no emotion. "Where is my brother?"

"He has been told you are here."

"Then why do I not see his face?"

"Find him in his quarters. Ask him that question."

She did not move.

Abner turned to face those who had gathered, among them the elders of Israel and certain men of Benjamin, and addressed them.

"Hear me. Some of you long for the days when Saul protected Israel. Others of you, and I know this because you have told me so, seek David to be king over you. Now I tell you that the time has come. The Lord has spoken to me of David, saying, 'By the hand of my servant David I will deliver my people of Israel out of the hand of the Philistines and out of the hand of all their enemies.' "

"Amen and amen," a gray-bearded priest intoned, and the people took up the word, chanting, "David! David! David!"

CHAPTER SIXTEEN

So it was that Abner, and his men with him, came to David in Hebron. The priest, Abiathar, made a sacrifice, the smoke rising to God from the altar and from braziers where a great feast was prepared. The men of Judah embraced the men of Benjamin. Maidens danced in praise of the Lord. There was wine from the king's own stocks and much singing and a fistfight or two—not necessarily between former enemies.

Through it all, Michal sat in state on a throne beside that of David, although the king did not join her there but circulated among the people, for he was one of them, and he returned the love that they gave him.

A great cheer went up when Abner formally pledged himself to David with ringing words and soaring voice.

Urnan smiled indulgently. "They do like to make

speeches, these Hebrews," he remarked to his family, all of whom except Sunu—who was out with his scouts —were gathered around him.

"Soon I will arise and go," Abner was saying, his great voice carrying to the furthermost limits of the square. "I will gather all Israel unto my lord the king that thou mayest reign over all."

When it was David's turn, his pleasantly modulated voice carried as well as Abner's harsher one, and his words were received in awed silence. He spoke of peace and of a free and united Israel. Drawing Abner to his side, he embraced him, saying, "Go, then, my friend, in peace—and by the grace of God, together we will triumph."

But first there was wine to be drunk and food to be consumed. It was two days before Abner and twenty of his men marched out of Hebron to begin the task of recruiting all Israel to David's banners. As it happened, Abner's way led him to the northwest; thus he did not encounter either Sunu's mounted patrol or Joab's legion marching back to Hebron from a great victory.

David had assigned a special house for Michal's use. Aside from a formal public greeting he had not yet spoken to her when, excusing himself from the feast in Abner's honor, he sought out the daughter of Saul in her quarters.

Michal had changed from her public attire and was dressed in a diaphanous, flowing gown of white linen that revealed the womanly shape of her hips and the length of her legs as she rose to meet David at the door of her bedchamber. He halted in midstride, smitten all over again by her beauty.

"I had forgotten how fair you are," he said.

Michal was silent. She stood as still as a cedar pillar, staring at him.

"May I come into your chamber?" he asked.

"Since I am a mere woman," she said coolly, "I am yours to command."

David shook his head. "Not like that. Not like that."

She turned, walked over to a chair, and sat, crossing one leg over the other to expose a shapely ankle.

"How, then, my lord?" she asked.

"When last I saw you, you were concerned for me," he said. "You had made an effigy of fleeces and pillows in my bed to confuse your father's assassins."

"That was a long time ago. Now my father and my brothers are dead because of you."

A look of pain crossed his face. "Never because of me," he said fiercely. "I did not wish your father's death, and I have missed my friend Jonathan sorely."

"You made civil war against them," she said angrily. "You took with you the flower of the Army of Israel, leaving my father weak—so weak that he fell victim to Galar and the Army of the Five Cities without hope of victory."

"Not by choice," David argued. "What would you have had me do? Stay in Gibeah and die at the hands of Saul's assassins?"

"And now you have debased my last living brother," she said, ignoring the question.

"On the contrary, I have offered to share the kingdom with him."

"Oh, come now, David. You shamed him. You didn't want me back simply for the sake of the love we once knew. You made your condition to Abner to humble my brother—and me."

"Not true. I have missed you."

"Because of you, I was subjected to the sight of my husband—my *husband*—rending his clothing and weeping like a child as Abner's men carted me away from him."

"In the silence of the night, when I lost you, I shed my tears as well," David said.

"But you were not subjected to the shame of seeing the man to whom you had been given—given as if

you were an animal to be traded for gold or advantage
—lamenting and bewailing his fate for mile after mile."

"I cannot be held responsible for something over
which I had no control."

"But you seized control over me, didn't you? Had
I any choice?"

"I hoped you would be pleased," David said,
spreading his hands.

"Pleased? To be kidnapped from my home by a
man who made war on my father? To be snatched from
the bed of my husband—poor, weak thing that he was
—and paraded as a trophy to your harem?"

David's face was grim. "Shall I send you back to
your husband, then?"

She smiled for the first time. "It will not be as easy
as that for you, David. I am a king's daughter. I am not
blind to what is happening. Would you be rid of me so
blithely? Do you want to send me back to a defeated
man who pays tribute to a soon-to-be-defeated king?"

"What I would is to keep you with me, in love and
in a position of honor."

"Among all of your other wives," she said. "You
missed me so much that you took how many others?
Three?"

"I think I'm justified in saying you have no basis
for criticizing *me*," David said. "I have been told you
went to the bed of Phaltiel without protest—with some
willingness, in fact."

Michal rose from the chair and walked to a window. A breeze wafted her perfumed hair and rippled
the material of her gown. David moved to her and put
his arms around her. She made no objection, nor did
she protest when he denuded her of the clinging garment and paid tribute to her beauty with lips and fin-
gertips. When he went into her, she met his thrusts
with an eagerness that surprised him, and, matching his
every passionate movement, reached her own peak
even as he did. The act was accomplished with gusto
and with every indication that she was experienced in

the matter of taking her own pleasure while giving her partner his due.

She slept. He lay beside her. She had changed so much. He remembered the shy virgin coming to his bed tentatively and with wide, frightened eyes. The act just completed had not been the performance of a demure young girl but that of an adept, sensuous woman. He felt a mixture of jealousy and lust. Some other man had helped her develop that skill at making love. But, ah, the way she answered his need!

He felt a tightening of his groin. He woke her with his mouth hot on her taut stomach. With a moan of desire, she buried her fingers in his tightly curled hair and pulled him to her moistened lips.

Wives and daughters who had waited patiently at the gates of the city escorted Joab's army through the streets, rejoicing with tambourines, with dancing and chanted praise to God, and with songs to honor the bravery of the men of Judah. The arms and armor of the defeated Trans-Jordanians were piled in a great heap in the square before David's palace.

Mara was among those who celebrated. She watched Sunu, sitting his horse straight and strong, leading his troops at the forefront, and she was quivering with impatience when finally she was able to push close, elbowing her way through an adoring crowd. Spotting her, Sunu leaped off his horse, and Mara threw herself into his arms. There before God and the people she was kissed so thoroughly that she grew dizzy and had to cling to her husband until the weakness in her knees dissipated.

"I am so happy!" she exulted.

"Not as happy as I am to see you."

"We will not be parted again."

"If that is God's will."

"The war is over."

He put his hand under her chin and tilted her face

up. She beamed at him. "Abner, the son of Ner, came
to the king while you were away—"

"Abner?" Sunu cast a quick glance in the direction of Joab. "Abner was here?"

"To pledge his loyalty to David. Now he has gone
to bring all of Israel to the king."

"Little dove, wait for me by the two pillars. I must
speak with Joab."

"Whatever it is you must say to Joab can wait,"
she said, pouting.

"Trust me, it can't," he said, pulling away.

But when he reached Joab, it was clear that he
had already been told. He glowered at Sunu. "You
have heard?"

"Yes."

"Come, we will confront the king with this thing."

"Joab, give it some thought."

"Come or not," Joab said impatiently, striding
away.

Sunu hurried to catch up with his commander, and
he was at Joab's shoulder when he reached David's
side. "I am told that you had Abner within your power
and that you let him go from you."

"The son of Ner has pledged to us," David said.
"Rejoice and be glad, my friend, for there will be no
more fighting between Hebrews."

"He came to deceive you," Joab said angrily. "I
know the man. Did he not take the life of my brother,
Asahel?"

"Let the past bury its dead, Joab," David implored. "Think of the good of all Israel. Abner has
made a pact with me, and without his support, Ish-
bosheth is no longer a factor. Soon you will fight at
Abner's side against our true enemy, the Philistine."

"I have brought you great spoils," Joab said. "This
day I have brought you news of a great victory. We
don't need the help of the murderer Abner. We have
beaten them, him and his would-be king, and now he

seeks to save his miserable life by seeking alliance with you."

"Joab, hear me," David said firmly. "In the coming battles, when we face not only the Philistines but the other old enemies of our people who occupy the land promised to Abraham by God, we will need Abner. Forgive the past. If you can't love him, at least do not hate him."

Joab was moodily silent. David walked away to go among the troops—patting this man on the back, taking this man's arm, examining a slight wound, always smiling and praising. Joab watched him for a few moments, then turned to Sunu. "I will not fight alongside the man who killed my brother."

"My friend," Sunu said, nodding toward David, who was surrounded by a knot of men, "think twice before you ignore the wishes of that man. See how they adore him. They would follow him into the jaws of death. He is our king, and my advice to you is to obey his wishes."

Joab grunted noncommittally. Then, replacing his dour mood with one of good cheer, he said, "Sunu, go to your pretty little wife. Forget for a while the sting and clash of battle."

Sunu grinned. "That order I will gladly obey."

When Sunu was out of sight, Joab went off and found a trusted lieutenant, then gave him certain orders. Within the hour four men on fresh horses rode out through the gates of Hebron toward the northwest. They were able to follow the progress of Abner and his men by talking with people along the way, finally overtaking them where they were camped by the well of Sirah.

"Abner, it is David's wish that you return to Hebron," Joab's man said.

"But I am on the king's business," Abner protested. "How am I to rally all Israel around him by going back to Hebron?"

"I do not question the king's orders," the lieutenant said.

Abner sighed. "Very well."

He and his twenty men walked back to David's city, while Joab's messengers traveled by horse, giving Joab ample warning of Abner's arrival so that he was able to intercept Abner's party at the gates.

"We are well met, Joab," Abner said. "I have wanted to explain to you what happened that day after the battle at the Pool of Gibeon."

"And I have waited long to speak with you," Joab said. "Come aside with me that we might have privacy to talk man to man."

Abner sent his troops on into the city, then strolled with Joab along the city wall. "I begged your brother to turn back," he told Joab as the two men walked side by side. "I made allowances for his youth and for his fiery blood. I gave him more than one opportunity to leave off pursuing me. Even then, had he been less skilled as a swordsman I might have been able to spare him when he forced me to fight, but he was too good to be brushed aside." He stopped and turned to Joab, a look of entreaty on his face. "To save my own life I had to kill him."

"And for that you die!" Joab abruptly barked, thrusting a dagger into Abner's side just below the fifth rib.

Abner was half-paralyzed as the blade entered his vital core. He seized Joab's wrist weakly with both hands and looked down with startled eyes as blood poured out onto the hand of the man who had dealt him the fatal blow.

"This blood is for Asahel," Joab said grimly. He twisted the blade and shoved it deeper into Abner's pounding heart. The older man went limp, and as he fell his weight jerked the knife from Joab's hand. Joab retrieved the weapon and cleaned its blade by stabbing it repeatedly into the sandy ground. He left Abner's body lying beside the wall.

*   *   *

David was seated on his throne when the corpse was carried into the king's reception room on a litter by Abner's troop. "See what Joab has done!" cried one of the men.

David sprang to his feet. "You know that he has done this thing?"

"Yes. It was none other than the captain of all your armies," said the spokesman for Abner's grieving entourage.

"Believe me, men of Benjamin," David said earnestly, "I and my kingdom are guiltless before the Lord of letting the blood of Abner ben Ner."

"But it was done by Joab, your captain."

David's voice was terrible, his anger great, for he saw endangered his hard-won alliance with the men of Benjamin, saw endangered his plans to drive the Philistine and all others from the Promised Land.

"Let this sin rest on the head of Joab alone and on all of his father's house!" he thundered. *"Let there not issue from the house of Joab one womb that will bear children, and may all be leprous or crippled or be slain by the sword!"*

David held out his arms to Abner's men. "Come," he said, lowering his voice, "join me, all, in weeping at the grave of this good and noble man." He looked over and saw Eri and Urnan. "My friends," he said to them, "do me this service. Gather men about you and prepare a fitting place for Abner with a monument to mark his rest."

Urnan nodded in acknowledgment.

"And you, my people," David went on, "rend your garments and lament this man who would have stood with us. By your tears demonstrate our goodwill toward Abner and those who followed him, and join me in prayers to God that the grievous sin of one man will not poison the alliance that Abner made with me."

"Make it right, David!" one of Abner's men shouted.

"In God's name, I would if I could." David's eyes filled with tears. "But can I do more than place God's curse on the house of Joab? No, I cannot."

"I think, Father," Eri whispered in Urnan's ear, "that we are seeing a consummate politician in action."

Urnan gave his son a quick, sly smile. "That's close to blasphemy," he whispered back.

"God will not allow Abner to go unrevenged," David was saying, "but it will be God's work, not mine, for the kinsmen of Joab, the sons of Zeruiah, of Joab himself, of Abishai, and all the others have more power than I, a poor shepherd. But God will bring punishment down upon their heads in time."

Urnan nudged Eri. "Before God begins to speak to him, as he did to Samuel, let us go and prepare a place for Abner."

They made their way out of the palace and, with the help of several men in their employ, readied Abner's burial site.

At Abner's interment, David wept at the grave. Even Abner's men were touched, and they pledged their loyalty to him. Among the citizens of Hebron, only Joab was not present to pledge his fealty to the king.

CHAPTER
SEVENTEEN

Kaptar, Master of the Horse and royal armorer to the king, lifted the august personage of his young half-brother into a boat and positioned him in the bow. Sheshonk stood proudly, a slight figure endowed with natural poise and an air of command. He held a net in his hand as Kaptar punted the boat into the edge of a great papyrus marsh. Guards and attendants followed in separate boats at a distance designed to allow the king's boat to approach unsuspecting waterfowl silently.

"Be ready," Kaptar whispered. Sheshonk looked over his shoulder. Kaptar pointed to his right and steered the flat-bottomed boat in that direction with a skillful push. The bow broke into a small opening in the marsh, and a half-dozen startled waterfowl flapped noisily into flight, but not before the young king had sent his net sailing out to snare a pair of the birds. Wings entangled, they were borne down into the water by the weight of the net.

Sheshonk yelped with pleasure.

"Did you see me, Kaptar? Did you see that I did it just as you have shown me?"

"I saw, little brother. You did well."

"We will have them roasted," Sheshonk said, "and you will eat with me."

Kaptar laughed. "I'm hungry already."

"More," Sheshonk said, "we need more."

It was a pleasant day for the hunt. The blessings of the sun god were warm on their bare backs, although winter was on the land and the blazing temperatures of summer were moderated. In the close environs of the papyrus marsh sweat glistened on Kaptar's muscular chest as he poled the boat along easily. Once a crocodile came close to investigate this invader of his domain. Kaptar struck the beast a smart rap between the eyes with the end of his pole, and the great lizard disappeared in an angry swirl of water.

When a dozen fat ducks were lying in trussed shock on the bottom of the boat, Kaptar turned back toward the point on the bank where the king's chariot awaited along with an extensive entourage. Servants gathered up the stunned ducks, a few of which protested noisily as they were carried by their legs, wings flapping.

Sheshonk said, "May I drive, brother?"

"Of course." Kaptar picked the king up and swung him into the chariot. A slave held the heads of the two spirited horses while Kaptar gathered the reins and put them into the boy's hands.

"Ha, ha!" Sheshonk called, slapping the reins. The slave had to leap to one side when the horses sprang into a run in one quick burst of motion, their hooves pounding the rich black earth.

The brothers reached the palace far ahead of the rest of their entourage. As Kaptar and Sheshonk came up from the royal stables, the boy sitting on Kaptar's shoulder, Musen the Libyan met them. In the two years that Kaptar had been a fixture at the court, his stepfather had come not only to trust the armorer but to like him. Kaptar's devotion to his half-brother was touching. Musen was never concerned when the boy he believed to be his son was with the smith.

"A feast tonight, Father," Sheshonk called out happily. "Tell him, Kaptar. Tell him."

"Here we have a mighty hunter of waterfowl," Kaptar said as he lowered Sheshonk to the ground. "He captured no less than a dozen splendidly fat ducks."

"You should have seen me, Father," Sheshonk said gleefully.

"I'm sure you were quite impressive," Musen said. He lifted his eyes to Kaptar. "By the way, you should know we are to be honored by a visit from an official representative of the Amon priests of Waset."

"Oh, no," Sheshonk groaned. The young king was not fond of sitting through the formalities of a state visit. "Kaptar and I want to go hunt lions."

Musen laughed. "You're a bit young to hunt lions," he said indulgently. "Kaptar has his duties, as do you."

"Oh, well," Sheshonk said with a shrug. "It's all for the good of the Black Land, I suppose."

Kaptar's heart twisted, for the way Sheshonk shrugged reminded him of his mother. The boy's concern for the good of Egypt would have pleased her.

Walking together, they reached the palace and entered. Sheshonk was sent off with the grandmotherly kinswoman of Musen who acted as his governess.

"Who comes?" Kaptar asked the Libyan.

"A priest close to the throne. His name is Nehri."

Kaptar nodded. "I know him."

"In your capacity as Master of the Horse you shall be his official host."

Kaptar nodded again. He did Musen's bidding

without objection. He was biding his time, waiting until his half-brother was old enough—waiting until everything was ready to fall into place. And then he would exact his revenge for his mother's murder.

The delegation from the south arrived four days after the coming of their advance messenger. The priest Nehri was accompanied by his household, which was rather unusual for a court official on a state visit. Among the members of Nehri's family was a stately daughter of eighteen years, tall, elegantly slim, dark of eye, and fair of face. Her beauty reminded Kaptar of his mother. Her name was one that sang in the ear: Nefernehi, the Beautiful One of the South.

Neither Musen nor Kaptar learned the reason for the state visit during the round of formal ceremonies. Nehri spoke resoundingly and long of Kaptar's regard for his brother, Sheshonk. In turn, Kaptar, speaking for the King of Lower Egypt—for this occasion, the empty title "King of the Two Lands" was omitted from Sheshonk's formal designation—returned assurances of love and respect. But his attention was divided. The dark, flashing, kohl-accented eyes of the Beautiful One burned into his consciousness.

The meal for the evening included roasted duck. The young King of Lower Egypt announced proudly that he himself had provided the birds. Nehri applauded and praised Sheshonk.

"Kaptar helped me, though," Sheshonk said, reaching out to touch his brother's arm affectionately. "Didn't you, Kaptar?"

Kaptar's eyes were being held by the dark orbs of Nefernehi.

"Didn't you, Kaptar?" Sheshonk asked again.

Kaptar started. "Forgive me, brother. I was—" He paused.

"The royal armorer was daydreaming," Sheshonk said.

Nefernehi smiled with secret knowledge.

The feast was accompanied by wine and the rich beer of the delta and by a troupe of Nubians who performed amazingly athletic dances. When the banquet was ended, Nefernehi was escorted to her sleeping chamber by her chaperones, thereby removing Kaptar's focus of fascination. Sheshonk nodded sleepily in his chair.

Kaptar glanced at the boy king, then stood up, declaring, "Lord Musen, honorable Nehri, friends all. My brother is young and needs his rest. The king blesses you and bids you enjoy."

He gently touched Sheshonk's arm, and the boy smiled gratefully and stood as well. Music accompanied their passage. A woman's voice, reedy and melodic, followed them out of the banquet hall. Sheshonk walked at Kaptar's side until they were some way down the corridor; then he halted and held up his arms. Kaptar picked him up and carried the young king to his chamber, where his Libyan female attendants were waiting.

Leaving his brother, Kaptar made his way to his own bedchamber. Having drunk his share of wine and beer, he fell asleep almost instantly.

He awoke with a hand on his shoulder. Immediately his hand closed hard around a wrist.

Musen grunted with pain. "Easy, my son, don't break my bones."

"It is you," Kaptar said, sitting up.

"I have learned something that will interest you," Musen said.

"Hold, I will light a lamp."

"No. It will take only a minute." He paused momentarily, then said, "After you and Sheshonk left us, Nehri at last divulged the reason for this visit of state."

"Which is?" Kaptar's mouth was filled with a vile taste, and his head ached from too much wine, food, and beer.

"It did not escape my notice that you had eyes for Nehri's daughter."

"She is worthy of a man's attention," Kaptar agreed.

"Don't you think it somewhat unusual for a man to bring his household with him on a state visit?"

"It is odd, yes."

"He brought all—wife, servants, others of his children—so that he might also bring the Beautiful One."

"So?" Kaptar asked.

"Nehri's master, Thure-Amon, has in mind an alliance by marriage."

"No!" Kaptar said quickly, his heart skipping at the thought of Nefernehi becoming the wife of another, even a child king. It took just seconds, however, for him to assign priorities to his concern. He forgot his attraction to the Beautiful One and thought only of his promise to his mother and to Kemose. "True, she is beautiful, but she does not have the blood of kings. She is not for Sheshonk. My brother, the king, will marry a princess of the blood."

Musen chuckled. "It is not Sheshonk for whom Nefernehi is intended. It is you."

"Me?" Kaptar gasped as a thrill of desire filled him.

"It seems, Kaptar, that Thure-Amon was not convinced by your assurances that you have no desire to wrest the Amon throne from him. By marrying you to the daughter of a man who has no connection by blood to any of the old ruling families, he declares to the Two Lands that Kaptar is not deserving of aspiring to the throne of Upper Egypt. Nehri is a worthy man, and he has no little wealth, but he is a commoner. He has risen to his position at the side of Thure-Amon by the strength of his sword arm."

"Yes, I can see Thure-Amon's reasoning. The new king of Upper Egypt does not sit securely on the Amon throne."

"Indeed, we have learned only recently that blood has been shed by a claimant to the throne who challenged the high priest. He paid for his attempted regicide with his own life."

"I am not surprised," Kaptar said.

"How does this proposal from Nehri strike you?"

"She is—" Kaptar paused, at a loss for words as he pictured the graceful movements of the Beautiful One's legs under sheer linen as she walked. In the darkness of the room Musen could not see the pleased smile that spread across his face—but he probably heard it in his voice. "She is the most desirable woman I have ever encountered."

Musen clapped his hands. "Ha! Then Nehri is to be rewarded with success for his mission."

"It would appear so," Kaptar said, his smile now widened to a grin.

Musen left the chamber, and Kaptar sank back on his bed. He didn't think he'd be able to sleep for thoughts of Nefernehi, but he did.

When he awoke, it was with a fuzzy head. He swam in an artificial lake outside his quarters, dressed himself in fine white linen, then went in search of Nefernehi. He found her in a palm-shaded courtyard with her female attendants. She smiled when she saw him but did not rise from her couch.

"Send them away," Kaptar said, indicating her attendants.

"Yes," she said. "Go."

When they were alone, he pulled a stool near her couch and sat down.

"So you have been told," she said, looking at him with a disconcerting directness.

"Yes."

"I will confess to you in all honesty that I am not pleased," she said.

He felt a stab of pain. "That saddens me, for I could not be more pleased."

"Thank you. I will, of course, obey my father's wishes."

"I'm surprised by your candor. There must be a

reason for it. There is someone else for whom you care?"

She nodded. "His name is Kot. He is the son of an old friend of our family, a grain merchant. I have dreamed since childhood that I would be his bride one day."

"I thank you for your honesty."

"Since we will be man and wife, I owe you no less."

"Consider this," Kaptar mused. "If I reject this union, will you then be able to go to your childhood love and become his wife?"

Tears came to her eyes. "No."

"Why?"

"Because his father, like mine, is ambitious. Because he has already been forced by his loyalty to his father and his family to take as his wife the daughter of a landowner with whom his father wanted a business alliance."

Kaptar nodded his understanding. "There would be some advantages to being my wife. You would want for nothing. You would be a part of the intimate court of a king."

She sighed. "I don't disdain such things, Kaptar. I only wish it were you that I love, truly I do. You are quite beautiful."

He made a startled sound. She laughed. "Yes, we women do talk that way about men. If it embarrasses you to be called beautiful, I'm sorry."

"It's an unexpected application of the word," he said. "I have reserved it for you from the first moment I saw you."

She lowered her eyes modestly. "As I said, I will obey my father. If you will have me, knowing where my heart lies, I will consider myself honored."

"So be it, then." He took her hand in his. "Will you give me a chance to earn your love?"

"I will be a good and dutiful wife to you," she said, but there was no gladness in her voice.

"I could ask for nothing more."

He left her then and made his way to the throne room, where he found Musen and Nehri. Sheshonk, wearing the miniature crown of the Two Lands, was playing hounds and jackals with one of the young Libyan girls of his entourage.

"We were just speaking of you," Musen said. "Nehri is eager to hear your response to his overture of an alliance between his family and yours."

"Lord Musen," Kaptar said with a smile, "I have come to ask for a private conversation with my future father-in-law so that we might become better acquainted."

"Excellent," Musen said, slapping Kaptar on the back. "I'll leave you two to arrange the details."

Kaptar escorted Nehri out to the gardens, where they walked under date palms heavy with fruit. "I have talked with Nefernehi," Kaptar said.

Nehri looked concerned. "My daughter has not yet outgrown all of her delusions."

"Fear not. We arrived at an understanding."

"She does not know her own heart. You will find her to be warm and affectionate. And all the women of our family are fecund. She will bear you many sons. You have my gratitude, lord, for overlooking my daughter's childish fantasies."

Kaptar looked at the man sharply, and his voice was harsh. "While I am grateful to you for bringing me such a gift, I deplore your unconcern for the feelings of your daughter."

Nehri's face turned red. "It is a father's duty to guide his daughter into doing what is best for her future well-being."

"Does the crown sit so uneasily on Thure-Amon's head that he must resort to such petty doings as this?"

"Please, lord, do not speak disrespectfully of my king," Nehri said nervously.

Kaptar assessed the man. "Come, Nehri. You served my uncle. You were his friend. You could not fail to be aware of his dreams of a united Egypt. Why, then, this sudden loyalty to Thure-Amon?"

"A wise man is loyal to he who holds that wise man's future in his hand. Yes, I knew Kemose, and I loved him. Once I shared his dream that you would sit on the throne at Waset, that you would be the instrument to bring about the reunion of the Two Lands. Now I see only strife and disunion. A mere boy sits on the throne of Lower Egypt, a puppet of his Libyan father."

Kaptar looked around with concern. "Those are dangerous words," he cautioned.

"It is always dangerous to voice one's true opinion of a king. Do you think I enjoyed being ordered to use my daughter, the flower of my life, as a trading piece in Thure-Amon's game of intrigue?"

Kaptar halted, took Nehri's arm, and turned the older man to face him. "Like my uncle, I bewail the loss of Egypt's glory. I think that you feel likewise."

"With all my heart."

"You knew that my uncle had despaired of seeing the north conquered by force to bring all of the Black Land under the rule of the Amon priests at Waset."

"Yes."

"The man who will bring glory back to the Two Lands is now just a boy," Kaptar said, watching for a reaction.

Nehri sighed. "So Kemose would have said, for he predicted that the Libyans would triumph."

"And for some time my brother will have me at his side."

"Egypt could do worse than to have a nephew of Kemose looking after her."

"One day an army will ascend the Nile, and Sheshonk will be hailed in Waset as king of the Two Lands. I would like for you to be prepared to welcome him and to become a part of his plan for Egypt."

"When you are my daughter's husband, our families will be one," Nehri pointed out.

Kaptar smiled. "Then let us join in union sooner than later."

The Egyptian's love for ceremony was displayed once more when Kaptar, Prince of Upper Egypt, Priest of Amon, Armorer to the King of Lower Egypt, and Master of the Horse, took to his breast as wife the Beautiful One of the South, Nefernehi. After the pomp and ritual, Kaptar surprised his new bride by taking her for a waterfowl hunt on the river with her new brother-in-law, King Sheshonk. He surprised her further when, after the evening meal, he escorted her to a bedchamber in his quarters and then left her there to be tended by handmaidens. She lay awake for hours, expecting him to come—and was most surprised when he did not.

The following morning Nehri and his official delegation set off up the Nile to take the news of the success of his mission to Thure-Amon.

In the days, weeks, and months that followed, Kaptar was delighted to find his wife to be not only beautiful and innately intelligent but intellectually curious as well. However, her education had been that of a woman: negligible. Kaptar sought to amend that. Nefernehi took to the teachings of a scribe-priest with an enthusiasm that saw her swiftly master the art of reading and writing. When she pumped Kaptar for his knowledge of the rich history of Egypt, he edified her gladly. They walked the hot and barren sands admiring and wondering at the ancient pyramidal tombs of the great kings of the dim and distant past, speculating on the mysterious visage of the sphinx. She could not get enough of hearing of the great ones—Narmer and Khafre and Menkure and all those who followed—but she was most fascinated by the story of the queen with whom she shared a praenomen.

"Take me there, to their forgotten place," she asked, not for the first time, as once again she listened while Kaptar recited what little he knew about the Heretic, Akhenaten, and his beautiful queen, Nefertiti.

"One day," he promised.

Nefernehi quickly captured the heart of young King Sheshonk, as well. Considerable jealousy was aroused in the king's private quarters when it became apparent that he preferred the company of his new sister-in-law to any of the female relatives of the man he called father. And if he had the fortune to be in the company of both Nefernehi and his brother, the Master of the Horse, any attempt to interfere risked an almost adult burst of royal temper.

And so the months passed swiftly. At last Musen came to Kaptar to say, "It is time to repay the honor of a visit of state that was conferred upon us by Thure-Amon. I'm sure your wife will welcome the chance to see her father and her other relations."

"I am to be the emissary, then?"

"The brother of the king will be able to talk with many people in Waset," Musen said, nodding. "There are rumors of strife in the south, Kaptar. I want to know if it is true. Should we find that the competition for the Amon throne has produced sufficient weakness . . ."

Kaptar felt a chill. In his heart he knew that sooner or later a Libyan army would sweep into the southern land and fulfill the final ambition of Musen, but he was not emotionally prepared to face that eventuality.

He took his leave and made his way to his quarters, where he gave Nefernehi the news of their impending visit. As Musen had predicted, she was most pleased at the prospect of visiting her family. Sheshonk, on the other hand, fell into a royal sulk.

"I fail to understand why I cannot accompany my brother and my sister," he said, pouting. In a more childish voice, he whined, "Why can't I go, Kaptar?"

"Because, my little king, this is to be a mission by a delegation of state, not a royal visit." He straightened Sheshonk's tunic. "It would not be politic to put the king of Lower Egypt in the hands of his rival, would it?"

"True. I certainly wouldn't want to have to stay there in the south," Sheshonk said. Brightening somewhat, he added, "I have talked with men who say that the waterfowl hunting is far more rewarding in the marshes of *our* delta."

"Far more rewarding," Kaptar agreed with a straight face.

"Hurry back, Kaptar," Sheshonk said plaintively. "And you, Beautiful One."

"He takes after his big brother in being a flatterer," Nefernehi said, laughing.

"But you *are* beautiful," Sheshonk said. "When I am old enough to pleasure you, I shall have my brother sent off to the land of cedars on a mission, and while he's gone I will steal you away from him."

Nefernehi hugged him, lifting him off his feet. "You could do it, too."

"But I won't—really, Kaptar," Sheshonk said, winking at his brother.

A messenger proceeded ahead of the royal barge by swift dhow to announce the coming of the delegation from On. Aboard the barge, Kaptar and Nefernehi continued their custom of separate rooms, for Kaptar persisted in honoring a vow that he had made to himself, which was unknown to Nefernehi: He would not come into her bed until he was invited not only because of wifely duty but because of love.

There were times when Nefernehi wondered at her husband's strange behavior. It was obvious to her that Kaptar adored her. He never tired of being in her company, and he showered her with gifts. Because of his legacy from Kemose he was a very rich man, and he was more than generous with beautiful things wrought of gold and silver, ivory, lapis, and jeweled glass. There were times when a touch from her hand could make him tremble. At such times he would find an excuse to leave her, and more than once she was tempted to call him back, to plead with him to forget the things she had said before they were married. However, she was young, and there was romance in her heart, and she reveled in the sweet melancholy of lamenting her lost childhood love. She was content with Kaptar, and no royal queen could have had a more luxurious life, but sometimes in the dead of night she awoke with a hunger inside her knowing that something was missing in her life.

As they floated down the Nile, Kaptar pointed out the place of the Heretic and his queen, telling her in hushed tones how his mother had spoken to him there on that haunted and barren plain. She shivered. "Will we stop here?"

"No, because we are expected in Waset," he said. "But we can stop on the way back, if that is your desire."

"Yes, please," she said.

"I have been told there are empty tombs there in the desert," he said, pointing toward the red, arid cliffs that ringed the valley.

"Why were they hated so, the Heretic and his queen?" Nefernehi asked, her voice subdued and almost lost in the chant of the counter of strokes for the oarsmen, the murmur of the river, the sigh of a wind moaning around the canopy that sheltered them from the late afternoon sun.

Kaptar had no answer.

"And their tombs," she whispered. "They are empty?"

He nodded.

"Tomb robbers?"

"It is said that nothing remains save broken pieces of a great sarcophagus."

"Did the tomb robbers drag their mummies out of their resting place and cut into the binding to recover the heart scarabs and other treasures in the wrappings?"

"It is not known what happened to them."

"How terrible to think they were hated so much that they were ripped and torn and broken and scattered, their places of eternal rest desecrated and left empty so that their *kas* have no home and must roam that desolate place."

Kaptar put his arm around her when she shivered. Without thinking she leaned her head against his shoulder. His heart pounded. He felt her soft hip against his thigh, felt the warmth of her under his arm —and he had to tear himself away lest he begin to hope too much.

CHAPTER EIGHTEEN

The royal barge was moving slowly upriver through a countryside increasingly familiar to Kaptar when a surprised shout caught his attention. A group of pointing, jabbering men were gathered on one side of the craft. Kaptar went to see what the excitement was about. He looked down into the river and suddenly felt cold. A body was floating past the barge, facedown in the water. Kaptar recognized the colors of the uniform as those of the royal guard of the high priest of Waset.

"There! More of them!" someone cried.

Two more bloated bodies were being swept slowly along by the current.

"Great One," said the master mariner in charge of the barge, "is there a plague in the Southern City?"

"A plague that strikes only members of the high

priest's personal guard?" Kaptar asked pointedly. He ordered a slave to bring a grappling hook. When next a body floated close, he snagged the tunic and pulled the corpse to the barge. It rolled to reveal a grotesquely swollen stomach and a face of horror—nose, eyelids, lips, and soft areas of flesh had been eaten away by small, voracious fish—and Kaptar saw the shaft of an arrow sticking out of the dead man's chest.

"It would seem the disease that has dispatched these men has tips of iron," he said.

"Perhaps this is not an ideal time for a state visit," the master mariner suggested matter-of-factly.

Kaptar looked to the riverbank and took his bearings. "Not far upstream is a good beach. We should reach it before nightfall. We will tie up there until we can determine the state of affairs in the city."

From the condition of the floating bodies—some mutilated by crocodiles, not all in the uniform of the guard—Kaptar knew the men had been dead for at least three days. It took that long for a body thrown into the water to ripen and float. The number of dead told a grim story. Apparently so many had died that they had overwhelmed the ability of the living to care for the corpses properly, necessitating a wholesale dumping of them into the sacred river—a cruel but necessary action in a time of turmoil, since pestilence and plague festered and bloomed in decaying flesh. Moreover, there had been so many of the dead, it seemed, the giant reptiles of the river had become sated and were unable to consume this feast of plenty.

The broad river was at least temporarily clear of the bloated evidence of strife when the barge was made fast on a clean, sandy beach shaded by a line of sheer cliffs. Nefernehi watched silently as Kaptar removed his princely outer garments and dressed in the long, dingy robes of a commoner. She couldn't help but worry about her family in Waset.

"The master mariner has orders to cast off and head back downriver at any threat," Kaptar told her as he belted his sword around his dingy robe. "Don't concern yourself about me. I know this land. I can blend into the masses. If it should become necessary for the barge to return to On without me, I will catch up to you."

She gripped his arm. "Please, let me go with you! I must see my family!" Her face was pale. She bit her lip to keep it from trembling. "I can disguise myself, as you have."

He laughed. "My beautiful one, not even the most susceptible enemy would be able to envision you as a woman of the people. No man seeing you walk would take you to be anything but what you are."

On impulse she put her arms around him. "Be careful."

He allowed himself one liberty, for the first time letting his lips touch hers. Her eyes closed, and she answered his kiss with ardor.

He drew back from her and smiled. "For that I will be back," he told her softly. "The enmity of the gods themselves could not keep me away."

Then he turned and was gone, making his way up the eastern bank, past the mud-brick homes of the tillers of the land through fields that promised a rich harvest. There was no sign of trouble until he saw the magnificent temples of Ipet-isut, "The Most Select of Places," outlined against the moonlit sky. He approached the complex with great care. His heart leaped when he stumbled over something soft. A stench of death was stirred up by his foot. He saw a shaven head, a face covered with dried blood—a priest. The servants of Amon had not been spared the violence that had swept the Southern City.

The long, glorious avenue of ram-headed sphinxes was deserted, the pavement shining in the light of a full moon. He found himself inside the enclosure of the sacred place without incident. No lights, no signs of life were evident as he made his way toward the Great Temple of Amon. He turned into the hypostyle hall and froze when he caught a glimpse of movement, then advanced through the forest of columns with his hand on the hilt of his sword. It was not until he had entered the sanctuary at the heart of the temple that he saw a flickering light.

"Who dares trespass in the holy of holies?" a voice demanded.

"A priest of our god Amon," Kaptar said.

Three robed figures stepped out of the shadows. One of them picked up an oil lamp and lifted it to look into Kaptar's face.

"Great One!" he whispered fervently. "It is you!"

"Mutmoses," Kaptar said, recognizing the priest even though his features were distorted and shadowed by the cast of the oil lamp, "we are well met."

"My prince, I pray to Amon that you have come to restore order to Waset and to the temples of the gods," the priest said.

"Tell me what has happened."

Mutmoses bowed. "First we must retire to a safer place. There is no law in the city. Chaos is all-pervasive. Looters roam freely, even into the temples of the gods." He gestured ahead. "Come."

Kaptar followed. Far back in the complex, hidden in an isolated corner of the temple of Amon-Re-Harakhty, the three priests escorted Kaptar to a bench beside a heavy bronze door, which was closed.

"Now you will tell me," he said.

"There has been no real stability in Waset since Kemose, may he live, joined the gods," Mutmoses explained.

That surprised Kaptar, who said, "When I left it seemed that Thure-Amon was in control."

"Thure-Amon is dead," Mutmoses said. "Nehri threw his body into the river."

"Nehri?" Kaptar asked in amazement. "By the gods! It was Nehri who started civil war among the priests of Amon?"

"It is Nehri who sits in the palace," said another of the priests. "But it is an uneasy throne under him."

"I would think that the blood of a commoner who usurps the ancient crown of Upper Egypt would go cold in his veins at the very thought of his own arrogance," Kaptar said.

"There is a faction led by Mentupe that has not pledged support for Nehri. They have taken refuge in the temples of Ipet-resyt and on the west bank. It is only a matter of time before they attack the city."

"Then they are fools," Kaptar said. "If Musen knew the condition of this city, he would dispatch an army this very day."

"Do we face that danger?" Mutmoses asked.

"Not immediately," Kaptar replied. "Nehri is in the palace?"

"Yes. If it is your intention to go there, it would be best to wait for morning. The streets are ruled by the rabble in the absence of the sun god."

"I have this," Kaptar said, patting his sword as he got to his feet.

He was escorted by the priests back to the entrance of the Great Temple. "May Amon watch over you, my prince," Mutmoses murmured as he left.

Kaptar was forced to use the sword all too soon, for he had barely set foot in the city when he was accosted by two men armed with cudgels. He dispatched one quickly, showing no mercy, appalled as he was by the lawlessness that had taken over the city of his birth. The other robber fled and was not worth the chasing.

Guards stood in the light of torches at the approaches to the palace. Kaptar stepped from the shadows and announced himself, then waited while an officer was summoned. The officer recognized him, and he was immediately escorted into Nehri's presence. Seated on the gilded chair, the priest was dressed in the linens of a king. Beside his throne was the crown of the Two Lands, and lying next to the crown were the scepter and flail, symbols of royal authority.

Seeing Kaptar, Nehri hurried to meet him, throwing his arms around him and declaring, "We are pleased, but we admit that we are surprised."

Kaptar felt a surge of cynical amusement; on Nehri's lips the royal "we" was an affectation.

"It seems, Father-in-law, that we picked an interesting time to return your state visit to the city of my brother, Sheshonk."

"An auspicious time, my son," Nehri said gravely. "As the nephew of Kemose you will be able to draw support to me."

Kaptar made no comment.

"But you said 'we.' My daughter—is she with you?"

"She is safe. The royal barge of On awaits downriver. Fear not. It is well protected by members of Sheshonk's royal guard."

"The gods be thanked," Nehri said. "We will send for her at once. Will you go, my son, or shall I dispatch one of my officers with a message from you to assure your men that it is your wish?"

"First, is it safe to bring Nefernehi into the city?"

"Safe? Of course."

"A moment ago you admitted you needed support. I am told by the priests that an army led by Mentupe may attack at any time."

"Nonsense," Nehri said angrily. "Lies. My enemies magnify the worth of this upstart priest who dares question my right to the throne."

"Which raises an interesting question," Kaptar said. "Tell me, Father-in-law, how you acquired the right to the throne of my uncle and my ancestors."

Nehri's eyes narrowed. "You are the husband of my daughter. But you are either with me or against me."

"Oh, I would rather have you rule than have the likes of Mentupe claiming divinity," Kaptar said.

"Do I have your pledge?" Nehri demanded.

Kaptar drew his sword and held it with the hilt in

front of his face, blade upward. "By this blade I pledge that I will do nothing to dispute the right of my father-in-law, Nehri, to the throne of Upper Egypt."

Nehri beamed. "My eyes hunger for the sight of my beautiful daughter. Let us send for her immediately."

Kaptar nodded. Nefernehi longed to see her family. He would remain vigilant and be ready to cast off at a moment's notice for the safety of the river should fighting break out. "Give me stylus and parchment, and I will send my orders to the master mariner," he said.

Nehri snapped his fingers, and the writing instruments were quickly brought. Kaptar seated himself in the position of a scribe and marked his message. Nefernehi would be able to read the hieroglyphs as well, thanks to the education he had helped her obtain. He would be waiting with Nehri's soldiers to make sure that the waterfront was secure when the barge arrived and to help clear the streets if necessary.

As it turned out, the streets ran with blood before morning when looters threatened the royal area and Nehri set his guards to killing any wretch who could not outrun spears, swords, or arrows. The dead were being cleared away—a fresh feast for the crocodiles of the sacred river—when Kaptar led a company of hand-picked guards to the waterfront to await his wife.

Nehri, wearing a war helmet, stood at Kaptar's side.

"It grieves me," Kaptar said.

"I know, as it does me."

"The blood that stains the Nile should be that of the Libyans."

"Be with me, Kaptar," Nehri begged. "Together we will fulfill your uncle's dream. We will send you back to On with a great army to punish those who would take Egypt's glory for themselves."

"Nehri, I gave up that dream long ago. You know that I have pledged fealty to my brother."

"But does that not make you an enemy of your

native city, of Upper Egypt, and the Amon priest-hood?"

"It makes me a loyal subject to my brother, in whose veins runs the blood of kings."

Nehri frowned but said nothing more.

A shout went up as the golden barge appeared. Nefernehi was standing on the prow, her filmy white garment pressed by the breeze against her shapely legs. She was so breathtaking that Kaptar momentarily forgot the troubles plaguing his native city.

The barge docked, and Kaptar escorted his wife off. Throwing protocol to the wind, Nefernehi ran into her father's arms, needing to be reassured that all was well with him.

A triumphant procession carried the royal entourage back to the palace, where a feast had been prepared. While acrobats performed and lovely, nubile slave girls danced with their charms hidden by nothing more than the most transparent of materials, Nefernehi and her father sat with their heads close together in conversation. Nefernehi's own mother was dead, but her father had other, younger wives and several children of tender years, and Nehri caught her up on all of them.

The day was just past half its length when a uniformed officer came striding into the banquet hall, seeking Nehri's ear. The self-made king listened to his officer's message, then leaped to his feet, motioning to Kaptar to join him.

"Mentupe is attacking," Nehri said urgently. "He has ferried men across the river from the west in boats and is moving out of the Ipet-resyt temple complex in force."

"Can you hold him?" Kaptar asked.

"His men are being slaughtered at the water's edge," said the officer who had brought the news.

"Kaptar, stand by me," Nehri implored.

"Where do you fight?"

"Against Mentupe himself on the avenue of the

human-headed sphinxes," Nehri said, reaching for his sword.

"The palace is protected?" Kaptar asked.

"By my finest men. Come."

Kaptar lingered, looking down at Nefernehi. There was concern on her face, but for whom? For her father?

"Must you go?" she asked her husband.

"I must do my best to prevent damage from being done to the holy places," he replied, pleased by her apprehension for him.

He hurried to his chamber and strapped on leather armor and his sword, then followed Nehri and his officers to the avenue of human-headed sphinxes. One attempt by Mentupe's forces to break out of the temple area had been turned back, but at a cost that made Kaptar wonder how long Nehri could continue to fight. The dead littered the grand promenade that led toward the gate and the towering pylon of Ramses the Great. Kaptar and Nehri arrived just in time to join in desperate battle as Mentupe sent his forces to march in two wings around either side of the great temples.

The men leading the attack were fresh troops. They smashed into Nehri's defense lines with howling challenges and clashing swords, spears, and shields. The shrieks of the dying rose over the field of battle, accompanied by the desperate hacking and slashing of gasping, panting men who were afraid of death but more afraid of being called coward, more terrified of deserting what they believed a just cause than of being martyred to it.

Slowly Kaptar was forced backward. Again and again his sword delivered the spurt of arterial blood, sought out vulnerable flesh under a foe's shield. All around him the enemy fell, but so did Nehri's defenders until, as the sun turned red in the west, exhaustion and attrition left only a few men to face the arrival of a new force of desert archers closing in from the river.

"They have broken through!" Kaptar gasped as he drew near Nehri. "We must fall back to the palace!"

"No! Stand with me," Nehri said. "We will stop them here."

"There are too many of them. Order your men to fall back slowly. We will take up a position around the palace in more favorable circumstances."

"We will slaughter them here," Nehri said stubbornly. He lifted his sword and called out an order to charge. Without looking back, he ran forward. No man moved to follow him. He died in a hail of arrows that found first his legs below his shield and then, as he sprawled to the pavement of the avenue of human-headed sphinxes, his sides and his belly.

"Fall back!" Kaptar yelled. "Keep order! Fall back to the palace!"

They reached the palace to find it under attack from the river. Kaptar's hastily rallied force struck the enemy from the rear, and there was a great carnage. Mentupe's forces from the Ipet-resyt temples, well blooded by the spirited defense, delayed their arrival. The body of troops who had landed from the river were slaughtered between the royal guard in front of the palace and Kaptar and his men.

In a moment of quiet, Kaptar hurried into the palace and sought out Nefernehi. She flew into his arms. "The gods are kind," she whispered. She lifted her mouth to his. It was good. So good. He dreaded what he had to do as he broke off the kiss and held her at arm's length.

"Your father is dead," he said reluctantly.

"I knew," she said in a careworn voice. "My heart told me so. The gods know that I will mourn him, but I feared that it would be you as well."

Before Kaptar had time to think about the import of her words, he saw his master mariner enter the hall. "Ho!" he bellowed, waving his arms. As the master mariner neared, he asked, "Is the barge secure?"

The master mariner nodded. "As yet we have not

been drawn into the fighting. The invaders came
ashore upriver from our position. Come with us,
Prince. We must look to the safety of our people and
the barge itself. I shudder to think what would happen
if the rabble succeeded in boarding us."

"How are the streets?" Kaptar asked.

"The street rats are hiding in their holes while real
men are fighting," the master mariner said with a
sneer.

A great sea of sound crashed on their ears—
shouts, the clash of arms, the sounds of hysteria and
destruction and desperation.

"What about your family?" Kaptar asked Nefernehi.

She did not have time to answer. The fighting
erupted into the hall, with the defenders of the palace
falling back. Kaptar grabbed Nefernehi's hand and led
her and the master mariner to a concealed exit. They
ran down long corridors that eventually led past the
harem, finally slipping out of the palace alongside some
former queen's pleasure lake and then into the streets,
which were eerily deserted. Fires were burning somewhere, the acrid smoke eddying in the close streets.
The sounds of the battle around the palace diminished
as they reached the waterfront and ran toward the
barge.

The men of Sheshonk's royal guard lined the rails,
and a few of them were on the wharf, weapons at the
ready, glaring threateningly at a growing crowd of ruffi-
ans armed with a variety of makeshift weapons. The
rule of law in Waset had been suspended. Kaptar was
breathing hard when he carried Nefernehi up the gang-
plank and set her down on the deck. The guards on the
wharf swarmed aboard while the master mariner
shouted orders. Lines were parted with the slash of a
sword. A flock of arrows halted the silent surge of the
mob toward the gilded, treasure-laden barge. There
were screams of pain and shouts of frustration as a
second hail of arrows sent the rabble scurrying for

cover. The barge moved more swiftly as the oarsmen added their momentum to the force of the current. Behind them Waset burned, flames reaching for the sky.

They were soon passing the northernmost reaches of the city. To Kaptar's great sorrow he saw looters swarming over the temple complex at Ipet-isut. The Most Select of Places was adding its own smoke to the smutted sky. Kaptar groaned when he saw flames and dense clouds issuing from the place where the priests had stored and preserved the knowledge of the past. Books of parchment burned hot and fast, and nothing could be done to save them because there were hundreds of the rabble, perhaps thousands.

"Please, don't," Nefernehi whispered to him, seeing tears form in his eyes and roll down his soiled cheeks. "Please don't weep, my love."

"It is the history of the sweet Black Land that burns," Kaptar said mournfully. "The records of the great kings, their deeds of valor and their names, the words of the gods as transcribed by uncounted generations of priests."

"Stop, my love, for you make me weep with you," she said.

He looked at her with surprise. "Twice you called me your love."

"Yes," she said with a sad smile, tears trickling down her cheeks. "And I curse my foolish heart for not realizing it long ago."

He crushed her to his breast, and his breath caught in his throat at the delicious scent of her. He then held her at arm's length, looking into her face. "Is it true? Can it be true that you have come to love me as I have from the first moment loved you?"

"Oh, yes, yes, yes," she whispered, lifting her mouth hungrily to his.

"Then," he whispered back, his lips brushing hers, "whatever else has happened, whatever else is lost, I have gained that which I have desired more than anything else in all the Two Lands."

So it was that, in a riot of emotions, Kaptar finally knew his wife in a luxurious bed in a gilded chamber aboard a royal barge constructed for a king. Her passion matched his, and the love was strong—so strong that they became one a second time and yet once more in the cool hours of morning.

True to his earlier promise to Nefernehi, Kaptar ordered that the barge be stopped beside the parched wasteland where once, long ago, a king had given his devotion to one god and one god alone. With an escort of guards, they walked the sands littered with the debris of a great city that had been deliberately destroyed by the king Horemheb in a frenzy that seemed to Kaptar, as he remembered the priestly writings in the temple library, to be out of proportion to the actions of the Heretic. With the aid of two scruffy guides from the one poor village at the river's edge there on that desolate plain, they found tombs in a dry wadi in the eroded vastness of the desert. Ancient vandals had eradicated the name of the king whose body had lain in the smashed and broken sarcophagus that now littered the floor.

"She was not here," Nefernehi announced in a quiet voice.

They were standing hand in hand in the inner recess of the tomb. The air was stale, the heat debilitating, the light of flickering torches uncertain.

"She was not here," Nefernehi repeated.

"You speak of the queen?"

"The Beautiful One Who Is Come. She did not die with her husband."

"What god tells you this?" Kaptar asked, perplexed.

"I just know. I know that she was never in this terrible place."

Kaptar shivered. "We can never be sure," he said. "Only the Amon priests knew the name of her king, and all of their knowledge was burning in flames as we left Waset."

"Lord," said one of the guides nervously, "there is nothing here but bad air and evil presences. We must seek the light."

"Yes," Kaptar agreed.

"Wait," Nefernehi said. "Hold your torch just here."

She bent to pick up a carved scarab half-hidden in the debris and clutched it in her hand.

They made their way out of the dim tomb and breathed deeply of the heated desert air, silently thankful that they were alive. Nefernehi handed the scarab to Kaptar. She had cleaned away the dust. A royal cartouche was carved into the stone.

Kaptar mouthed the syllables softly, then said the name aloud. "Akhenaten," he said. "The Heretic's name was Akhenaten."

"Lord," said one of the guides in a frightened voice, "that name is evil and is never to be spoken, lest all the gods strike you down. Save yourself. Throw away the thing that bears his evil name."

Nefernehi took the scarab from Kaptar's hand. "I will risk the anger of the gods," she said.

"But I will not risk losing you," Kaptar said, seizing the scarab. He threw it as far as he could. It landed among fallen scree along the side of the wadi, bounced once, then blended into the colorless rock. Nefernehi uttered one small sound of protest, but made no objection when Kaptar took her hand to lead her back toward the barge.

CHAPTER NINETEEN

A soft touch on his shoulder awakened Sunu from a sleep made satisfyingly deep by a certain amount of pleasant exertion involving an always-willing Mara.

"Someone calls," his wife said.

The small tapping sound that had awakened Mara came again. Sunu got out of bed quietly, pulled a tunic over his nakedness, and found the hilt of his sword. He padded out of the bedchamber, through a room where coals still glowed on the hearth, and approached the entrance to their house in Hebron.

"Who's there?" he asked through the door.

"Joab," came a furtive-sounding voice.

Sunu opened the door. The figure was wrapped in a cloak; a hood hid his face. Seeing the gleam of Sunu's blade in the light of a dim, cold moon, he threw back his head covering to reveal himself.

"Come in," Sunu said.

Joab entered the house quickly. "Don't light a lamp."

"Come. Sit near the fire," Sunu offered. He selected a handful of small twigs and coaxed them to flame by blowing on the glowing embers, then added more wood as the small blaze grew. Joab held out his hands to savor the warmth.

"I count you as my friend," he said.

"Rightly so. And I you."

"What has David said of me?"

"Since his speech designed to placate Abner's supporters in Benjamin, nothing."

"Nothing?"

"More than once I have been tempted to bring up your name, but I didn't consider the time to be right."

"That's why I'm here," Joab said. "I came to ask you a great favor."

"You have only to name it."

"Speak with David. Tell him this: that I am his kinsman, the son of his sister."

"I don't think he needs to be reminded of that," Sunu said.

"Perhaps not, but tell him just the same. Tell him likewise that my brother who died at Abner's hand was also the son of his sister. Remind him that Abner defied him, he who was anointed by God, and made every effort to raise Ish-bosheth above him."

"Joab, surely the king knows all this. I know he loves you. But you must admit that you acted precipitously in killing Abner just after he had made an alliance with David."

Joab muttered something indistinct into his beard.

Sunu shook his head. "You didn't simplify the king's task of uniting Judah and Israel, my friend."

"If we men of Judah stick together," Joab grumbled, "we can unify the tribes with this." He patted his sword.

"I want no part in continued strife among my

grandmother's people," Sunu said. "It's time we turned
our blades to better use, against the Philistines."

"Sunu, speak to David on my behalf," Joab said,
his voice hinting at his desperation. "He has cursed me.
He has laid a vile condemnation not only on me but
upon my house and my descendants. And for what?
Because I killed a man who slew countless numbers of
our countrymen, including my brother."

"I will do as you ask," Sunu promised.

"Where can I go if I am not a part of this cause
headed by my uncle?" Joab asked, spreading his hands.
"What is there to do if I can't be at my uncle's side
when at last he drives the enemy from the promised
land?"

"You will be there," Sunu said. "Although you displeased David and made things difficult for him, it's my
opinion that his harsh condemnation of you was for the
benefit of the Benjamites who mourn Abner. I will
speak with David, and you will be back at your old
command soon. Of this I'm sure."

"Pray God you're right."

"You will sleep here," Sunu said, rising from the
hearth.

"Yes. God knows that I am tired."

Sunu showed Joab to a spare room and saw to it
that he had ample coverings for his bed. Back in his
own bed he cuddled up to Mara for warmth.

Joab was still sleeping when Sunu finished breaking his fast with sweet dates, cheese, and bread.

"When he awakens," he told Mara, giving her a
kiss good-bye, "tell him to wait here for me."

First he went to his father's house, where he found
Eri preparing to go to the forges. Sunu told him of
Joab's request.

"Walk easily," Eri warned. "Don't come between
David and his purpose."

Sunu shook his head. "May God prevent me from
making that mistake."

"Perhaps Joab should simply bide his time," Eri suggested. "The death of Abner will not be forgotten, but the memories will become less and less keen. When the nation is united in fighting a common enemy, then Joab will be able to find his place again."

"I said that I would speak with David about him. I will keep my word."

Eri nodded. "And what will you say?"

Sunu had been planning his approach since first awakening. "It would be desirable to know the mood of the Trans-Jordanians and Ish-bosheth, now that Abner is dead. I'm going to suggest that my troop make a reconnaissance to assess the situation, and I'm going to tell the king that I would feel more confident if I had with me a man of experience."

"That man being Joab."

Sunu nodded.

"It might work. David will listen to any suggestion that might forward his purpose."

"You wouldn't like to come with me when I seek an audience with David?" Sunu asked with a wry smile.

"You have only to ask," Eri said.

Sunu's relief was evident. "I have asked."

The king had them admitted immediately. David was dressed in a fresh white tunic. His hair was bound with a leather band that stood out dark against his forehead, but an errant tangle of curls tumbled free almost to his eyebrows. He greeted his old friend Eri with an embrace. To Sunu he said, "You have read my mind."

"How so?" Sunu asked.

"I was just about to send for you. I would like for you and your men to ride north, the object being to penetrate the lands over the Jordan to assess the feelings of Ish-bosheth's supporters."

Eri winked surreptitiously at Sunu, who was trying to keep a straight face.

"Am I to make contact with Ish-bosheth?" Sunu asked.

"No. Talk with a few countrymen. Question some of his soldiers—without bloodshed, if possible. I don't think it's quite time to establish contact with him."

"I would ask a favor," Sunu said. He threw a quick glance at his father.

"Speak."

"There is a man of experience who would be willing to accompany me."

"His name?"

"Joab."

David's eyebrows shot up. "He is here? In the city?"

"Lord . . ." Sunu hesitated.

David waved an impatient hand. "You need not fear that you are betraying him. He is my sister's son. He acted rashly and out of passion, and he has caused me no small amount of concern—but he is of my blood." He nodded. "Take him. As a matter of fact, you'll be doing me a favor to keep him out of sight for a while. Just tell him that I am not desirous of making open war on Ish-bosheth at this time, so I will be pleased if he'll keep his blade sheathed if at all possible and refrain from killing off any more of my allies."

"Thank you, lord," Sunu said, unable to suppress a grin.

"That's all?" David asked. "Do you have everything you need?"

"We are ready. We'll ride before the sun is high."

Eri turned to leave with Sunu.

"Stay with me, Eri," David requested, "unless you have pressing business."

"The usual. I was on my way to the forges when my son asked me to come with him to see you."

"To act as a buffer between the young warrior and the cruel king?"

"You *can* be intimidating," Eri said.

David laughed. "Let me walk with you."

"My pleasure."

The morning was bright and brisk. As they left the palace area, guards saluted. In the streets people hailed the king, some bowing before him. A woman came close to touch his sleeve.

"David," she whispered. "David."

"May God bless you, sister," David said.

"God has given us a king," the woman said, kissing his hand.

In Mahanaim, a man who was also called king retired to his bedchamber, an upper room of the modest building that served as the palace, upon hearing of the death of his army commander. The news made Ish-bosheth sick at heart, for Abner was his kinsman, his main support, and the stiff backbone of what was left of the Army of Israel. Now he was gone. Michal was gone, as well, given to David by Abner without so much as a protest from the king, her brother.

Though it was but noon, Ish-bosheth threw himself across a bed, and merciful sleep came to him to ease his troubles for a time.

Outside the door of the king's chamber a servant sat on a bench, her duty being to prevent anyone from disturbing her master. The day had warmed after a chilly morning. The harshly bright winter sun came in through a window, making the narrow corridor hot and close. The woman's head bobbed once, twice. Her heavy eyes closed; her head dropped to her chest as she leaned back in sleep. She did not awaken as a door slowly opened at the end of the hall.

Two men, brawny warriors of Benjamin, crept toward the sleeping woman. One lifted his sword, and the servant's repose became the eternal sleep of death.

Quietly, furtively, the two men opened the door to Ish-bosheth's bedchamber. The king slept on. One of the men moved forward quickly and with one great blow of his sword almost severed the head from Ish-bosheth's body. It took but a second blow to complete the job. The assassin stood back, breathing hard. Blood pooled atop the bedding, but soon the great gushes of red stopped pumping. Not a muscle had moved in Ish-bosheth's body, so quickly had he died. The house of Saul had been depleted once more, leaving as the principal vessel of the Tall King's blood one small, crippled boy: Mephibosheth, Mara's brother.

The killers wrapped Ish-bosheth's head in a fleece and left the palace. They escaped unnoticed and were soon out of the city, riding southward in haste. As they traveled far into the night, they talked about the rewards that would be theirs when they presented their grisly trophy to David.

"I will say this," said Baanah to his brother Rechab. "I will say, 'Great king, we, the sons of Rimmon, whom you know as the patriarch of a Benjamite family of high rank, have given you the crown of Israel.' "

"We will not ask for riches," said Rechab, "only for rank and the chance to gain great wealth as captains in David's army as he drives the Philistines from Israel."

So they talked and dreamed as they completed the journey to Hebron.

Since his arrival in Hebron from Mahanaim with his wife and granddaughter, Urnan, the smith of Shiloh, had found himself more and more in demand by the king—a situation he was not entirely confident about.

"More than once I heard your words of advice to Saul," David told him, "and never did I hear you give false counsel. I need you at my side, old friend."

"But you have the Levite priests and those who have marched with you since you fled Saul's court," Urnan argued. "I serve you best by turning out the weapons you will need when you march north."

"The priests look after the welfare of my soul. And those who have marched with me speak best with

their swords in their hands." David smiled. "You, old
friend, have a particular wisdom unmatched by any."

So it was that Urnan was with David when a her-
ald announced the arrival of two Benjamites from
Mahanaim with an important message for the king.
David, too restless to sit on his throne, was pacing the
floor when the sons of Rimmon were allowed to enter
the room. Urnan was seated on a stone bench against
the wall, an uncomfortable perch that he was already
anxious to abandon.

"Great king," said Baanah, holding out before him
a fleece from which emanated a powerful, horrific
stench, "we have come to place before you the crown
of all Israel."

David's face went blank. He cast a quizzical look
at Urnan. The smith shrugged.

"I am Baanah, son of Rimmon, and I speak for my
brother, Rechab. Perhaps you recognize the name of
our father, for he is of the first rank in Benjamin."

"First rank in Benjamin is of lower position than
the most junior infantryman in the Army of the Five
Cities," David retorted. He held up his hand for silence
as Baanah's face darkened with resentment at the insult to his father's name. "Not that I scorn you or your
father."

"Be assured, lord, that we will fight with you,"
Baanah said.

"For which you will be welcomed. But you say you
have come to place the crown of Israel on my head."

"Yes. We do it thusly," Baanah said proudly. He
knelt and spread open the fleece.

Though the miasma of rotted flesh curled David's
lips, his eyes were terrible as he beheld the head of Ish-
bosheth, son of Saul.

"Accept this gift, lord," Baanah said, "as a favor
from the sons of Rimmon. We ask only—"

"You fools!" David thundered. His voice, which
could be so soft and melodic when delivering a paean
to God or one of the old love songs of his people, filled

the room with an anger that froze the blood of the two brothers.

"Please, my lord," Rechab said, groveling on his knees and speaking for the first time. "We will not be greedy in asking for reward, but—"

"Have you not heard what was done to the man who claimed to have been the instrument of delivering Saul from his pain?" David asked, his voice now a chilly monotone. "Don't you know what fate awaits the murderers of a king?"

"But, my lord . . ." Baanah protested.

"You don't have the looks of men who would be brave enough to face a son of the Tall King," David snarled. "What did you do? Did you creep upon him from behind?" He glared at Baanah. "Or perhaps you fell upon him while he lay asleep in his bed." The look in the man's eyes told David he had hit upon the truth.

Rechab was white with fright. "But hear us, lord. We did it only for you."

"What evil did Ish-bosheth to you?" David shouted. "Were you really witless enough to think I would be pleased to learn you have murdered your master? Did you really think I would take kindly the death of a king at the hands of such filth as you?"

David turned to his captain of the guard. "Take these insects away and see to it that it takes a long, long time to erase this blot on my honor. Stated plainly, I want these misbegotten wretches to know torment before they find the ease of death."

The two brothers wailed their bewilderment and shock as soldiers seized them and dragged them away. Urnan rose from the bench. David's eyes were hard as the stone itself as he looked at the smith.

"Was I too harsh?" he asked. "Unreasonable?"

"Kings have never liked the idea of regicide," Urnan said placidly. "Saul's downfall began when he spared the life of a king, remember? Just as you can imagine yourself lying in your bed like Ish-bosheth, completely at the mercy of assassins, so Saul could picture himself in the place of the king he'd been ordered by Samuel to kill."

David's eyes narrowed angrily. "Sometimes you look too deeply into a man's soul," he muttered.

"Did not a certain king—a young king by the name of David, I believe—command a lowly smith to be at his side to share his humble thoughts with that king?"

David's face softened. "Forgive me."

"There is nothing to forgive."

"Urnan, have someone come and take . . . this," David said, looking down at the severed head.

"Certainly, lord." Urnan went to the door and looked into the hall. The guards were dragging the two brothers away. From the other direction came Michal. She was dressed in blue, with a paler blue undertunic. Combs of silver graced her ebony hair, and her eyes were outlined in the Egyptian manner. Urnan quickly stepped out of the room and closed the door behind him.

"I know those men," Michal said, looking at the prisoners. "Why are they in custody?"

"I think, lady, that the king wants to speak with you," Urnan said.

She made to step past him, but he blocked her way to the door. She looked at him quizzically.

"He will come to you," Urnan said.

"I will know what is going on," Michal said imperiously.

Behind Urnan the door was flung open. David paused when he saw Michal. She looked past him and saw the severed head. The eyes were glazed open and the mouth gaped, but the face was recognizable as that of her brother. She put her hand to her mouth as though to stop the sound that nonetheless escaped, a harsh, keening moan of agony. She managed to cut the scream short.

"Those two, those who were being dragged away . . ."

David nodded. "They will be punished."

"So now they are all dead. All of my brothers," Michal said. "Now you rule by right of survival, is that not true, *great* king?"

"If you feel it will lessen your grief to demean me, do so," David said sadly. "But not when such behavior embarrasses a friend."

"I hear and obey, *my lord,*" Michal said. "Now, if you will excuse me, I will see to it that my brother's remains receive their proper respect."

"He will be given the rite of burial that is his due," David said. "But this is not the work of a woman."

"It is always woman's work to grieve her kinsmen who die in one war or another." Michal tried to push past, but David stopped her by putting his hands on her arms.

"Leave us," David said. "When he has been decently treated I will summon you."

She turned and walked away with her head high and back straight.

"Will you see to it, please?" David asked Urnan, looking quite ill.

"I will," Urnan said.

The severed head was placed in a gilded chest. After administration of the customary rites by Abiathar, the high priest at Hebron, it was interred in the grave of Abner so that the two kinsmen were together in death.

Now, one by one, there came the principal men of the Hebrew people to David in Hebron. Each man represented hundreds, even thousands. They came with sweet words: how they had esteemed David during Saul's lifetime, how it was general knowledge that David had been chosen of God by Samuel before the prophet's death.

"Save us," they begged their king. "Save the land from the Philistines."

As they arrived, each man was feasted and treated

with honor. Each man was told by the king, "Go with my pledge, and bring all the people unto me. Bring all who have shields and spears, all who have the bow and quiver, all who wear the sword."

They came in their hundreds, in their thousands. They came from the tribe of Simeon, over seven thousand of them, and from Levi under Jehoiada the priest. Ephraim's tribe was mighty and came in numbers, and there were men of valor from Manasseh and Naphtali and Issachar and Zebulun and Gad and Dan and Asher and from Manasseh beyond the Jordan. They came in their multitudes, all save the men of Benjamin, where, because of the murders of Abner and Ish-bosheth, many still sought someone from the house of Saul to rule over them. They came with corn and wine and stores of food, with their shields and spears, with their headpieces and swords, their bows and arrows. Some few had warhorses, and there were a handful of chariots to be integrated into David's well-trained mobile forces.

Sunu and Joab heard the news of Ish-bosheth's death several days after the event. Having gone so far, it seemed of little profit to return to Hebron to take news that, they were assured, had already been delivered to David. They rode northward and began a survey of Philistine positions on the edge of the coastal plain.

When they and their men finally returned to Hebron after a cold, endless time of harassing isolated Philistine outposts in the north, they had to make their way through a great host camped around Hebron.

"David has done it!" Sunu shouted joyously, for he could see the banners of all the different tribal units. "He has gathered all of the nation."

A nervous Joab accompanied Sunu into the city. They went directly to the forges, where they found Eri directing frenzied activity. Winter was moderating, and the swift change of season would begin almost any day. Eri embraced Sunu with affection.

"I see preparation for great things," Sunu said.

"When will we march against the Philistine?" Joab asked eagerly.

Eri held up his hands. "Do I look like a king that I can answer such a question? Since it's customary for the commander of a returning reconnaissance force to report to his leader, perhaps you should ask David the same question—and then share his answer with me."

Sunu laughed and turned to Joab.

"I will stay with your father," Joab said, answering the unasked question.

Sunu noddded. "I understand. I shouldn't be too long."

In fact, he had to wait for over an hour to meet with David as a dozen important tribal leaders were admitted one or two at a time to the king's audience chamber. It was late and the sky was darkening when at last Sunu marched in and saluted.

"You have returned just in time," David said. "What is the condition of your troop?"

"Fit," Sunu replied.

"But tired, I imagine."

"Not too tired to lead the army's way to the north. I have, lord, a detailed mapping of the Philistine frontier outposts."

"Perhaps they'll be of use another day. When your men have enjoyed a little rest, you will ride north—but not toward the Philistine outposts."

"The city of Beth-shan, where General Galar is headquartered?" Sunu asked. "That is your destination?"

"Don't be so impatient," David said with a fond smile. "I, too, long for the day when we face Galar's legions once more, but I fear we are not ready. You saw an army camped around the city."

"Yes."

"How did they look to you?"

"Undisciplined," Sunu said truthfully.

"We will not risk another defeat such as that suffered by Saul at Gilboa. For a while longer we will allow the Lords of the Five Cities to think we are friends. In the meantime, we will complete a small job left unfinished by our ancestors back to the time of Joshua."

"Jerusalem, then."

"Can you think of a more fitting location for a capital city that will be the point of unity between Judah and Israel?"

"Ahh," Sunu said, with sudden understanding.

"Ahh," David said with a smile. "You will take a good position on the hills around Jerusalem, there to make note of comings and goings for me to study when I arrive with the army."

"When can we expect you?"

"I will announce my coming with drums and trumpets. You will know, and the Jebusites will know. You won't fail to hear the angels shouting when the Army of God begins the work of claiming *all* the land promised to Abraham and his seed."

"One thing, lord . . ." Sunu said hesitantly.

"Let me guess. Joab."

Sunu nodded.

"You may tell my nephew he is to remain here, in the city."

"But, lord—"

David held up his hand. "To take command of the troops who will make the assault on the Jebusite walls," he finished.

"Yes, sir!" Sunu said, grinning. He saluted, turned smartly, and ran to deliver the good news to Joab.

Soon after that he was in his own house, in the arms of his Mara, and there he stayed for three straight days and four straight nights—for had the king not ordered him to allow his troops to rest?

CHAPTER TWENTY

Sheshonk had grown tall. At the age of twelve, just short of official manhood, his head reached to Kaptar's shoulder. He was long of leg and fleet of foot and prided himself on being able to outrun his older brother. It was obvious the two were products of the same womb, for in each face there was evidence of the beauty of their mother.

When in public or in his room of audiences, Sheshonk was every inch the king, and his half-brother was nothing more or less than Master of the Horse, armorer to the king, and the king's most trusted adviser. When the two were alone, however, which was as often as the king could arrange it, Sheshonk's adoration of his older brother allowed for a relationship that ignored the king's exalted rank. The boy strained his developing muscles to greater strength in panting, tumbling wrestling matches with the iron-muscled armorer; he coaxed Kaptar into racing across the sands; and he led the way, laughing and teasing his slower sibling, to a cooling plunge in a pleasure lake.

It was a good time for the Egyptian son of Urnan. Not only did Kaptar enjoy a lofty position, he was the envy of the court for the beauty of his wife. He had eyes only for Nefernehi, and the fact that she remained childless did not upset him—though it would have been a joyful thing to hold in his hands a child of his seed from the womb of the Beautiful One. While still at his uncle's court in Waset he had experienced that pleasure more than once, but the results of his unions with various women were officially children of the king. He thought often of his one son, born to a charming lady of the dance—a boy with the dark, curled hair of Kaptar's Mesopotamian ancestors and the paw print of a lion marking his left hip. But his life as a prince of Upper Egypt was a thing of the dead past. Just as he himself had never seen his own father, the smith Urnan, his son by the lithe and passionate dancing girl would not see his sire until that time when an army of Libyan mercenaries marched upriver to make Waset and the south a part of Sheshonk's kingdom.

The world could be cruel, and numerous people of Kaptar's acquaintance liked to dwell on the inequities of life. Oddly enough, most of those who did so were Libyans. Egyptians took a longer view of the trials of the world, making them secondary to the primacy of eternity. Had Kaptar been so inclined, he could have wasted valuable time and energy bewailing the fact that he had never had a father. He could have mourned the loss of his mother and could have tortured himself endlessly with the knowledge that she had died at Musen's hands, her place in eternity robbed when her body was mutilated and fed piecemeal to the crocodiles of the sacred river.

However, Kaptar had long since reconciled himself to his duty: to keep his word to both his mother

and his uncle, Kemose, to do all that was in his power
to make the young son of his mother and a common
Egyptian soldier ruler of the Two Lands, not just the
Libyan north. In the fullness of time, he knew, the god
of the dead would accomplish that which Kaptar's oath
had prevented—the death of Musen.

That long-anticipated event came soon after
Sheshonk's twelfth birthday, at a time when the brothers had left the city to travel with only a small entourage to the Giza plateau. Once there, Sheshonk
ordered the courtiers and his senior advisers to remain
on the royal barge, since none of them were good
enough horsemen to keep up with such skilled riders as
the king and his Master of the Horse.

In fact, Kaptar himself was hard put to match the
king, for Sheshonk was a natural horseman with an un-
canny eye for judging the worth of a particular animal.
Not only could he outride Kaptar, he always chose a
superior mount.

Kaptar lagged behind as they rode toward the
mighty monuments to the glory of the ancients in that
place where the kings of the Fourth Dynasty had been
sleeping for two thousand years. He caught up with
Sheshonk, who had dismounted in the shadow of the
Sphinx.

"Brother, we should have brought water," the
young king said, wiping his forehead, as Kaptar dismounted, as well.

A sly look on his face, Kaptar removed a woven
reed basket from its place behind his seat on the horse.
"It's neither your superior horsemanship nor your superior horse that enabled you to best me so badly. It's
the weight of *this* that prevented me from catching
you," he joked.

"Good old Kaptar, always dependable," Sheshonk
said, laughing and diving into the reed basket to find a
container of wine and a chunk of bread.

They ate and drank in the shadow of the great
god. Sated for the moment, Sheshonk leaned back

against a bank of sand, put his hands under his head, and looked reflectively up at the jutting chin of a long-dead king.

"Tell me again, Kaptar, about Thutmose, he who heard the voice of the god. Was it the second or third of that name?"

"The fourth Thutmose, as a matter of fact."

Sheshonk sighed. "Sometimes I think the Black Land is cursed with too much history. So many kings. So many centuries." He sat up and pointed toward the three tombs that rose dramatically into the sky. "They call me a king, but I could never build a tomb to match any of those—not even the lesser ones that lie in the desert beyond the great ones. I will never have my face carved on the body of a lion so large that it defies the imagination in its immensity." He sighed again. "I couldn't even afford to do what the fourth Thutmose did."

"You will do a great deed," Kaptar said firmly. "You will make the Two Lands one again."

"Into a Libyan land," Sheshonk said. "Doesn't that bother you, Kaptar?"

"No, because you're my mother's son, and there is Egypt in you."

"But I am half-Libyan."

Kaptar was silent. To alleviate his own feelings he said, "Once, at midday, a royal prince sat down here where we are now, in the shadow of this great god. He was tired, he slept, and in his dreams the god spoke to him, saying, 'Hear me, Thutmose, for it is I, your father, Harmachis-Kheri-Ra-Atum. I will give you my kingdom, the good Black Land, the Two Lands of the sacred river. You will wear the white crown and the red crown, and the Black Land will be yours in its length and breadth.' And the prince asked, 'What is it that I must do, father of my fathers?' And the god answered, 'I am ill, my son. The sands sap my strength as they cover my body. Free me of this burden, and all that I promised will be yours.' "

Sheshonk looked up at the underside of the huge chin. "Speak to me, god of the past. Ask me a favor and I will do it." He looked at Kaptar. "So he cleared away the sand and he became king. What have I done, Kaptar, to deserve to rule one half of this land?"

"The hot, rich blood of Egypt is in you."

"And in you," Sheshonk said. "But, then, I don't suppose you've ever been spoken to by a god, either."

"No," Kaptar said with a chuckle.

They fell into a companionable silence. The sun beat down on the eternal sands and gleamed radiantly off the white, smooth sides of the pyramidal tombs.

"Kaptar . . ."

"Umm?" Kaptar answered sleepily.

"I want to do more than clear the sand away from some ancient monument."

"You're young. You'll have your chance. I've told you that you will unite the Two Lands."

"I want to regain the empire."

Kaptar sat up. "A worthy ambition."

"I want hymns of praise for me carved into stone, as they were carved for the third Thutmose."

"Your memory is improving."

"Oh, I remember him." He recited in a quiet, melodic voice, " 'I have come, giving thee to smite the princes of Zahi. I have hurled them beneath thy feet among their highlands. I have come, giving thee to smite the Asiatics and the western land . . . Keftyew and the lands of Mitanni tremble because of thee.' "

"Very good," Kaptar said, "although you left out a few lines."

"What I left out isn't important," Sheshonk said. "I want Amon to compose a hymn to me."

"Why don't you recite the rest of the hymn, where Thutmose smites the Libyans and the Sand Dwellers?"

"You chide me for my Libyan blood, and yet you are the son of a foreigner."

"No, I do not chide you for having Libyan blood," Kaptar said. He longed more than anything to be able to tell his brother the truth, but that was not practical, for to Sheshonk's knowledge he was Musen's son, and he had a strong love for his father.

"I want to have them see me as they saw Thutmose—a jackal, swift-footed, stealthy, roving the Two Lands and reaching out to bring back to Egypt the glory that she has lost."

That, Kaptar thought with immense pride, *is not a Libyan talking.* "First Upper Egypt, great king," he said aloud.

"Be with me, Kaptar. Be at my side."

"That is my place, my king and brother. I will be ever at your side."

"And when we march out of the Black Land to smite the Asiatics, to make the land of Mitanni tremble at our approach, lay down arms, and beg to be a part of Egypt once more, you will ride with me?"

"I will be there, O great conqueror."

Sheshonk sat up suddenly. "Did you hear anything?"

"No."

"Nothing?"

"Nothing." Kaptar cocked his head. "What did you hear?"

"A voice calling my name. A voice telling me to return to the city as swiftly as possible."

Kaptar shivered. Sheshonk leaped to his feet and threw himself with one bound onto his horse. "Hurry, Kaptar, hurry!" he shouted as he urged the spirited animal into a plunging, sand-kicking run.

Musen died in great pain while gasping for breath and clutching his chest. His body was still warm when Sheshonk came running into the room to look at the attending priests with accusation in his eyes. The young king fell to his knees and clasped the dead Libyan's hand in his. He stayed in the room for a long time after telling the priests to leave him alone with his father. When he came out, Kaptar was waiting for him.

"I grieve for him, Kaptar," the boy said. "My heart hurts so that I can't think. Think for me. Do that which should be done. See to it that my father receives the honors to which he is entitled."

"I will," Kaptar said with a bow.

"Come to me when all the plans have been completed," Sheshonk said, not sounding grief-stricken at all.

Kaptar personally and carefully chose the priests who prepared Musen's body for transportation to the house of the dead. He saw to it that certain arrangements were made before the sarcophagus left the palace on its doleful journey. All the Egyptian ceremonies and traditions were in play, for as Kemose had once said to Kaptar, the Libyans wanted nothing more than to have the status and prestige of being Egyptians. The body that was to be transported to the house of the dead by the Amon priests selected by the High Priest Kaptar would be treated for seventy days and then placed in a prepared tomb with all the honors due the father of a king. Meanwhile, the body of Musen the Libyan, the man who had deprived the princess Tania of eternity, would be separated into its various parts, and in the dark of night, legs, arms, head, heart, and organs would all become food for the river crocodiles. Since many of them lived long lives, it was quite possible that Musen would be a meal for the same reptiles who had devoured the flesh of Tania so long ago.

Kaptar felt lighter in his heart when, later that day, he found his younger brother taking a meal in the women's quarters. Although Sheshonk was not long past puberty, he had taken quite enthusiastically to the pleasures offered by the sweet, soft bodies of his several wives and the women of his harem. He had sought their company to take his mind off the sadness of his father's death.

"Come, Kaptar, take food with me," he said.

Kaptar made a selection of fruit and seated himself.

"Take more than food if you have the appetite for it," Sheshonk said with a self-conscious smile as he indicated the women of his house.

"The royal sarcophagus has been carried to the house of the dead," Kaptar said.

"It makes me shiver to think of it," Sheshonk said. "Do I have to go there, Kaptar?"

"It will not be necessary."

"But when it is done, I will have to perform the ceremony of the opening of the mouth, won't I?"

"Yes."

"Will he stink?"

"No. He'll be well swathed in linen and spices. He will smell only of incense and perfumes."

"Good. Kaptar?"

"Yes?"

"I want intelligence on the lands of the former empire."

"Getting men into the southern lands beyond the First Cataract would present certain problems, since Upper Egypt lies between, and Mentupe is rather hostile to us."

"But we can send emissaries to the Peleset and to those peculiar people who fight among themselves in the hills," the king pointed out. "And to the Asiatics."

"If it is deemed worthwhile, I think we could reasonably expect an official emissary to survive such a trip," Kaptar said dryly.

"It is my wish, Kaptar," Sheshonk said. "If I am to have a hymn composed by Amon carved into stone in my honor—if I am to be the instrument of restoring the glory of empire to the Black Land—then I must have intelligence about our potential enemies. I must know who rules and with what strength. Once we had communications with our allies all the way to Kadish and beyond. Now a dark silence leaves us in ignorance."

It was only a boy who sat so straight in his chair, Kaptar knew, but he spoke with the voice of a man—

and with the ambitions of a man. *Well, little brother,* he
thought as he wiped the juice of a ripe fruit from his
lips with a dainty cloth, *what have we here? What manner of man is this to be, this fruit of my mother's womb,
this seed of Egypt?*

"See to it, will you, brother?" the king said, and it
was not a question.

"It will be done," said the Master of the Horse
and the king's closest adviser. Even as he spoke he was
remembering with bittersweet emotions the way his
mother had often described Urnan the smith. And for
a moment he was a child again asking, "But when the
king exiled him from Egypt, Mother, where would he
have gone?"

He could almost hear his mother's voice, remembered vividly the look of sheer yearning in her eyes as
she said, "I think he would have gone back to the land
of his first wife, for he always held hope that the son of
his youth was still alive somewhere in the hills of that
country or on the plains of the Peleset."

Yes, with the favor of the gods, an emissary of the
king of Lower Egypt could travel to the Philistine cities, to the cedar coast, and perhaps even into the hills
of the interior and return in safety. And with very special dispensations from all of the gods, perhaps that
emissary could locate one particular man—a man with
the paw mark of a lion on his flank.

Little brother, Kaptar said to himself, *you have set
me a fine dilemma.* To seek his father in that far land
appealed greatly to him, but that would mean leaving
Nefernehi behind. He would have to balance carefully
the merits of the one against the loneliness of the
other.

But even as he said the words to himself, he knew
which course he would take.

Epilogue

～～～～～～～～～～～～～～～～～～～～～～～～～～～～

At the time of the change of seasons, nights could be cool in the land of God's chosen people. The family of the scholar's sister was all together in the main room of the stone house on the side of a hill looking across the Valley of Hinnom toward the City of David. A fire burned low on the grate. A plate of cakes made sweet and heavy by dates and honey was almost empty, and the savory smell of the evening meal—meat had been served to honor the visit of the rabbi—lingered in the room.

The scholar listened for a moment to the sounds of the countryside, the call of a night-hunting bird, the contented bleat of a lamb from the cote backing the stone wall of the house, a sigh of wind. His nephew, the oldest son of the family, sat at his feet, waiting patiently for the storytelling to continue.

"Will you have another cake, Uncle?" asked the oldest daughter, a nubile girl with the dark eyes and ebony hair of the descendants of Abraham.

"In all things, moderation." The scholar nodded sagely. "Perhaps if David had remembered that adage and lived by it, he would not have been denied the joy of fulfilling his ultimate dream."

"But, Uncle," the boy protested mildly, "wasn't his dream to reunite Israel?"

"That was his original goal, boy," the scholar said.

"Well, he forged a vast empire. He made a mighty slaughter against the Philistines . . ."

"That is true," the scholar said. *"He defeated the Army of the Five Cities and sent them running back to the coastal plain, and never again did they pose a serious threat to Israel."* He lifted a finger and smiled behind his grizzled beard. *"But did you know, my son, that David's personal guard was made up of Philistines?"*

The boy shifted uncomfortably. His uncle had a knack for knocking his thoughts askew.

"He called his royal guards the Cherethites and the Pelethites. They were mercenaries from the great cities of the Philistines, from Ashdod—where Saul and his young friend Eri tricked the Dagon priests into sending the Ark of the Covenant back to Israel—from Gaza and Ashkelon, from Ekron, and from Gath, the city of giants. They came from all the cities of Philistia, these mercenaries, and they served under the command of Benaiah, son of Jehoiada."

The scholar put his hand on his nephew's head. Most of his words were directed to the boy. He had hopes for his nephew. Soon, God willing, the boy would come to the city and begin his study of the Talmud, the sacred books of the law, thus extending the family tradition of service to God through one more generation of Levite priests.

"Since David needed to consolidate his position, to build and train an army, it is understandable, isn't it, that he began his drive toward the empire of God by eradicating a festering sore from the heart of Judah?" the scholar asked. *"Why do you suppose he chose to attack the city of the Jebusites?"*

"As you said this afternoon, Uncle, Jerusalem was an excellent site for his capital, since it lay near the border of Judah and Benjamin."

"And?"

"And because the Jebusites had resisted Joshua successfully. The fortress was so strong, not even that mighty

warrior of God could bring down its walls, and the Jebusites continued to defy the will of God."

"Uncle . . ." said the oldest daughter in a shy, soft voice.

"Speak, child."

"I understand why the Philistines were our enemies, for they subjugated Israel and robbed the people of their substance, but why did God tell his people to slay all the others?"

The scholar nodded. "You are a woman, and your heart is soft. You wonder why, for example, God felt it desirable—you might even say fair—to give this nation of Israel to Abraham when there were already people on the land."

"Canaanites," the boy said.

"It does sound harsh," the scholar said, "unless one has studied the sacred texts and understands that no worthy nation was ever condemned to extinction by God. He gave this good land to Abraham and his seed because those who were on the land practiced abominations. Had you been born a Canaanite, dear girl, you might well have become one of the whores of the temples of Baal."

The girl gasped in shock.

"Oh, yes," the scholar elaborated, "for Baal was a heathen god of fertility, and to prompt the false god to make the land, its animals, and its daughters fruitful, his worshipers performed sexual unions. Each heathen shrine was staffed with gedeshim and gedeshoth, with male and female attendants, for this purpose. It was for such abominations that the Canaanites were cursed by the One God and doomed to extinction."

The scholar paused for a moment, smoothing his beard with his hand. Then he continued, "A study of the sacred texts tells us that it was excesses of the flesh that doomed all of the peoples who were conquered by David in those years following the death of Abner and Ishbosheth. The enclaves of Canaanites in the north at Megiddo, Beth-shan, and Taanach worshiped the phallic symbols of the so-called earth goddesses and practiced the *obscenities of Baal. The Moabites were the product of the incestuous union of Lot and his daughters, who tricked Lot into lying with them after God destroyed the corrupt cities of Sodom and Gomorrah; and the Moabites continued to propagate these evil practices. It was likewise with the Ammonites and the Edomites. They had been seduced by the followers of the heathen gods into sexual practices that could not be condoned by God or a godly people. And so, one by one they were slaughtered before David's armies until even Damascus was his, and his empire extended from the Euphrates River to the borders of Egypt."*

"He was truly a man of God," the boy said.

"Yes," the scholar agreed, "but in the final analysis he was a man and heir to the temptations of the flesh."

"You speak of the beautiful Bathsheba," the girl said in her hesitant voice. "But could he be blamed for falling in love with her when he saw her at her bath?"

"Ah, but was that the first time the Shining King saw Bathsheba?" the scholar countered.

"I think so," the girl said.

"Was he a blind man, then?" the scholar asked, shrugging as he spread his arms. "The father of Bathsheba was one of David's counselors, and her grandfather was also close to the king. Her family home was next to the palace. Doesn't it seem likely that David knew Bathsheba before he saw her on the rooftop at her bath? And doesn't it seem odd that this woman would pick a spot directly below the king's window to display her charms so indiscreetly? Could it be that there had been encounters between the king and Bathsheba prior to that fateful day when David turned his eyes to his window?"

The scholar put his hand on his nephew's head again. "What was David's weakness, boy?"

Having only recently begun the metamorphosis that comes with puberty, the boy understood the answer only in theory. "His weakness was that most common of human failures: He fell prey to the desires of the flesh, to the

*same compulsion that brought the heathen Canaanites to
the Baal temples to participate in their immoral acts."*

"So it was," the scholar confirmed. "And thus it was
that the hungers of the flesh deprived David of his final
ambition: to build a temple to the Lord in Jerusalem.
Perhaps had he not betrayed Uriah—husband of Bathsheba, a godly man although he was born a heathen—
perhaps had his sin been no more than that of adultery—
But who knows? We know that Uriah the Hittite was good
and loyal, one of David's thirty mighty men, a man who
obeyed God and his superiors. We know that he received
the ultimate wrong from the king who was anointed by
God, and we know that David was never able to fully
atone for having ordered Joab to send Uriah to his death.
Not all the prayers, not all the songs of praise that came
from the heart of the Shining King, not the psalms that
enlighten us and make our hearts glad, not even his service to God's chosen people could erase the stain of
Uriah's blood."

"Tell us how Solomon continued David's work and
built the temple," the girl begged.

"Egypt," the boy added eagerly. "What of Egypt?"

The scholar laughed. "I just saw my son-in-law yawn
with his need for sleep."

"The work of a farmer begins with the sun," the man
of the house said.

"And yet these two," the scholar said, "want to hear
about Solomon and about Egypt. In fact, the two are in-
tertwined, the Wise King and the Black Land."

"And Kaptar, Child of the Lion," the boy said. "Did
he help his half-brother conquer Upper Egypt?"

"I fear all those questions will have to go unan-
swered," the scholar said. "At least until we have slept
and done our work and gather here again before the fire."

"Ohh," the boy groaned in disappointment.

"Until tomorrow night," the scholar promised.

"You will tell us about Egypt then?"

The scholar nodded. "And about the boy king
Sheshonk, who sent wives to Solomon. About Kaptar and

*his Beautiful One and how he came to know his father,
Urnan, the smith of Shiloh; and of Eri, son of Urnan,
and his son, Sunu, who smote the enemies of Israel at the
side of the Shining King."*

The scholar's bed had been laid out. He found it to
be soft, the covering just right for the coolness of the night.
He could look up through a window and see the stars—
the same stars that had shone on Abraham during his
long trek from Ur through the Promised Land to Egypt
and back again; on Joshua; on Samson and Deborah,
Judges of Israel; on the ill-fated Saul and his four sons;
on David and his many wives and sons; and now on the
Wise King, who, in his golden palace, was a symbol of the
goodness of God and the glory of Israel.

The scholar's prayers that night were brief, for he was
tired from his journey that day. He prayed for his family,
for the poor who are always with us, and for the king, lest
he, like those who had occupied the throne before him,
fall from grace and through his punishment bring strife
and suffering to Israel once more.

The Children of the Lion—Book XIX
TRIUMPH OF THE LION
by Peter Danielson

David, once a lowly shepherd boy, has seen his great dream come to fruition: he has united the tribes of Israel and Judah, whose elders now proclaim him king. Political triumph and personal tragedy mark his long rule as he leads his army in victory against the rampaging Philistines, establishes his capital in Jerusalem, and orders the murder of an innocent man in his adulterous pursuit of the sultry Bathsheba.

Three generations of Children of the Lion— Urnan, Eri, and Sunu have served as armorers, warriors, and confidants to both David and his illustrious predecessor, King Saul. Now they will be called upon not only to assist David in his military exploits but also to counsel him in affairs of the heart.

Meanwhile, Kaptar, the son Urnan has never seen, embarks on a dangerous journey from Egypt to find his father, relying on intuition and ingenuity to combat Philistine raiders and overcome other deadly obstacles along the way. Then Leah, Sunu's lovely half-sister, discovers that she possesses the same mystical powers that have blessed—or cursed—the Children of the Lion through the centuries. Her newfound gifts could be used to great ends . . . or twisted to destroy the house of David forever.

Look for *Triumph of the Lion,* Volume Nineteen in the CHILDREN OF THE LION series, on sale in December 1995 wherever Bantam books are sold.

FROM THE PRODUCERS OF WAGONS WEST

THE CHILDREN OF THE LION

Extraordinary tales of epic adventure. A saga that creates anew the splendor and sweeping panorama of desert kingdoms aflame with the excitement and passions of the world's earliest legends.

___26912-7 **THE CHILDREN OF THE LION** $4.99/$5.99 in Canada

___56145-6 **DEPARTED GLORY** $4.99/$5.99 in Canada

___56146-4 **THE DEATH OF KINGS** $4.99/$5.99 in Canada

___56147-2 **THE SHINING KING** $4.99/$5.99 in Canada

ACROSS UNTAMED LANDS THEY FORGED
A LEGACY THAT TIME WILL NEVER FORGET!